Some Like It Scandalous

"But you definitely must try harder to act like you're seducing me," she ___ ___ not feeling the slightest bit ___ ___ ___ the knees or w___ ___ ___ re being swept of ___

___ ___ he dropped the ___ ___ ___ ent on giving her a tas___ ___ ___ medicine. "Let's fix that immediately.

"You don't have to do it *right now*—"

He gave her his wolfish smile. Then he leaned in close to whisper in her ear, but words failed him for a second. She smelled *good*. It was that heady fragrance. And her skin was smooth and dewy and just lovely. Hers was a complexion that begged to be caressed. That was just the skin politely exposed; he idly wondered about the rest of her . . .

Finally, he remembered what he meant to say. Something romantic and seductive. Two could play at this game of irritating each other profoundly. "What do you say we return to that gazebo and see if it's empty so we can be alone?"

"To do what, exactly?"

"Get to know each other better. Intimately."

Had they been alone he might have kissed her earlobe. Desire flared when the thought occurred to him.

Thank God they were not alone.

By Maya Rodale

The Gilded Age Girls Club
SOME LIKE IT SCANDALOUS
DUCHESS BY DESIGN

Keeping Up with the Cavendishes
IT'S HARD OUT HERE FOR A DUKE
LADY CLAIRE IS ALL THAT
CHASING LADY AMELIA
LADY BRIDGET'S DIARY

The Bad Boys and Wallflowers Series
THE BAD BOY BILLIONAIRE: WHAT A GIRL WANTS
WHAT A WALLFLOWER WANTS
THE BAD BOY BILLIONAIRE'S GIRL GONE WILD
WALLFLOWER GONE WILD
THE BAD BOY BILLIONAIRE'S WICKED ARRANGEMENT
THE WICKED WALLFLOWER

The Writing Girls Romance Series
SEDUCING MR. KNIGHTLY
THE TATTOOED DUKE
A TALE OF TWO LOVERS
A GROOM OF ONE'S OWN
THREE SCHEMES AND A SCANDAL

Maya Rodale

Some Like It Scandalous

❋ THE GILDED AGE GIRLS CLUB ❋

AVONBOOKS

An Imprint of HarperCollinsPublishers

SOME LIKE IT SCANDALOUS. Copyright © 2019 by Maya Rodale. All rights reserved. Printed in the United States of America. No part of this book may be used or reproduced in any manner whatsoever without written permission except in the case of brief quotations embodied in critical articles and reviews. For information, address HarperCollins Publishers, 195 Broadway, New York, NY 10007.

First Avon Books mass market printing: July 2019

Print Edition ISBN: 978-0-06-283883-4
Digital Edition ISBN: 978-0-06-283881-0

Cover design by Guido Caroti
Cover illustrations © Paul D'Innocenzo2018

Avon, Avon & logo, and Avon Books & logo are registered trademarks of HarperCollins Publishers in the United States of America and other countries.

HarperCollins is a registered trademark of HarperCollins Publishers in the United States of America and other countries.

FIRST EDITION

19 20 21 22 23 QGM 10 9 8 7 6 5 4 3 2 1

For the ladies who wear red lipstick
And the gentlemen who read romance

Some
Like It
Scandalous

Prologue

*M*iss Daisy Swan was not pretty. In the unlikely event that there was any doubt, her peers—fellow children of Manhattan's four hundred finest families—took it upon themselves to point out that hers was not a face that would launch one ship, let alone a thousand. Her nose was a trifle too large, her eyes a smidge too close together, and her mouth unfashionable. At present she was a gawky, ungainly girl of thirteen, with all the despair, yearning, and awkwardness that came with it. Yet Daisy harbored hope that one day she would become a woman who made the world look twice at her—in a good way—and want to know more.

While the other children in her social set played a rambunctious game of tag in the park, Daisy took a seat under the shade of a tree and did her best not to draw attention to herself. She had procured a copy of *Wells's Principles and Applications of Chemistry*, which lay open upon her lap, and which she was currently pretending to read.

In fact, she was eavesdropping on the nearby cluster of governesses and thinking her peers were fools to be running around rather than getting this crash course on the trials and tribulations of womanhood.

Their conversation included what to do about rakes and mashers who accosted one on the streets (a swift jab of a hat pin did the trick) and there were skin problems to solve, gripes about one's time of the month, fashions to discuss, and debates about whether or not to rent one of those new apartments downtown. Oh, and the gossip! Who was handsy, who was having an illicit affair, who drank too much or worse.

Daisy barely knew about being a girl, but she was learning all about being a woman.

She spared a glance for her fellow children running around in the blazing sun, ruining their complexions, and playing silly games when this was where the real action and drama was, even if it was only secondhand.

Among them was Theodore Prescott the Third.

He possessed a kind of beauty that made her heartsick.

All those luscious golden curls wasted on a

boy. Her hair couldn't decide if it was blond or brown but it had definitely made no attempt to do anything other than hang there, despite the best efforts of her maid, Sally. Daisy was outrageously jealous of Theodore's hair. He probably didn't even brush it. He probably didn't even *try* to look so good.

His eyes were large, dark pools of ocean blue and fringed by impossibly dark lashes with just a *hint* of curl. His mouth was almost cherubic. His beauty was almost feminine and it was *definitely* wasted on a boy, who had no need to be pretty like a woman did.

Daisy already knew that a woman's currency was her beauty and it didn't matter what a man looked like.

So when she looked at Theodore Prescott the Third, she seethed with jealousy.

Daisy straightened when she saw that Theodore was coming her way. She froze, book still open in her lap, as those blue eyes fixed on her. Her brain and her gut started sounding alarm bells.

He smacked her arm. "Tag. You're IT."

"I've always wanted to be the it girl," she replied. It was a rather witty, cheeky retort, she thought. One that wouldn't sail over his head if he was smarter.

He wasn't smarter. "Now you have to chase me."

Chasing meant running and running meant

sweating and panting and sunburn and all sorts of unappealing physical things that she would be teased about.

"I'd rather not," she demurred.

"What are you doing that's more important?"

"Reading. Eavesdropping. Not making a spectacle of myself."

They were having a whole entire conversation now—a stunning and unexpected turn of events. It did not escape the notice of the other girls, who closed ranks and surged closer as if to protect their golden boy from the gawky bluestocking he was speaking with.

"Besides, I think you have enough girls chasing after you already," she said.

Enough was apparently not a concept that appealed to Theodore Prescott the Horrid. No, he wanted *all* the girls hankering after him.

He leaned forward. *Wells's Principles and Applications of Chemistry* was wrenched cruelly from her hands by someone who could have no possible interest in it.

"Hey!" Daisy lunged for it.

Theo tossed it to his friends, two vile, spoiled boys named Daniel and Patrick, whose fathers reaped fortunes from coal and oil. They laughed, tossing the book back and forth between them, shouting, "Keep away from Daisy!"

Keep away from Daisy! Keep away from Daisy!

It was the stuff of nightmares, that chant.

They were perilously close to the duck pond, leaping from logs to rocks and back to the muddy shore. If they dropped it, she would have to buy another. She'd already had a row with her mother about whether it was appropriate reading for a young lady.

As the awful boys laughed with malicious glee while tossing her book between them, Daisy confirmed with one thousand percent certainty that she despised Theo, his friends, and all her classmates, who were cheering at this new "game."

And then it happened.

Daisy didn't know how exactly—it was all a blur. One minute she spied an opportunity to grab her book, one second later she reached for it, and all of a sudden she was falling backward.

Arms flailing. Lungs seizing. Heart stopping.

She landed with a splash in the duck pond, among the reeds and bright green duckweed floating on the surface.

She was soaking wet and covered in pond scum.

Beside her, a duck quacked.

And then, to her everlasting mortification, so did her classmates.

Quack! Quack! Quack!
Keep away from Daisy!
Quack! Quack! Quack!

Honestly, she couldn't decide what hurt more, the laughter or the feigned quacking or the sharp rock she'd landed on.

One voice rang out above the others: "Ugly Duck Daisy!"

It was Theodore Prescott the Horrid, smirking as he destroyed her life with three little words.

Keep away from Daisy!

Ugly Duck Daisy!

Quack! Quack! Quack!

It was then that Daisy decided hers would be a different path going forward. She would cut ties with her peers as soon as possible, for theirs was not a society she tremendously enjoyed and why should she run herself ragged, seeking their approval when all they'd do is *quack* at her?

She would never put herself on the marriage mart, subjecting herself to the appraisal and consideration of mean and petty men like these and the women who sought their favor. If that meant she would be alone, a spinster, so be it. No one would be able to hurt her. And who knew what she might accomplish when free from petty and pretty distractions?

And Daisy knew with utter certainty that she would hate Theodore Prescott the Third with every breath in her body until her dying day. Starting today.

Chapter One

Twelve years later
New York City, 1895
854 Fifth Avenue

*A*t the age of twenty-five, Miss Daisy Swan was still not pretty. Her nose was still a trifle too large, her eyes a smidge too close together, and her mouth inspired no man to raptures. Despite the secret, fervent prayers of her teenage self, she had not transformed from an ugly duckling into a beautiful Swan like her mother and sisters.

Perhaps on a good day, in the right light, and at a certain angle, she might be considered handsome.

Few young women wished to be considered handsome, at best, on a good day.

When one was handsome at best, and unmarried at the age of twenty-five, one anticipated spinsterhood.

Daisy was *quite* looking forward to it: she would soon complete her studies at the recently established Barnard College and, free from the expectation of marriage, would be able to pursue a life of independence. Then her life would *really* begin. This was all she'd ever wanted, ever since she'd been thirteen.

"Daisy, we need to talk," her mother said.

"Hmm." They were in the parlor of their town house on Fifth Avenue, overlooking Central Park. Daisy was happily reading a chapter on *Advanced Topics in Inorganic Chemistry* while idly sipping unsweetened tea.

"Daisy," her mother persisted. "We need to talk about your future."

"I have one year left of my studies. And then I shall discuss my future. That is what we agreed upon."

Daisy had hoped to delay discussions of marriage until she was so firmly on the shelf that no one would have hope of her making a match. She would then take her degree from college and . . . do something with it. She had ideas about creating and selling products for women that would make them look and feel beautiful. Daisy just wasn't quite sure how to go about it yet. She thought she had more time to figure it out.

But she had underestimated her mother, Mrs. Evelina Swan, who clearly had other ideas. Worse yet: she harbored ambitions.

"Yes, darling. But . . . hmmm."

Daisy was aware of her mother doing that thing she did: pursing her lips and giving the faintest hum that a more foolish or hopeful person would interpret as agreement. Daisy knew better.

"Mother, you are making a sound that indicates you no longer wish to be bound by our agreement. I'm fervently hoping that's not the case."

"You're always so blunt, darling. It's hardly attractive."

Her mother set down her tea. Daisy looked up from her book.

"I hardly see the point in making myself attractive. Especially when I am alone in the privacy of home with my mother, who is supposed to love me unconditionally."

"You know I do, Daisy."

Her mother did love her, even if she was nothing like her sisters. Rose, Camilla, and Lily were golden-haired, blue-eyed replicas of their mother. The four of them thrived on gorgeous gowns, small talk at parties, and champagne. They lived and breathed for soirees, nights at the opera, romantic intrigues, shopping the Ladies' Mile. Her sisters, of course, had all married well. One had even snared an English Viscount.

That just left Daisy. The ugly Swan sister. The one named after a weed.

"What do you wish to discuss, Mother?"

"Theodore Prescott."

"The second or the third?"

It was a distinction of the utmost importance.

Theodore Prescott the *Second* was one of Manhattan's most celebrated millionaire tycoons. His was a legendary rags-to-riches story; after humble beginnings working in a factory, he eventually came to own the factory. And another and another until he forged his own massive fortune in iron and steel. It was said that Prescott Steel was single-handedly supporting the new, towering Manhattan skyline.

With his impressive wealth, good looks, and brooding intensity, he was considered one of the more eligible bachelors of his day. His fortunes and status had been elevated when he married Miss Maribel Gold, the reigning beauty of her day.

But tragedy soon struck when she died shortly after the birth of their son.

Theodore Prescott the Second never remarried; instead, he threw himself into his work and doubled his fortune several times over. Widely respected, incredibly wealthy, and still one of the most handsome men in Manhattan—if one liked that distinguished, older-gentleman look, and many women did—he was still considered a catch and there was no small trail of broken hearts left in his wake.

But his son, Theodore Prescott the Third, was a menace.

He was the worst of the age: all excess and idleness and the enjoyment of inherited wealth.

Oh, he was a darling of Manhattan high society. A man that good-looking, that rich, so impeccably dressed and charming, would naturally be universally adored. Hostesses clamored to include him, and pretty young ladies aspired to be seated next to him at dinner. He and his friends—who Theo had dubbed the Rogues of Millionaire Row, and the press had adopted—used Manhattan as their playground and it seemed all they did was play. Nights at the theater, dalliances with opera singers, horse races in Saratoga, weekends yachting in Newport . . . The list of frivolities went on and on.

The gossips found him endlessly fascinating.

But to Daisy he was and would always be the boy who christened her Ugly Duck Daisy, a name that had plagued her ever since, and, as such, her mortal enemy.

Meanwhile, up the street . . .
901 Fifth Avenue

THEODORE PRESCOTT THE Third thought that the less said about the Saratoga Scandal, the better. But in this he held the minority opinion. It was all anyone who was anyone wanted to talk about, the newspapers especially.

His father, certainly, would have something to say about it.

Theo settled in for a lecture.

But first his father fixed him with that legendary

and nearly deadly stare. It had reduced seasoned businessmen into quivering, cowering messes who agreed to whatever demands he made. That stare, along with his father's sharp intelligence and enormous appetite for risk, had built this sprawling wood-paneled library, this massive house, this fortune.

One day Theo would inherit the library, the house, the fortune.

But not The Stare.

Whereas his father was tall, broad, and bearish, Theo was more like a lion: sleek, fair, and idle most of the time. The father took a perverse pleasure in looming over others and used his size and stature to intimidate. The son preferred to flirt. The elder Prescott loved nothing more than visiting his factories; Theo found it all rather sooty. Though they were father and son, they were as alike as night and day.

Much to the despair of his father.

As Theo was well aware.

"Theodore."

"Father."

"You've really done it this time. For the first time I don't even know where to begin."

"We could skip the conversation entirely," Theo offered. "Or we could cut to the part of the conversation where I apologize, admit that what I did was wrong, and promise not to do it again. Or at least not get *caught* again."

He flashed that grin that usually got him out of trouble, but his father missed it as his eyes were closed and he seemed to be counting back from ten under his breath. Probably praying for the Lord to save him from his indolent son.

"We could do that. But then I suspect we'd be back here in a month's time. Best to have this conversation now. Before it's too late."

"It was just a little mistake."

"It was not a little mistake. It was a monstrously expensive mistake." His father continued, "My expectations for you were always simple. Follow in my footsteps. But at your age I had already earned my first fortune. And you are . . ."

"The handsomest devil in Manhattan, last I checked," Theo quipped, in an attempt to lighten the mood. It was *heavy* in here. "According to *The New York World*, ladies everywhere, and the mirror."

"You are vain, Theo. You spend too much time on frivolous amusements. Your clothes, your friends, your ladies, your scandals. You have nothing to occupy you and you have no purpose."

This was not technically true. From a young age Theo understood that his one purpose was to follow in his father's footsteps, and to ruthlessly devote himself to the steel business. Unfortunately, he had absolutely no interest in the making and selling of steel, wrangling with workers over wages, or enduring the dirt and noise of the factory. This was not a calling in life that he wished to answer.

The problem was that he didn't have an alternative.

Theo knew what he liked: scintillating conversation, the thrill of seduction, beauty and style, and the finer things in life. He liked women. As far as he was aware, there was no industry that wanted his eye for beauty, or his talent for talk. He had no idea how to take what he was good at and enjoyed and turn it into a business that would earn a fortune of his own and thus his father's respect.

In the meantime he went yachting in Newport.

He consorted with actresses backstage on Broadway. He flirted his way from Fifth Avenue ballrooms to Bowery haunts and back again.

"The situation in Saratoga has made it clear. If you are not beyond redemption already, this is my last chance to make a man out of you."

He also went to the horse races in Saratoga. He consorted with actresses there, too.

His father was standing now, taking deliberate strides across the room. One was tempted to call it pacing, but his father's determined movements were not compatible with the aimlessness that pacing implied. No, this striding was for effect. To mesmerize. To demand one always keep watch and dominate the room. To impress his superiority and power over the other.

"Now, wait—"

"This is my last chance to mold you into a man we can both be proud of. A man of purpose. A man of accomplishment. You know that I do not fail, Theodore."

Theo was not opposed to becoming a man of purpose or accomplishment. But he was very opposed to what his father said next.

Meanwhile, at 854 Fifth Avenue . . .

"MARRIAGE!" DAISY SPIT out the word. Her mother had just included the words *you* and *Theo Prescott the Third* and *marriage* in the same sentence. And she was *serious.* "I am shocked. Horrified. Nauseated."

"Enough with all the vocabulary words, darling. You know men don't like women smarter than them."

"Which is why men are idiots, starting with Theodore Prescott the Third. I swear that man has tissue paper for brains."

"He's very charming and very handsome. Those blue eyes. That golden-blond hair. Very well dressed, too. That boy has an eye for a good suit and wears it well."

Daisy rolled her eyes.

"But he's also an utter wastrel, mother. He and his pack of friends are a bunch of spoiled, mean-spirited blights upon the city."

"You aren't still upset about that afternoon in the park all those years ago?" Just the mention of it made Daisy's anger flare. "That was years ago. A lifetime ago, practically."

It may have been a lifetime ago, but it felt like just yesterday. Laughter like that wasn't something a girl ever forgot. It was burned in her memory and inscribed in her soul.

"Indeed, it was years ago, Mother. More than a decade, in fact. And yet people still call me Ugly Duck Daisy. Just last week someone quacked when I went into supper."

Her mother mumbled something about boys being boys and getting over youthful indiscretions. Daisy was not inclined to agree. Mean boys grew up to be mean men and *youthful indiscretions* had a long half-life.

"I'm not still upset about it, if that's what you think, Mother. But when a man shows you who he is, believe him. Theodore Prescott the Third has shown that he cares only about appearances and impressing his idiot friends. The most recent example of which is the Saratoga Scandal. But there is no point in discussing this. I have no intention of marrying anyone, least of all Theodore Prescott the Third. I will eat my hat, feathers and hat pins and all, before I walk down the aisle to *him*."

"Daisy, I *really* must urge you to reconsider."

Her mother sipped her tea nervously. She refused to meet her daughter's eyes, piquing Daisy's curiosity.

"Why, Mother? Why must I consider an arranged marriage of mutual loathing?"

"I think you two might have some chemistry together . . ."

"That is patently false and absurd. You're the one who consoled me every time he, or his friends, or all the popular people teased me or excluded me. What is the real reason?"

And now Mrs. Evelina Swan was adding a heaping spoonful of sugar to her tea and taking a second bite of a sandwich. These were things she never, ever did—she was forever on a restricting regime—unless she was very upset indeed.

"What have you done, dearest mother?"

"Well. Theodore Prescott the Second and I were seated together at Mrs. Astor's dinner last week. Of course we talked about our children, given that you and Theo are the same age and did grow up together, in a way. After young Theo's trouble in Saratoga . . ."

No.

Daisy closed her eyes.

No. No. No.

Theo was in trouble and she was to be his penance.

"He thought marriage to the right woman would be just the thing for his son. Someone sensible. Disciplined. Unswayed by frivolity. I thought he might marry you."

Meanwhile, at the Prescott residence . . .

"I've decided what you need is a wife," Theodore Prescott the Second said to his son, who startled at the suggestion. Theo adored women, but so far none of the beautiful debutantes whose company he enjoyed could hold his attentions and affections for more than a fortnight, let alone the rest of their lives.

"I don't think marriage is the answer—"

"The right wife will force you to settle down and become serious about something. The right wife will keep you in line. You need someone sensible. A no-nonsense type of woman. Someone who will manage things for you."

"Are you advertising for a wife or a governess?"

His father fixed him with The Stare. "A wife."

"Clearly the stuff of romance and fantasies."

"I have just the woman in mind."

"I'm breathless with anticipation."

His father gave him a strong look of disapproval. Which cut all the more because all Theo ever wanted was his father's approval.

"You might as well tell me the name of this paragon of management whom I am to make my bride," Theo said, forcing himself to sound bored, when in fact his heart was thundering with rage and disappointment. He was being fobbed off, like last season's suit. Because his father was too busy with other more important things than his son—like making even more money. They did not need more money.

"Miss Daisy Swan."

Daisy Swan?

Theo's jaw dropped. Was his father out of his mind?

Theo took one look and saw that, no, his father was not insane or joking.

No one had ever uttered a more swift and immediate "no" than Theo in that moment.

"And why not?"

Theo didn't know how to *say* it. He wanted his father's attention—and maybe even his approval—for who he was, not who he married. He wanted to be wanted for who he was, flaws and all. He didn't want to be *delegated* to someone else, especially a bride he didn't choose.

Especially Daisy Quacking Swan.

But Theo did not know how to say these things. He could scarcely make sense of the feelings inside and articulate them in his mind, let alone put them into words that he would say aloud. To his father. Who was famous for intimidating people with just a stare. Theo had a first-rate education—he went to Harvard, even—but it had not included talking about his innermost feelings to the man whose approval he sought the most.

But his father was staring at him—that stare!—and he had to say *something*.

"She's not quite my type."

"On this we can agree. Your type tends to be breasty and breathy, with champagne for brains. Your type tends to inspire you to commit acts of grand larceny and disturbing the peace."

He was referring to Annabelle Jones, his costar in the Saratoga Scandal. She was a celebrated stage actress with whom he had absconded on a stolen horse and carriage owned by one of Saratoga's wealthiest men. For reasons he dared not breathe a word of.

His father leaned against the desk, leaned toward his son. "I think, speaking father to son, that you should try a new type."

Maybe. But Daisy Swan was not the solution.

He loved the social whirl while she preferred to stick her nose in a book. She was smart and she made sure everyone knew it. When she did attend parties, she stuck to her group of friends in the corner reserved for spinsters, suffragists, crones, and eccentrics. She even occasionally cast disapproving glances toward him and his fellow Rogues and the beautiful, stylish women who surrounded them.

Daisy wasn't exactly beautiful. He didn't consider her desirable. He hadn't considered her in that way at all, really. Theo did have some notion of actually *wanting* to be with his future wife.

But the thing he really disliked about Daisy Swan was her way of making him feel frivolous and vaguely silly. Ornamental, even. Not unlike how his father made him feel, come to think of it.

Theo did not want to spend the rest of his life shackled to a woman who thought him frivolous and vaguely silly.

"You cannot simply spend your days and nights living a life of idle amusements at your club with your questionable friends. I suppose it is my fault for allowing you to persist in the belief that you could. I thought you needed more time to develop a head and appetite for business but to my great regret, I fear you never will."

In other words, Theo was a hopeless case.

"This is my last chance to be a good father to you."

His father punctuated this with The Stare.

"This is my chance to make you into a man we can both be proud of."

"How about sending me to the army instead? Or downtown for a stint in the Tombs?"

He was only half joking.

"You will marry Daisy Swan. Or you will be cut off."

The twist of the knife was that all Theo ever wanted was his father's approval, though he so often settled for his attention. Getting his antics in the gossip columns was one of the few ways to get Theo the elder to lift his head from his desk and to step away from his business and give his son his undivided attention.

Was marrying Daisy Swan what Theo had to do to finally secure his father's good opinion? Or was marrying him off to a responsible, managing woman his father's way of washing his hands of Theo forever?

"I think I might have a purpose after all," Theo remarked as he stood and made his way to the door. "*Not* marrying Daisy Swan."

Meanwhile, at the Swan residence . . .

"I won't do it," Daisy said flatly. "Nothing in the world could compel me to even consider shackling myself to anyone I didn't love, let alone someone I loathe."

She had seen and heard enough to know that marriage, if not undertaken in precisely the right circumstances and with exactly the right person, would be a prison sentence. So many society women had married to advance their status and it made them miserable. There were not enough diamond brooches and ropes of pearls in the world to compensate for despising one's spouse.

Besides, Daisy had things she wished to do in life and nowhere on her list was marriage to a man like Theo, who would ignore her and embarrass her and invite his awful friends over to their home to tease and embarrass her there. She would have no respite.

Call her crazy, but Daisy thought she deserved better.

She thought she deserved love.

And if not that, then at least her independence. And she was *so close* to being an undeniable spinster, with all the freedom it promised.

Daisy looked out the windows and saw storm clouds gathering, heavy and dark in the sky, and it fit her mood perfectly.

"Now, darling, he's so handsome. His father is rich. Society adores them both."

"Not after what happened in Saratoga."

The newspapers spilled gallons and gallons of ink on his latest exploit. She'd heard that it involved a midnight dash on a stolen thoroughbred. With an infamous actress of some renown and a bedsheet wrapped around them both.

Very little was left to wonder.

Yet society managed to discuss it endlessly.

Marriage to her must be his penance and punishment. They probably wanted her to reform him. As if she didn't have better things to do with her time! As if she didn't have plans and ambitions of her own that did not involve the reformation of wayward rogues.

"Daisy—I beg of you to consider it."

Something in her mother's voice made Daisy turn away from the window, away from the storm clouds, away from her thoughts. "Why? What is the real reason, Mother?"

Her mother crossed the plush carpet to shut the engraved oak door to the parlor in their Fifth Avenue mansion.

"We need the money," her mother said in a low voice.

"Father is wealthy. His brokerage firm manages the fortunes of the wealthiest families in Manhattan. My sisters have all married well. We live in one of the finest residences in the city and count ourselves among Mrs. Astor's Four Hundred."

"We *will* need the money."

"You better explain everything."

"I cannot say," her mother exclaimed, while anxiously gripping the folds of her antique rose silk dress. It was a Worth gown, from Paris, to be treated with the utmost care. "Your father is involved in something . . . oh, *nefarious* is probably too strong a word but . . . I don't fully understand it. I've only overheard things. I know it's bad, Daisy, and so I need to see *all* my girls wed before the scandal breaks. Otherwise, what will become of us?"

"I'm sure we'll be fine. We have friends. We could go live with one of my sisters. I'm sure Rose, Camilla, or Lily would love your company."

"If you don't marry soon, you might not have a prayer of a decent marriage at all. Ever."

Excellent. "What if I don't wish to marry?"

"You must. There's no ladylike way to support yourself otherwise."

This was not quite true and Daisy knew it. Women all over the city worked in factories and as seamstresses, writers, servants, or other lowly positions that, admittedly, were not done by a woman of Daisy's station if they could help it. She wasn't above doing such honest work, but she knew there were other women who supported themselves by their wits and talents. Madam C. J. Walker owned her own business selling hair care products for women. Just last month she had seen the estimable Elizabeth Perkins Gilman speak on women's suffrage—she'd supported her family for decades by giving speeches and publishing a newspaper. Why, last year her mother redecorated their town house with furnishings purchased from Mrs. Ayer of Sypher's Antiques. And those were just the ones she knew of, off the top of her head.

Her mother may not wish to acknowledge such women, but Daisy looked to them like a beacon. They gave her hope of making her own dreams come true.

But this was not a conversation to have while her mother was in such an agitated state.

"What has Father done that would bankrupt

us so completely?" Daisy asked. He was the president of a brokerage firm and incredibly sought after for his wisdom and investment advice and consistently generous returns. He spent most days at his office and evenings at his club. When she was younger, her father had often discussed business in her presence but since she made her debut, she'd been left to her mother's care.

"I cannot say," her mother said.

"You owe me an explanation, Mother. You can't ask me to do something like this without a full explanation."

"When I say I cannot, I mean that I can't explain—I don't quite understand it. It's all very complicated and quite possibly not even legal. I overheard some things, you see, and when I mentioned it to your father, he said our situation was dire and that I should make sure our girls are taken care of sooner rather than later."

"What did you hear? What did he say?"

Her mother repeated some choice words, like *fraudulent* and *investment* and did her best to explain what seemed to be a dire situation.

"Oh, damn," Daisy whispered.

Jack Swan was not exactly a family man. He was forever busy with his work, his schemes, his whatever he did that kept the family in luxury. No one ever asked questions—as long as her mother had the latest fashions and Daisy's tuition was paid, they had no reason to question the source of the family's wealth.

But maybe they should have.

They definitely should have.

If her mother had the right of it. Daisy had learned at a young age that her mother wasn't as flighty as people often assumed her to be.

"Until then we need to keep up appearances. You must marry, and soon, and it must be someone like Theodore Prescott the Third. Or else—"

Marriage to a powerful man—submerging herself in his name and social standing—was the obvious thing to do, the easy way out of any scheme or scandal. She would be somewhat protected from the worst of a scandal, and her mother would be at liberty to take an extended tour of the continent until the worst of it blew over. But Daisy would have to live with him— Theo—as his wife. Forever. Marriage was a shortsighted solution.

And Daisy had other ideas.

She, too, harbored ambitions.

She saw, perhaps, another way.

"I won't be used as a pawn," she said. "I will not sacrifice the rest of my life because of one potential scandal. If the situation is really dire," Daisy continued, "I shall find another way. I could earn the money."

"This isn't your scheme to make and sell

complexion balm, is it? I have told you, Daisy. No respectable woman would be seen buying it, let alone wearing it." Her mother closed her eyes and groaned. She had resumed lying on the fainting couch. "And how will it look for one of Manhattan's finest families to have a daughter engage in trade?"

"I thought we were facing catastrophic scandal. Who will care at that point?"

"It will only make things worse. Besides, you'll never make enough to keep yourself in the style in which you were raised."

Yes, the standards were high—they lived in one of the premier residences in Manhattan and moved in the best circles. But Daisy could point to other women who had earned such fortunes—Madam C. J. Walker. Or her dressmaking friend, Adeline Black, who was well on her way to doing so. Or—and this was a scandalous thought in the present age—Daisy could be happy with *enough*. Society bored her. One only needed so many dresses.

"Maybe I don't need to live in the style in which I was raised."

"Even *if* you embarked on your mad scheme, Daisy, you'll need your good reputation and social standing to convince the women of society to try your silly product. You must marry him! It's the best way, the only way, to ensure your future."

One look in her mother's eyes revealed that Mrs. Evelina Swan was committed. She truly feared for the looming scandal and would do anything to avoid it or protect her daughter from it.

But Daisy had gotten one thing from her mother, if not her looks: the same stubborn streak and iron will. "I refuse. I simply won't do it."

And with that, she stormed out.

Unfortunately, she did so without her coat. Or hat. Or umbrella.

The sky was a putrid, purple gray, thick with menacing clouds, and promised an unholy deluge of rain. It was only four o'clock in the afternoon but the world was shrouded in the darkness of a later hour. It was a dreadful time for storming out of the house in a self-righteous fury and forgetting one's things. But one could not sheepishly return for them and attempt to slink out of the house again.

It would ruin the effect and lessen the point: she was determined to live on her own terms. By her own wits.

Even if scandal was about to hit.

Even if her family was about to fall apart.

Even if it was about to storm.

She would not marry a man with whom she shared nothing but a mutual loathing.

This was not what she wanted from her one and only life.

Once she had entered the gates for the park, just steps from her home, she had successfully stoked those sparks and embers of anger at the situation into a full, roaring blaze of fury.

The park was desolate as wiser, less furious people scurried to seek shelter from the coming storm.

Defiant, Daisy turned her face up toward the sky, relishing the cooler air on her hot skin, which was never normally exposed so brazenly to the elements.

Her complexion was her one true vanity. Daisy had no apologies for it, either. Whatever her features might be, her complexion was the stuff of envy: smooth, luminous, unblemished, and soft to the touch.

She took great, great care of her one beauty.

She thought she might even make a fortune of her own from her one vanity.

With her face upturned and her eyes closed, Daisy didn't see him until it was too late. They came face-to-face before she could take another path, or turn around and march back from where she'd come, or fling herself in the duck pond. Just like old times.

The devil himself.

Theodore Prescott the Third.

Chapter Two

Central Park

*I*n no uncertain terms, beyond a shadow of a doubt, Daisy Swan was the last person Theo wished to see right now. Because Theo was having the worst day of his life, there she was, stomping through the park with the grace and elegance of a deranged dowager in high dudgeon.

Circumstances were such that it was impossible to avoid each other.

Their eyes met.

There was a rumble of thunder. It was not distant.

"You." She breathed the word like it was an accusation of murder.

"You," he replied in kind.

At that exact moment, the sky cracked open and unleashed a deluge.

She shrieked in shock, in outrage, in anger.

And then she ran toward the nearest shelter—

a gazebo nestled among some foliage. It was a popular spot for lovers.

Because the basic biological instinct to seek shelter in a storm apparently outweighed his desperate wish to have nothing to do with Daisy Swan, Theo followed her.

"You are the last person I wish to see right now," she said. Nevertheless, he leapt up the steps and joined her in the gazebo. The roof protected them from the rain, but the open sides still left them exposed to the elements.

Theo glared at her for a long, hot second. His father wanted him to wed and bed this rain-drenched and scowling creature who wanted nothing to do with him. Impossible. Not even for his father's approval—because the thing he wanted even more than that was something like a tender connection with another human. Not that he could ever *say* that without mockery from his peers. Not that he could ever find that with this sharp-tongued spinster.

"I assure you, the feeling is mutual. Was it your idea, Daisy?"

"Oh, you think this is some grand plan for a bluestocking spinster to land one of the city's most eligible bachelors?" She scoffed. "You may have difficulty conceiving of this in your undoubtedly sleep-deprived and alcohol-addled male brain, but I have no wish to marry you."

Good, Theo thought.

To hell with her, he thought.

And *me, too.*

Being eaten alive by reptiles was preferable to marriage with a woman who looked at him like he was insignificant, unworthy, and unwanted, which was the way she looked at him now and every other time they'd met ever since they were children.

But he also thought, *Why not?*

He was handsome, everybody said so. He came from wealth. Was impeccably dressed. He was sought out at parties, a coveted dinner table companion, and never wanted for the flirtations of beautiful women.

Miss Daisy "Ugly Duck" Swan could do no better than him.

So what did she want, then?

He did not care what she wanted, he told himself, and refused to consider it.

"Well, I don't want to marry you, either," he said. "Being lost at sea on a raft without food, water, or a hat would be preferable."

"I would rather be stranded on the Alps in nothing but my unmentionables and wet stockings."

"We are in violent agreement," he said. He watched as she turned away to stick her head out of the gazebo. The rain was lashing down furiously. "Why are you sticking your head out like that?"

"I am trying to determine if I would rather risk drowning in a rainstorm or catching my death of a chill than stay here with you."

"Don't let me keep you."

"I could say the same. You must have very, very important things to attend to."

The sarcasm in her voice did not go unnoticed. They both knew that he had no important business to attend to, unless one counted calling on the popular ladies of the Four Hundred with whom he enjoyed friendships and flirtations— all of whom were insufficiently managing to be considered a suitable wife for him.

After all, he thought with some sarcasm, they were all just as pretty and flighty as himself.

Maybe he would rather go down to the factories and learn the business than marry her.

He *hated* the factories.

"Oh, come on, Daisy. I'm not so awful that you won't spend a quarter of an hour bickering while waiting out a rainstorm? This is one of those summer storms that will be over in a moment."

"You are awful enough that I do not wish to be caught in a compromising position with you. Which this may be construed as, given our current situation."

They were unwed and alone, not a chaperone in sight. And their parents were determined.

"Good God, you're right."

"It's a perfectly evil but genius plan to wed us.

You are in trouble after that Saratoga business and—" She stopped short and caught her words before they left her mouth. "And my mother wishes to have all her daughters wed. I assume your father and my mother have conspired."

"A pox on whichever hostess sat them next to each other."

"We can agree on that at least."

"God, what if they send someone out searching for us?" He pushed his fingers through his hair in frustration; it was already a mess from the rain so why not?

"They couldn't have known that we would both storm out in an uproar."

"They are fools if they thought we would simply agree to their outrageous plot."

"Given their aims, this would be too good an opportunity not to seize. Finding us here like this. My mother has ideas. And reasons."

Mothers always did. There was no more fearsome adversary than a woman who harbored matrimonial ambitions for her child. They were almost as fearsome as his father.

"And you, Daisy?"

"What I have are other plans that do not involve you," she said coolly. In spite of himself, Theo was curious, but he would die a slow death before inquiring.

"I also have other plans," he said loftily, to sound just as important.

She looked skeptical. Which was infuriating. Perhaps she *was* in league with his father.

"I have plans to tour all the opera houses of Europe," he said. It was the first thing that came to mind.

"Opera singers, you mean," she corrected. Because she already thought him a rogue, Theo winked at her. She rolled her eyes.

"Well, I have plans to commit myself to an insane asylum," he replied, drawing up to his full height and stepping closer to her. "It seems preferable."

"I have plans to trek through the desert dressed in full mourning attire. Sounds so much more pleasant than marriage. To you."

She took a step forward and jabbed him in the chest with her finger. They were now so close he could feel the heat and fury radiating from her.

"I thought it might be more fun to spend an extended stint in the Tombs with an incomplete deck of cards," he retorted.

"What are we *actually* going to do?" she asked, stepping away.

"Not get married, *obviously*," he replied.

"Yes, but *how*?"

"How are we going to *not* get married?" Baffled, he replied, "I should think it's easy. We just don't do it."

"You shouldn't think. It doesn't suit you. It'll give you wrinkles on that pristine and perfect forehead of yours. Have you met your father or my mother? They are worthy adversaries. They have *reasons*."

He gave a short exhale, a huff of vexation. Why? Why him? Why now? Why *her*?

Also, he did *not* have wrinkles.

Because of the Saratoga Scandal. Because he'd caused a scene with the wrong kind of woman one too many times, he now needed to present himself with the right kind of woman. The sensible, managing kind who will make him into the sort of man his father could be proud of. Or at least not embarrassed by. It was what he wanted, at a price he didn't want to pay.

"Let us gather the facts," she said, keeping her firm control of the conversation. "Our parents wish for us to be wed to each other."

"Yes."

"We have no wish to do so."

"Right. Correct. Scientific fact. Gospel truth."

"And I have other plans."

"Same," he said, even though he did not have other plans. He really ought to get other plans, immediately.

"As long as we are *not* engaged, they will make every effort to throw us together," she said as she started to walk in circles around him as the rain continued to lash down. "We will find ourselves seated next to each other at suppers, stuffed in opera boxes together, forced to dance at parties.

We shall constantly be at risk for entrapment, discovery, scandal. It will make life unbearable. To say nothing of the inevitable parental nagging."

She was pacing now, back and forth before him, like a general plotting a battle or a sleuth outlining the facts of a murder. Like his father in his study, earlier, determining his plans. He watched her warily out of the corner of his eye. Her hair was a sopping-wet bedraggled mess and her dress wasn't much better. Her lips were moving as she mumbled to herself.

In fact, if he took her down to Bellevue right now to have her committed, it was likely no one would question it. Theo was seriously considering it—he assumed one could not marry a person committed to an insane asylum—when she said the craziest thing yet.

"And thus, the logical thing to do would be to claim an engagement," she declared. "To simply agree."

Wait.

What?

Theo startled, stood straight. He had not been listening.

"Now, wait a minute here—"

"Hear me out, pretty boy." She raised a hand to silence his protests. "If our parents think that we are acquiescing to their wishes, they'll leave us alone to pursue our other plans and interests. In fact, we can use the excuse of seeing each other to pursue those other interests. You did mention having other plans, did you not?"

She was warming to her idea now. He could see it. Her cheeks were flushed. Her eyes were bright. Why, she was almost pretty, all alight with her own genius.

She was also mad. Insane. Off her rocker. A danger to his liberty.

He really ought to have her committed.

"You are forgetting about mothers and weddings," Theo pointed out. "They love to plan them. Purchase things for them. Commission gowns and trousseaus. Reserve the church and invite hundreds of people to witness the blessed event. This scheme could quickly and easily get out of control. Especially if we are not paying attention because we are doing other things."

She opened her mouth to protest, but stopped. "As much as agreeing with you physically pains me, I must admit that you do have a point."

"How magnanimous of you."

"Look at you with the big words."

"I went to Harvard, you know."

"Of course I know that. Everybody does. Harvard people have a way of working it into conversation. I'm just not sure that you attended classes while you were there."

"If this is your way of wooing me to your cause, I can see why you're a spinster. It's one thing to have a sharp tongue but—"

"But what, pretty boy?"

"Nothing. Never mind."

"You were about to say that I'm not pretty enough and I have a sharp tongue and you cannot risk being wed to me for the rest of your life because how could you endure looking at or listening to me? And goodness, what will they say at the club?"

She feigned mock horror.

"They will say you're the luckiest girl in New York to be wed to a handsome, wealthy charmer like me."

"Oh, please."

"We both know it's true."

"Depends on your definition of *luck*. A loveless marriage isn't mine. I ought to leave you to fend for yourself."

With that, she turned on her heel and walked resolutely out into the storm.

Good, Theo thought. *To hell with her.*

But she was already gone.

Chapter Three

Good riddance, Theo thought, as he strode determinedly through the park to his club. If he never saw Daisy Swan again in this lifetime, it would be too soon. The way she walked and talked in circles around him was maddening. He couldn't stand the way she gazed shrewdly at him through her stormy eyes, like she looked past his handsome face and fine attire and saw . . . nothing but a pretty face.

He was so much more than that. Good hair, for example. A lean, muscular body kept firm and trim by regular sport and clad in the finest from Savile Row. He was good at cards, an excellent companion for yachting and waltzing. If there was a best-dressed list, he'd be on it.

It was a short walk through the park—through the rain—to his club, a haven from managing fathers and maddening females and his present impossible situation. Theo's immediate plans involved drying off, having a drink, lamenting extensively about the situation to his friends, Daniel and Patrick, and then sorting out what to do.

Perhaps he'd come up with some occupation that would bring him such success that he could afford to disregard his father's wishes or maybe even earn his grudging approval.

Perhaps he'd think of someone else to marry instead. He and Miss Esme Pennypacker had an ongoing flirtation that could turn into forever. Or perhaps he and Miss Victoria Gould could finish what they'd started last summer.

Or not.

There was to be no respite. Upon arrival at The Metropolitan Club, the exclusive haunt for all the new money robber barons and their sons, Theo was stopped and informed, delicately, that his club membership had been suspended for reasons best not discussed.

Theodore Prescott the Second was rumored to be ruthless, and now Theo had his own taste of it. This was his father's heavy-handed way of forcing the match.

Marry Daisy Swan or you will be cut off.

If it was actually possible for a man to die of embarrassment, Theo would have expired on the spot in an explosive burst of guts, anger, and humiliation. Worse luck: he survived.

It was one thing to be gossiped about for one's exploits with an actress, one of his many infamous dalliances that portrayed him as a playboy who got all the girls. It was another matter entirely to be informed that he was not one of the great gentlemen of New York. And thus, the world.

It was one thing not to have the respect or admiration of his father—he'd never had that ever since it became clear that Theo wasn't some rough-and-tumble boy, destined to succeed his father as a ruthless steel magnate. But to be cut off from his friends and society, too—well, that was too much. He was the sort who thrived on the social whirl. Because first it was his club. Next Mrs. Astor's guest list. And then he was done. Finished in this town. Cut off from the friendly banter, sparkling laughter, and glittering parties that sustained him.

There was nothing he could do about it.

There was nothing else he could even do. No way he could think of to earn money to support himself without his father's money. It burned, that.

That burning gave rise to a peculiar new feeling; one might have called it determination or ambition. Being made so aware of his position of dependency stirred something within him. A determination to stand alone.

Theo vowed that he would find something to succeed at. Spectacularly. He would earn his own fortune, on his own terms. And then he would finally get his father's respect. He would never, ever be at anyone's mercy again.

But first, he needed Daisy Swan.

Before he hit the streets, he wrote a quick letter to her. Though he would die a thousand slow, humiliating deaths before admitting it, if he was stuck playing this game, he could do worse than teaming up with a smart girl like her.

Meanwhile, uptown . . .
854 Fifth Avenue

DAISY HAD ONLY been out for an hour, but it was apparently enough time for her mother to completely and thoroughly ruin her life. Or rather, to request a maid do it. For there, in the foyer, was her maid, Sally, carrying a box of items that looked suspiciously like Daisy's most treasured possessions.

"Where are you going with my things, Sally?"

"I'm so sorry, Miss Daisy," Sally said in her soft Irish accent, her eyes apologetic. "I'm only following orders."

Her mother threw open the parlor doors as if she'd been waiting for Daisy to return home.

"There you are, darling!" Daisy stood before her, her skirts dripping on the marble floor. "Did you have a nice walk? It looks like you were caught in the rain."

A nice walk.

Caught in the rain.

And now *this*.

"What is this, Mother?" Daisy asked, waving her arms in the general direction of Sally and the box she carried that all at once contained her greatest hopes, dreams, and chances. Glass beakers and dishes, her scales, her experiments in progress.

"Out with the old and in with the new, darling. It's just your chemistry supplies and . . . your experiments, I suppose we can call them. Rubbish, really."

"It's not rubbish. It's science." Daisy fought to keep her voice measured. Because it wasn't just science. "It is my life's work. My passion."

It was her *out*. Within the year she would be considered too old to wed *and* she would have a degree in chemistry, which would qualify her for some employment, though the opportunities would not be vast or lucrative. Because Daisy had even grander ideas.

She thought of creating products and selling them, a balm for the complexion, in particular. She would make womankind feel a little more beautiful *and* earn her own independence. If that wasn't happily-ever-after, she didn't know what was.

"Whatever it is, you won't need it when you're married," her mother said. "And you certainly won't have time for it while you're engaged. We have an announcement to plan, a wedding to throw. And your trousseau! Consuelo Vanderbilt has gold hooks on her corset and diamond-encrusted garters. I want nothing less for you."

"Mother, I need my chemistry supplies and experiments so that I don't have to get married. At all. Ever. To anyone. Especially Theodore Prescott the Third."

"Come now, Daisy. You're not going to support yourself with all those bits and bobs and science bits. You're a woman of a certain station. It's just not done."

But it *was* done. Martha Harper had opened hair salons that society women were starting to flock to. Adeline Black was taking society by storm with her new dressmaking establishment that made dresses with pockets. To say nothing of all the women writing for the newspapers. Nellie Bly. Jane Croly. And those were just the ones that Daisy knew. There were so many women striking out alone and succeeding.

"The world is changing, Mother. And I intend to change with it."

"Daisy, I just want you to be happy and I know that marriage is just the thing." Then, dropping her voice because Sally was still standing there, awkwardly holding the box and awaiting direction of what to do with it, her mother said, "Especially given what we discussed earlier."

What they discussed earlier was—and her mother had stressed this vehemently—not to be discussed. But suffice it to say, something had to be done about her future security and *soon*.

"If you truly wanted me to be happy, you would let me finish my studies and seek employment. Let me have a little more time before we discuss such things. In one year I'll be done with my degree and—"

"No." Her mother's tone was firm. Unyielding. Daisy knew her mother was stubborn but she'd never seen her like this. "You must marry Theodore Prescott the Third and *soon*. I know society, and I know there is no other way to survive this looming catastrophe."

Daisy leveled a hard stare at her mother. But Mrs. Swan was not dissuaded. Her beautiful mother, who serenely swept through life with a lilting laugh and a lovely smile, stood firm. There was a hardness in her eyes. "Listen to reason, Daisy. Even if you did wish to make a success of your scandalous idea, you'll need your good name and reputation to do it. And given the looming scandal, that means you'll need the Prescott name."

Blast, if her mother wasn't entirely wrong.

The butler, Groves, interrupted the stalemate between mother and daughter.

"Miss Swan, a letter for you." He presented a silver tray bearing a crisp white envelope flecked with raindrops.

With a huff of vexation, Daisy tore it open. Good Lord, it was from him.

Daisy,

Circumstances are such that, under duress, I have reconsidered your idiotic proposal and determined it is not, in fact, the worst and stupidest idea I have ever heard.

I'm in, are you?

Chapter Four

Mr. Theodore Prescott the Second, together
with Mr. and Mrs. Jack Swan, announce
the betrothal of their children, Theodore
Prescott the Third and Miss Daisy Swan.
—*The New York Times*

The next night
Mrs. Cooke's Ballroom

*T*heir agreement was simple: Daisy and Theo
would tell the world they were engaged with the
understanding that they would never, ever say *I
do.* There was no expectation that they would pretend to even like each other, let alone love. There
had been little—very well, *no*—considerations of
how society would respond to the news of their
engagement or what it would feel like to stand
up together in front of Manhattan's finest.

"Didn't quite think this through, did you?"
Theo murmured. Beside him Daisy's cheeks were
pink and hot with some combination of anger and

mortification. Someone in the crowd had actually quacked as they were announced. The rest of them just laughed softly. Some way to congratulate them.

Just tell them we're engaged, she said.

They'll leave us alone, she said.

We'll go our separate ways, she said.

He took the slightest comfort in the fact that she didn't know everything.

"You didn't, either," she retorted. And it was true. He, being fluent in the ways of society, should have anticipated this reaction and strategized. Vexed at the mistake and being called out on it, he replied without thinking.

"Well, you're the brains," he said. But it was the words he didn't say that were understood, that were unintentionally cruel. *And I'm the beauty.*

By mutual, unspoken agreement they retreated to separate corners of the ballroom at the first possible opportunity; she with her friends and he with his. They would probably never speak to each other again.

"Engaged, Theo?" Daniel guffawed. Again.

Daniel Thomas, whose family made a fortune in coal, was great fun to spend time with because he found the simplest things endlessly amusing and let it be known with his loud belly laugh. But tonight Theo found it irritating. Probably because he was on the receiving end of it for once.

"Just last week you were riding high, literally, with the most sought-after actress." Patrick Cavanaugh, heir to an oil fortune, smiled smugly. "And now . . ."

It was another sentence that didn't need to be finished to be understood.

"You're engaged to *her*."

They were three of Manhattan's most eligible bachelors. Wildly wealthy, blessed with good looks, and a devil-may-care spirit that many women tended to find irresistible. But not all women.

For the first time in perhaps ever, these three rogues looked across the ballroom to the corner where Daisy stood with her friends—the outcasts, the eccentrics, the not-quites. The distance between them was just the length of a ballroom and yet it seemed vast and insurmountable.

Daisy did not look like a woman happy to be announcing her betrothal.

"Lucky girl, huh?" Patrick said dryly.

"Lucky Duck!" Daniel shouted.

A burst of laughter that indicated Daisy Swan would henceforth be known as Lucky Duck Daisy. Which, given the circumstances, was cruel indeed.

"You'd think *she* would be happier to have landed *you*," Patrick said, somewhat confounded by the prospect of a woman who wasn't ecstatic to be wedding the likes of them.

Theo didn't quite understand it himself. But it had to be just her because soon enough, the rogues were surrounded by the prettiest, wittiest, and wealthiest debutantes in the city. The kind of girls that made all the others jealous. The girls enveloped them in a cloud of taffeta and tulle, perfume and soft laughter, and pretty pouts.

"What is so funny?" Miss Victoria Gould asked. "We heard you laughing from the far side of the ballroom."

"That Theo is engaged to Lucky Duck Daisy," Patrick said with a smirk. "Can you believe it? I can't believe it."

"So it is true! I thought it had to be a joke when I read it in the paper this morning," Miss Penny-packer said. She laughed. Theo did not.

"She doesn't look very lucky," Patrick said. "In fact, she looks like she's off to the gallows."

"But who wouldn't want to marry our Theo?" Miss Gould asked. She linked her arm with his, tilted her face up, and batted her lashes prettily. Theo struggled to remember why he didn't just run off with a pretty, wealthy girl like her. It would be so easy. But then he wouldn't have accomplished anything. His father wouldn't be proud of him. And all they'd have to talk about for the rest of their lives were parties.

Suddenly, he wanted more than parties.

"Lucky Duck Daisy, apparently," Daniel replied.

"This is your father punishing you for what happened in Saratoga, isn't it?" Patrick asked, lifting one brow with a knowing smirk. Like all the others, Patrick thought he knew what happened that night. But he had no idea.

"Looks like you got a lifetime sentence," Miss Gould quipped.

"If your father wanted you to get married, you could have run off with me, Theo," Miss Pennypacker cooed.

"Or me," Miss Gould added.

"Why didn't you call us, Theo?"

The girls swarmed around him with their perfume and questions. Theo did not have a good answer. He just knew that for the first time in his life, he wanted something more.

On the other side of the ballroom

THERE WAS A corner in each and every ballroom where those who wished not to be bothered with the preening and posturing that went on at parties gathered. After her disastrous presentation with Theo, Daisy plucked a glass of champagne from a passing waiter and made her way directly there. She held her head high and did her best to ignore the looks and stares as she passed. She was rather used to being ignored by most in society and already she missed it.

She took a sip and welcomed the company of

her friends: Miss Harriet Burnett and her constant companion, Miss Ava Lumley. Once upon a time Harriet had refused an unwanted marriage proposal—and found herself cut off from society as a result. She'd since inherited a fortune, and with the companionship of Miss Ava Lumley, a respected society woman, found herself back in the whirl of things.

"What on earth was that spectacle?" Harriet asked, gesturing in the general direction of Daisy, Theo, and the farce of a debut they'd just made.

"That was an act of desperation. Starring yours truly and my mortal enemy."

"I almost couldn't believe it when I read it in the paper this morning," Ava said. "But if it's in *The New York Times*, it must be true. And tonight's display only proves it."

"So you really are engaged?" Harriet asked, somewhat aghast. "To *him*?"

"Much as it pains me to say yes, I must. *The New York Times* has all the facts. We are engaged. In a manner of speaking."

Harriet's eyes lit up, understanding that something else was up. She stepped in closer. "What's the real story?"

For the first time all evening, Daisy truly smiled. This was why she loved her friends—because while everyone else in the ballroom thought that Theo was condescending to marry

Daisy, her friends believed that she was the catch and could do better than him.

"Our parents want the match. We do not. We are pretending to be engaged so that they'll leave us alone."

"Interesting strategy. But how are you going to get out of it?" Harriet asked. "Of course you are going to get out of it."

This, Daisy thought, was also why they were friends.

"Maybe you won't have to," Ava said. "This could be the beginning of a grand romance."

The three ladies burst out laughing at a most unladylike volume. Heads turned. People glared. How dare these outcast and eccentric women enjoy themselves!

"I cannot imagine a world in which Theodore Prescott the Worst and I live happily ever after."

"What will you do to get out of it?" Harriet wanted to know. "The stakes are too high to take this risk without a solid, foolproof, and fail-safe plan."

"I do have a plan," Daisy said. "But you'll have to wait until Thursday."

Chapter Five

One of the Rogues of Millionaire Row
is expected to wed the one spinster
Swan sister. Wagers are already being
placed on the outcome of the match.
—*The New York Post*

Thursday
Central Park

*T*he newspapers were not any kinder this morning as they reported on the disastrous debut and comical reception of the couple of the hour: the Millionaire Rogue and the Ugly Duckling. The newspapers and gossip columns were beside themselves sharing every last detail about their chilly behavior toward each other, anonymously quoting outrageous speculation about the reasons for the mismatch, and reporting on all the wagers made on the outcome. Odds were not in favor of *I do*.

Their parents were furious. *Furious.*

And embarrassed. Which only made them more furious.

Frankly, they weren't the only ones. Theo did have his pride, after all. He didn't know who he was without the good opinion of society.

Something had to be done.

And so, presumably at the behest of her mother, Daisy was seated by his side as Theo expertly navigated his carriage through the busy pathways of Central Park. Around them, people walked, picnicked, frolicked, and generally enjoyed the legendary green space.

Daisy wore one of those atrocious, large-brimmed hats that were the fashion these days. One could hardly see the woman underneath. Just . . . hat, perched upon dress.

Still, he'd wager that the expression on her face was one of: *What are we doing here? I no longer recognize my life and how does one make it stop?*

These were questions he also wanted answers to.

"It has been reported, in no uncertain terms, that last night was a disaster," he began.

"Ah, so you have read the papers. Or maybe your father had 'a word' with you the way my mother had 'a word' with me. In the unlikely event that it wasn't abundantly clear during each agonizing moment of the ball last night?"

"I told you, I went to Harvard. I am not an

ignoramus. I was well aware of the horror that was our debut. The newspapers this morning only confirmed it."

What she said next surprised him.

"It's just you're *so pretty*, Theo. One cannot expect you to be intelligent *and* be pretty."

"I am not pretty," Theo replied hotly. "Men are not pretty. If anything, I am boyishly handsome."

"Your father is handsome. In a distinguished, silver fox kind of way. *You* are pretty. Those blond curls. Those blue eyes. That pout of a mouth. Perhaps in thirty years you'll age into handsome."

"Let's not discuss my father. Especially like that." Theo was not in the mood to hear of yet another way in which he did not live up to his namesake. "How would you like it if we discussed your mother thusly?"

"My mother was once described as eighth of the ten most beautiful women in New York. Everyone discusses her thusly. I am *quite* used to it."

Theo did not mention the newspaper just this morning that had described Daisy in starkly opposing terms—"A woman who spent her evenings in the dim corner of ballrooms where the light suited her best."

"And then there's me," Daisy continued candidly. "So unlike her in every imaginable way. No, I wasn't dropped as an infant or acquired from a foundling hospital in case you were wondering."

"People don't actually say that." Theo glanced

at her. She was no Helen of Troy but she wasn't awful to look at.

"Oh, yes," she answered. "Many think it and more than a few have 'joked' about it. To say nothing of all the Ugly Duck comments."

Theo felt shame start to rise. He still remembered that day when he had come up with the name. It had felt good to make everyone laugh—but then he hadn't considered that they were laughing *at her*. He thought they were laughing at his wit. And he never thought the name would stick. He'd always had a knack for quips and nicknames. The Rogues of Millionaire Row, the Saratoga Scandal. And those were just the recent examples.

She continued, "Hardly funny, if you ask me, but I do see their point. Have you seen my mother and my sisters? Three nearly identical specimens of ideal feminine beauty. Those blond curls. Those blue eyes. That pout of a mouth. People cannot believe a creature so beautiful spawned someone who looks like me."

She spoke as if it was all very matter-of-fact. And he had to look. To confirm.

He merely saw hat.

A ghastly, wide-brimmed affair all aflutter with feathers and ribbons.

But they had grown up together. They'd spent the entire previous evening together. He knew what she looked like.

Sure, her mother and sisters were the ideals of female beauty and she was . . . not. Her nose was a little too much, her eyes perhaps a little too close together, her jaw more square than heart shaped. She turned her head and he saw her pink lips pressed firmly together.

That gave it away: she did not feel so matter-of-fact about her looks at all.

"You're very fixated on your appearance," Theo observed.

"How ironic that *you* should mention it. Why do you think that is? You were the one who called me Ugly Duck."

Theo winced at the memory. They had all been playing in the park on a blue-sky day, not unlike this one. Correction: he and the others had been playing but she refused to join the game. Like she was better than them. Like she had a purpose. Even then, he'd been jealous. His immature efforts to involve her, to bring her down to their level, involved teasing. With lasting consequences. He'd been an ass. There were no excuses to be made for it.

"I apologize," he said genuinely. "Ghastly behavior on my part. But in my defense, I was only thirteen. Everyone knows that thirteen-year-old boys are not exactly the high point of humanity."

"Thank you for your apology over a decade after the fact, when irreparable damage has been done," Daisy said dryly. "Now if only we could get everyone else to stop saying it."

"No one still calls you that," Theo scoffed, defensive. "It was *years* ago."

"It was in the newspaper this morning. *Ugly Duck Snares Millionaire Rogue.* Your friends quacked at me in the ballroom just last night."

Theo winced. Again.

"I'm sorry. I'm truly sorry."

"It is catchy. I would almost say that you have a knack for names and such."

Her compliment caught him off guard. No quick, sharp reply came to mind other than a simple "Thank you."

"You're welcome."

They fell into silence, and not an unpleasant one, either. It was almost a companionable quiet, where one felt at ease to notice their surroundings: the fresh green shoots of grass on the fields, the trees about to flower, the city folk all enjoying the greenery of the park.

For a brief, shining moment, it felt like they weren't mortal enemies.

That was when Daisy gasped.

"My goodness, we have done it! We have actually done it!"

"*It* being . . . ?"

"We have engaged in a civil, nearly polite, exchange. We have had a genuine conversation that wasn't a verbal death match. Pity no one was around to notice it."

"One hopes enough people have taken note of us together behaving somewhat pleasantly toward each other."

She sighed. "Otherwise, we shall have to do this again."

"Horrors," he deadpanned.

But Theo almost didn't even mean it. He was glad for the company, even if it was hers. He was at odds as to how to spend his afternoons without going to his club; his pride would not permit him to attend as a friend's guest. Which was beside the point; he'd learned everyone had gone up to sail at Belmont's place in Newport. One of those spur-of-the-moment, whirlwind plans hatched over drinks late at night and employed before anyone thought to send word to Theo in exile. He'd called on Miss Pennypacker, but she only wanted to ask questions about him and Daisy that he'd rather not answer.

Plenty of others remained in the city. Theo and Daisy both looked around. The park was full of people living their best lives, and that did not include observing a couple passing by in a carriage. Even if that couple was heavily featured in the morning newspaper. It was her hat—her big, atrocious hat—that kept her identity hidden and any interest at bay.

"We probably don't need to spend *that* much

time together," she mused. "In fact, there's really no need to convince anyone that we're in love or even in *like*. Which is a good thing. I doubt either of us has the acting skills to convince anyone of that, especially after last night."

"About that . . ." Theo began. Already, there was no going back to the way things were *before*. Theo had been cut off from his funds and left behind by his friends. All he had left was his reputation as a charming, sought-after, desirable man about town. He couldn't lose that, too; at least, not before he figured out something else to do with his life. A purpose.

"There's just the matter of my reputation to consider," he said.

"Do go on," she drawled, and he knew better than to think she actually cared but he continued anyway.

"It's bad enough that people think I have been rejected from the club, cut off from my funds, and forced into an engagement. But I can't have people thinking that I lack the good looks and charm to seduce *you*."

"Because I am not pretty or popular I should be grateful for your attentions, is that it?"

"That sounds worse than it did in my head."

"And what if you lack the charm to seduce me? What if I don't care about *your* good looks?"

She spoke in such a way to make it clear that he did indeed lack the charm, and his good looks did nothing for her. A pretty—or *handsome*—face was not enough. Neither were his fine suits or the way he filled them out with lean muscles honed from tennis. That was all he had to offer and she didn't want it. And there it was again: that burning drive to have something else, all his own, that no one could take away. But first . . .

"For the sake of my reputation, I think you should act like you're in love with me. A little bit. For appearances. It will help things when we eventually end our engagement, I think."

"Oh, shall I?" And her voice dripped with sarcasm. It oozed so much sarcasm, one could practically drown in it. It smothered a man to the point of suffocation.

Theo discovered that she was only just getting started.

"Perhaps, pretty boy, I'll start by resting my hand on your arm affectionately. I'll lean in close. I'll let my breasts accidentally on purpose brush against your arm. Maybe I'll murmur something wicked to you. Maybe I'll whisper something infuriating that will make you flush with rage, but everyone will think I said something wicked to cause you, a seasoned, scandalous rogue, to blush."

Worse yet, Daisy actually did these things to him. Her hands. Her breasts. Murmuring this wickedness. She was indecently close and he caught a faint but heady scent of something floral.

To his shock and horror, he was affected by these things.

Theo hardly liked her and had never considered her attractive. He hardly considered her at all, in fact.

But lo and behold, all she had to do was be *her*— a teasing, tormenting, confounding woman—and he was affected. In ways. Ways that were not merely physical.

"Or I could just gaze at you like some adoring sheep." She batted her lashes at him. It was more comical than alluring.

"If you aren't going to take it seriously—then never mind."

"My apologies. No issue deserves more care and consideration than a man's pride and reputation. I should not have made light of it."

Point taken.

"What is an adoring sheep anyway?"

"A poor choice of words, but I assume you get my point, Harvard. I could gaze at you like one of those young, innocent society girls or a young, innocent shopgirl or actress who firmly believes that fairy tales are real and a handsome prince will sweep them off their feet."

"I don't think you could gaze at someone like that even if you tried. Not even me."

"Is that a dare?"

"Only if people are watching. I should hate for such a performance to be wasted."

"You don't want a private performance, Theo?"

The words *private performance* made him think of . . . things. That one usually did not think of in the middle of the park, in the middle of the day, with a high-society woman like Daisy beside him.

But she had to tease him in a husky bedroom voice. It was anger that flared; or was that rush of heat and feeling indicative of something else? He didn't know; he didn't *want* to know. He wanted to continue his placid existence, unruffled by strange *feelings* for a woman he didn't even like.

"This really isn't necessary, Daisy."

"But I can't stop myself. You're just so pretty."

Lord save him.

Seriously. Please.

She was smiling at him now. Batting her eyelashes. Dear God.

"Is anyone watching?" she asked, not taking her eyes off his face. "Is it working? Because I just can't take my eyes off you."

"Stop. This is ridiculous. You are ridiculous."

"I'm just teasing you, Theo. When we are in public, I shall consider trying to pretend to be enamored of you for the sake of your precious reputation. Never let it be said that there was a living, breathing woman in Manhattan who didn't want you."

"Thank you." It was a hollow victory. He felt like an ass. She might flirt with him for appearances and it would mean nothing. Nothing, because she was a nobody and it meant nothing. What was *wrong* with him that he had even asked? Why did he care so much what other people thought?

"Besides, it will suit my purposes to have you acting somewhat enamored of me, as well."

"And what purposes are those?"

"Never you mind. But you definitely must try harder to act like you're seducing me," she said. "I'm not feeling the slightest bit breathless or weak in the knees or whatever it is girls feel when they're being swept off their feet."

"My apologies," he murmured. Then he dropped the reins and turned to her, intent on giving her a taste of her own medicine. "Let's fix that immediately."

"You don't have to do it *right now*—"

He gave her his wolfish smile. Then he leaned in close to whisper in her ear, but words failed him for a second. She smelled *good.* It was that heady fragrance. And her skin was smooth and dewy and just lovely. Hers was a complexion that begged to be caressed. That was just the skin politely exposed; he idly wondered about the rest of her . . .

Finally, he remembered what he meant to say. Something romantic and seductive. Two could play at this game of irritating each other profoundly. "What do you say we return to that gazebo and see if it's empty so we can be alone?"

"To do what, exactly?"

The lady was unmoved.

"Get to know each other better. Intimately."

Had they been alone he might have kissed her earlobe. Desire flared when the thought occurred to him.

Thank God they were not alone.

She turned away, nearly smacking him in the face with her hat and feathers.

"Those are some very seductive moves you have there, Theo. Very practiced. I don't think we need to act like we're in love—no one will believe that. We just need to strive for distantly polite or not outwardly hostile."

"Be still my beating heart."

"We needn't spend every waking moment together. Or any time at all, really."

"It's fine, I have the time," he said. One could only spend so many hours at the tailor. Especially when one's father was no longer paying the bills. He didn't know what else to do with himself, with his friends out of town.

"The thing is, I don't."

"What are *you* so busy with?" Theo asked hotly.

She smiled like a sphinx and said, "Wouldn't you like to know?"

Chapter Six

Rumor has it that Mrs. Evelina Swan
has reserved Grace Church for the
wedding of her daughter, Miss Daisy
Swan, to Theodore Prescott the Third.
—*The New York Post*

Later that afternoon
25 West Tenth Street

$\mathcal{T}$his situation with Theo had already taken too much of Daisy's time when she had other, more engaging, business to attend to. The business of getting *out* of her engagement, for one thing.

Daisy knew she could not actually marry him, but if the mood around the Swan household was any indication, Daisy knew she had to make other arrangements to support herself—fast. Her plans to develop and launch her cosmetics business would have to happen sooner, rather than later. She could not wait until after graduation. Her mother was rushing ahead with wedding plans at a furious, terrifying pace. She was eager to have Daisy settled before "the looming scandal" broke.

This just meant that Daisy had to move faster with her own plans. Which she did, over tea at a top-secret, ladies-only club meeting. They met downtown, at the elegant town house of their founder and fearless leader, Miss Harriet Burnett.

They being the Ladies of Liberty Club.

The membership was comprised of society women, school friends, and other women Harriet picked up along the way. Once upon a time Miss Burnett had been a debutante—just a year ahead of Daisy—but she had refused the match her parents had planned for her. When they cut her off, she sought employment by her pen and made a new set of friends. When her parents died, leaving her their fortunes, Harriet used her newfound wealth and position to create opportunities for women to achieve independence. No one, she thought, should have to choose between love and money.

She formed the Ladies of Liberty Club, involving her friends from society and her friends from the press, for the purposes of encouraging professional advancement for women. They helped women find good, honest positions that paid a decent wage. Or they pooled their funds and resources to help other women launch their own businesses. Most of all, they provided a community of like-minded ladies to support and encourage each other.

Daisy had been in the club for ages—she knew Harriet from her society days—and not once had she been nervous to speak with her fellow club members. But today was different. After watching one woman after another strive to launch her own business or embark on a career, it was now her turn to take the risk.

Today her hands shook just a little as she removed the various jars from her satchel and set them on the low table usually reserved for tea. The women gathered in close, intrigued.

"Well, there have been some delays, but I have finally achieved perfection."

"I'll be honest," a woman named Miss Parks began. "I cannot decide which intrigues me more—this eagerly awaited batch or the reason for your delays."

Daisy groaned. "You know the reason. You all must know. We don't need to discuss it."

Daisy had hoped that she wouldn't have to talk about *him* here, of all the places in New York. The Ladies of Liberty Club was where women met to discuss the business of women taking over the world, one woman at a time, not the business of matrimony. Lord knew Daisy got enough of that at home. While she was here, she didn't want to talk about *boys*.

Or boy, in particular.

Man, really. She had spent all afternoon next to him in the carriage and felt nothing but strong muscles filling out his impeccably tailored suit, which suggested that he didn't lead a life of entirely idle dissipation.

"Theodore Prescott the Third! Your future husband!" Miss Parks exclaimed. "What a catch."

"More like my past, present, and future nightmare from which I cannot wake," Daisy replied. "Between us ladies, we are only pretending to be engaged so our parents cease with their matchmaking. It's all a charade to allow me to focus on this," Daisy said, in an effort to bring the attention back to the reason she was here.

It was the reason she lived and breathed.

The reason she put up with Theodore Prescott the Worst.

The reason was presented in an assortment of mismatched, unmarked jars that Daisy had pilfered from around the house. She'd washed them and scrubbed the old labels off and lovingly filled them with a magical, miraculous concoction of her (mostly) own invention.

Complexion balm.

Yes. Complexion balm.

Most women relied on lotions based on an old family recipe whipped up by a servant, or something around the house (lard worked in a pinch) or simply endured dry skin and lackluster complexions. One didn't dare purchase a cosmetic without great risk to one's reputation so one could not buy it. Only the foolish made products that no one would risk buying.

And Daisy.

Because she thought that womankind deserved better. They deserved care and tenderness, even if only from her proprietary mixture of moisturizing ingredients. Daisy had taken her grandmother's old family recipe, passed down through generations, and improved upon it with what she had learned in her chemistry studies. She improved the texture, added fragrance, and tested the recipe until it really *worked* to make a woman's complexion seem like that of a goddess.

It wasn't just face cream. It wasn't just a moisturizing lotion. It was better than magic; it was science. It didn't just get the job done; it *performed*. It was her secret weapon. People could call her Ugly Duck Daisy until the rapture, but no one could honestly say that her skin wasn't flawless. This was the reason.

This was also the reason that all the name-calling in town hadn't bothered her *too* much. She had her one, undeniable beauty—her complexion—and she had a project that engaged her head, heart, and talents. She had things she loved about herself and something she loved to do. She had a wonderful circle of friends. That made all the rest matter a little less.

Miss Lumley glanced at Daisy, the balm, and back to Daisy. "This is the secret to your complexion?"

"Yes. My grandmother's recipe, which I have improved in the lab. It is tried and true and scientifically improved."

Daisy unscrewed a lid and passed it around. She took a dab from another opened jar and showed how to massage it into the skin.

"Just apply each night before bed for a fortnight and I promise you will see results. Smoother texture. Fewer lines. A brighter complexion. I have been using it diligently."

She was the only one.

She needed more.

She needed many, *many* women to buy it.

This little jar of ingredients was Daisy's way out—out of whatever looming catastrophe awaited her family, out of her fake engagement with a man she couldn't stand, and out of whatever middling and probably impoverished circumstances awaited a plain-faced and sharp-tongued spinster.

But even this group of ambitious, audacious women were hesitant to try it. One could practically see their internal battles between novelty and propriety.

"Well, given your complexion, Daisy, I shall try it," Harriet said, gamely reaching for the nearest jar. Daisy breathed a sigh of relief. Harriet was their ringleader and if she gave it her approval, then the other ladies would surely go ahead, as well. If they would only just try it, night after night, Daisy knew they would fall in love with it.

"But only on the condition that you tell us what the devil happened that you and Theodore Prescott the Third are engaged," Harriet added.

"We were shocked when we heard the news," Miss Parks said.

"We thought you could do better," Miss Archer added.

Daisy's heart swelled. This was why she loved her fellow club women. While her mother thought he was the best option, these women knew *her* better to know that she deserved better.

"He is very handsome—"

"One might even say pretty—"

"But we thought you might go for someone more . . ."

"Intellectual?"

"Accomplished?"

"Disciplined?"

"Motivated?"

Daisy cringed on Theo's behalf. True, he had never displayed an intellectual prowess that she was aware of (his precious Harvard attendance notwithstanding). And it was true that he had not any accomplishments, talents, or even hobbies of his own or apparent interest in acquiring any.

As far as anyone knew, Theo lived and breathed dissipation. A life of leisure. Idle pleasures. How boring.

"Our parents are keen on the match for . . . reasons," Daisy explained and hoped she wouldn't have to explain more. "He and I conspired and decided a pretend engagement will keep them from hounding us to be together. I only accepted his fake proposal when my mother chucked all my chemistry equipment because 'I would not need it once I was busy keeping house.' He only agreed when his father cut off his club membership and allowance."

"A fate worse than death according to the men in this town."

"It must be because of Saratoga."

Ah, yes. The Saratoga Scandal.

The *situation* was endlessly, breathlessly discussed in shocked and horrified whispers among polite society. The newspapers were constantly reporting on the rumors. But it was all speculation. No one knew the true story. But what was known was *bad*.

"I hope he told you the real story of what happened in Saratoga."

"We mostly avoid each other and when we are together, our time is spent bickering about who hates the other person most. There's really no time to discuss the inside story on this summer's greatest scandal."

She should have asked him about Saratoga. She had to get something out of this maddening arrangement.

"What is the Saratoga Scandal?" Mrs. Sanders asked and there were gasps all around.

"Do you not know?"

"I've been at Dr. Jacobs's for treatments. He forbids the news," she explained. Mrs. Sanders was frequently away on extended treatments for a mysterious ailment. Privately, Daisy thought she was just trying to escape her bear of a husband, but would never say so aloud.

"No one quite knows what has happened in Saratoga. But what is known is this—it involved an actress of some renown, a prized racehorse worth thousands of dollars belonging to a prominent politician, and a torn bedsheet."

The combination of actress, political figure, playboy, thievery, and sex was irresistible to society gossips.

"Paul Revere has nothing on him."

"He broke multiple laws including grand larceny. His father let him languish in jail for a weekend before bailing him out."

"And then do you know what he said? 'All in a day's work.'"

"As if he knows anything about a day's work," Daisy scoffed.

"So he is not who we expected for you," Harriet said.

"He is not who I expected for myself. Were it not for circumstances . . ."

"You could always refuse to wed at all," Harriet said softly. Pointedly.

The other club members fell silent, waiting and watching to see how Daisy might respond without insulting their friend and hostess, who herself had once chosen striking out on her own, penniless, rather than accept an unwanted match her parents had planned for her.

Daisy felt a rush of shame that she was not so bold. But she also knew that her mother was right—if she was going to implore on propriety-minded society women to risk scandal to buy her product, she needed her own good reputation to smooth the way.

"I *will* refuse to wed him, if it comes to that, no matter the consequences," Daisy replied. "But I have a plan. We are merely conspirators. Convenient and temporary allies. Nothing more. Ever."

"Well, do tell us your plan."

"You are looking at it. Wearing it. I am going to sell this complexion balm. Once I get established and can support myself, I shall have no need of a fake fiancé. But until then, I need help. And that is where I hope you ladies come in."

"Do you need investment?"

The Ladies of Liberty were known to pool their pin money and apply their membership dues to the support of female entrepreneurs. Their most recent investment had been the dress shop of Miss Adeline Black and it had been proven to be a success. The club was flush with funds.

"No, I don't need funds at this time. I have been saving my pin money in anticipation of this. But I do need good word of mouth."

This was no small request.

Purchasing a product like this wasn't done. For one thing it was so novel—nothing like it on the shelves—Daisy made a mental note that she also had to figure out how to get it on the shelves. In fact, she might even have to disguise it as a patent medicine. For another thing, it was verging perilously close to cosmetics, which were not worn by respectable women, as a rule. Blush, lip paint, kohl around the eyes—all marked a woman as wanton and disreputable.

It was to be expected that the Ladies of Liberty would hesitate. Truly. Surely. Of course. But Daisy firmly expected that after a moment or two of consideration, they would realize that together, with their collective status and power, they could change the way something like a cosmetic was perceived. If it was successful, it would open up new avenues for female employment and entrepreneurship.

They just had to change the world first.

"I would but . . ."

"It is somewhat scandalous to discuss. A woman's toilette is such an intimate thing."

"But we are discussing it right now."

"We are a special group. I would hardly mention it with the ladies from church."

"It's not like it's lip paint or powders or whatever actresses like Annabelle Jones would wear."

Annabelle Jones was the other principle player in the Saratoga Scandal.

"This is true. It is more discreet. We do all use something *like* this."

"I haven't tried it yet and I can already tell it surpasses what my lady's maid concocts for me."

Daisy began to feel something like despair at this tepid response. Some in favor, some not so much. But no one seemed ready to shout it from the rooftops.

She had assumed that she could count on her lady friends to support her because . . . it was her. Their friend. And because of the sisterhood. And because she had created a magical potion that would make them feel beautiful. These were all excellent reasons and yet . . . Miss Parks was holding a jar and evaluating it through narrowed eyes.

"I'm not afraid of vanity or scandal or personal conversation among friends," Miss Parks remarked. "But I'll say this. It's not very pretty."

Not pretty.

Of course. Words she knew by heart and hated with a passion.

"I wouldn't risk my reputation to be seen picking it up from a store display, for example. Daisy, if this is going to succeed, it needs to be so irresistible, so breathtakingly beautiful, that a woman will risk her most precious possession—her reputation—to be seen buying it. To leave it out on display on her dressing table, next to a silver brush and mirror from Tiffany's. To rave about it to her friends."

Daisy glanced from lady to lady and saw from their expressions that the packaging wasn't beautiful enough to overcome their reservations about being seen with it. And so they might use it—even now, she saw some ladies slipping the little jars into their purses and pockets—but they would not talk about it. They would not shout their love for it from the rooftops.

Just like her, standing next to Theo. She was the old jar and he was the fancy, pretty thing from Tiffany's. And that would be her fate for the rest of her life if she could not make this work.

Chapter Seven

The date has been set for the most unexpected
wedding of this season. If all goes according
to plan, Miss Daisy Swan will walk down
the aisle to Theodore Prescott the Third
in just two months. Having seen the
couple together, one does have doubts.
—*The New York Post*

Delmonico's Restaurant
Fifth Avenue and Twenty-Sixth Street

*M*rs. Evelina Swan had the ghastly idea that
Daisy, Theo, and their parents should enjoy
some sort of evening entertainment together to
bond them as families and, more likely, to show
off that despite all expectations her unmarried
daughter had snared the Four Hundred's most
eligible bachelor.

It would also make the match that much
harder to break.

And so, both Theodore Prescott the Second and

the Third were seated at a table with Evelina and Daisy Swan at Delmonico's, the opulent restaurant that was widely regarded as the best and was *the* place for Manhattan high society to be seen. The maître d', Pierre, showed them to a prominent table, visible to all other patrons.

"I'm terribly sorry," Evelina began with an apology, "but Mr. Swan won't be joining us this evening. Something came up with the brokerage firm. Mr. Prescott, I'm sure you understand how business trumps all other considerations."

Under his breath, Theo whispered, "He does."

"Pity, that," the elder Prescott said. "I was looking forward to hearing more about it. The returns have been excellent and I'm keen to know his secrets. Not that I *need* them, of course. My friends and I have all benefited tremendously from his investments."

"Oh, he won't spill those over dinner. He'd bore us ladies." Evelina Swan gave a fluttering laugh.

"I wouldn't be bored by it," Daisy replied. "I find business to be a fascinating topic of conversation."

"Daisy . . ." her mother warned.

"Well, that makes one of the children, at least," Theo's father quipped.

"Father . . ." Theo warned.

Oh, this dinner was going to be *splendid*.

There were multiple courses to be endured, of

New York Clam Chowder and the special Delmon-ico's steak. There was also wine, thank God. A waiter came around and filled everyone's glasses and Theo immediately took a sip.

"Oh, look at that woman's dress," Mrs. Swan pointed out. "What a ghastly color. What would you even call it? Some sort of purple or lavender, but that doesn't quite capture it, does it?"

"It is the color of a three-day-old bruise," Theo said after a casual glance in the direction of the dress in question. "One wouldn't think Worth would make such a dress."

"That's precisely it! What a gruesome but utterly precise description," Daisy's mother en-thused. "What an eye for color you have, Theo."

Daisy eyed Theodore Prescott the Elder over the top of her menu. There was no mistaking the tightening of his jaw, or the firm lines his lips displayed, as anything other than displeasure with his son. And *that* was putting it mildly.

Daisy suspected that it was not the maca-bre description that bothered such a supremely manly, masculine man, but the ease with which his son arrived at such a perfect description of something like a woman's dress. His son—his gorgeous son—had an eye for color, a flair for descriptive words.

And, Daisy thought privately, excellent taste in his suits.

A quick glance at Theo the younger—she could

not be caught looking—revealed to her that he was well aware of his father's opinion. The undercurrent of tension between father and son was nearly palpable. Daisy felt something like a pang of sympathy for Theo; while her mother despaired of her, she never disapproved of her. The distinction was slight, but made all the difference in the world.

A subject change was in order and Evelina Swan, ever the gifted hostess, noticed it and handled it adeptly. With her most winning smile, she turned and said, "Tell me, Mr. Prescott, about the plans for your new yacht."

Mr. Prescott, delighted with this topic of conversation, spoke at length about his new yacht.

Theo and Daisy took the opportunity to embark on a conversation of their own. Though theirs was more hushed, more urgent.

"Now that we are engaged and everyone knows it, I think it's time we start planning how to get out of it," Daisy began and Theo's bored blue eyes lit up with a spark of interest. He certainly was easy on the eyes.

"It seems we do have a point of common interest after all," he replied, as if they were merely discussing a shared hobby. "I suppose you have already come up with six different ways that all cast me in a horrible light."

"Wrong." Daisy smiled sweetly. "At least seven. Please do not underestimate me."

"I wouldn't dream of it."

"Do you want to hear the plan?"

"I am waiting with bated breath."

"At the right time, we simply tell our parents that we have decided not to marry and that no force on earth could compel us."

Theo paused, expectantly, for a half second before he rolled his beautiful blue eyes.

"Now, why didn't I think of that?" he drawled. "Your genius is unparalleled, Daisy. That didn't even occur to me—even with my Harvard education and first-rate tutors. Please, do tell how one determines 'the right time' because I'm ready now."

"Another week at least." She shrugged.

"Your specificity leaves much to be desired. It almost seems like you haven't given this much thought at all."

"On the contrary. It's a soothing, comforting fantasy as I fall asleep each night."

"You mentioned seven options. What's the next one?"

"Another option to bypass our parents would be to simply post an announcement in the newspapers."

He gave her a hint of a smile to signal his appreciation and approval of this plan. His eyes lit up with some thought. Daisy would never, *ever* admit it, but when he was thinking, she found him rather . . . attractive.

"*Theodore Prescott the Third and Miss Daisy Swan, together with their families, announce that the wedding will not be taking place after all,*" he said.

"Exactly. Very well phrased. You have a gift for words and phrasing."

He gasped in an exaggerated, dramatic fashion that immediately elicited a glance of disapproval from his father, who was clearly the stoic, inscrutable type who shuddered at any display of emotion either real or feigned.

"Why, Daisy, was that . . . a compliment?"

"Possibly. I must be losing my wits in my old age."

Their conversation was interrupted by the arrival of Mrs. Gould, who descended upon the group in a cloud of silk, feathers, giant ropes of pearls, and a diamond-and-emerald brooch that could take an eye out.

"How lovely to see the Swans and Prescotts dining together!" Mrs. Gould exclaimed. "Everyone has been talking about the wedding between these two . . ." Her voice trailed off as it was painfully clear that she meant to say "love birds" and stopped herself, as it was obvious they were anything but.

Daisy considered more accurate descriptions of her and Theo: *unconsenting adults, reluctantly conspiring enemies.*

As if her mother could read her thoughts, she leveled a warning stare across the table.

"Now, tell me, where will the wedding be taking place?"

"The ceremony will be at Grace Church, of course," Mrs. Swan answered.

Daisy and Theo exchanged a heated, pointed look. *There will be no ceremony.*

"The ceremony will be intimate—just five hundred of our closest friends and family," her mother continued.

"*Just* five hundred," Daisy remarked.

"The ball to celebrate the engagement will be held in the ballroom of my mansion, of course," Theo's father said. "What did I build it for if not to celebrate my son's nuptials?"

Daisy rather suspected that he built it to impress everyone with his wealth and the length and width of his . . . ballroom. But she kept that thought to herself.

"And what will happen after the wedding? Will there be a honeymoon? Of course you must go on a European tour or to Newport, at least."

Daisy and Theo exchanged another heated look: *There will be no after the wedding.* She sipped her wine, wondering at the strangely magical sensation of sharing a heated look with Theodore Prescott the Third. She told herself it was just the wine. Not the man.

"We haven't thought that far ahead," Theo replied.

"But Theo will come work for the steel business, of course," his father said.

"Of course," Theo said dryly.

"Why, Theo, that sounds hard," Daisy said with a feigned sweetness.

"It sounds like my personal nightmare," he murmured.

"I can just see you supervising all those long, hot, hard steel beams down at the factory," Daisy continued. His eyes flashed at her suggestiveness. "All those strong men, working with their hands. Sweaty from exertions. I can just imagine you among them."

"I would be in an office. Bored out of my mind," Theo said flatly. "If my father gets his way."

It was immediately clear to her that Prescott Senior wanted Prescott Junior to join the family business, regardless of the fact of how ill-suited his son was to the task and, more important, how much he clearly would rather drink poison or marry his mortal enemy than work there.

"Doesn't anyone want to ask me what I will do after the wedding?" Daisy inquired to the table.

"What a silly question," Mrs. Gould said with a laugh.

"Darling, *please*." Her mother's cheeks colored with embarrassment. Daisy sipped her wine and tried to cool that familiar surge of frustration and anger at the unfairness of the entire world that expected her to do as she was told—as if she were a child or a silly woman and not a human with a heart and head of her own.

Beside her, Theo noticed.

"We all underestimate you, don't we?" Theo asked in a low voice, for her alone.

"You, my parents, the whole world. Welcome to being a woman."

"I may regret these words, but I might confess to owning some small measure of curiosity about your aspirations that clearly do not include marriage or motherhood."

"Why, Theo, are you taking an interest in me?" She gave a deliberately dramatic gasp. But truth be told, it was an interesting and not unpleasant feeling to have and hold Theo's interest.

"The merest fleeting whisper of a hint of interest."

"But what will your friends say if they know you are interested in me?"

"Nothing good. Best to keep this between ourselves."

Mrs. Gould was now finishing up her gossiping—having gleaned the crucial details about the upcoming wedding, Prescott's new yacht, Jack's successful new investments, she could now proceed to the next table of acquaintances and pass it all along.

"Do have a good evening. The soup is excellent tonight. And Theo, Daisy—do attend my ball tomorrow evening. Everyone will be there, eager to see the couple of the hour."

"We need a better plan to get out of this," Theo said once she had gone. "Feel free to jilt me at the altar."

"It would probably be easier for you to jilt me," Daisy replied. "I am thinking of logistics, not my pride. Unfortunately, it's far easier for a man to get a train ticket and just . . . go. If my mother catches wind of such plans, she'll lock me in my room, like poor Consuelo Vanderbilt."

"Not exactly poor, was she?"

"No amount of money in the world makes up for marriage to someone you don't love," Daisy said.

In her twenty-five years, she hadn't yet found a man who made her heart flutter, her knees weak, or any of that romantic stuff. She hadn't met anyone whom she wanted to kiss and risk her future with. That didn't mean there wasn't someone out there for her. Of course she wouldn't settle for just anyone. She was fine enough on her own. And she hoped to be free to fall in love, not married to someone she loathed.

But how strange was it to be sitting at supper with Theodore Prescott the Third, speaking of love? They didn't even like each other. Her gaze connected with his and it wasn't awful. She found herself curious about him.

"It would be my pleasure to jilt you, Daisy."

"That's the most romantic thing you've ever said to me, Theo. When you wave goodbye from the train platform as you quit my life forever, I might weep with joy."

"You know, if I actually liked you I might be wounded by your words."

"I could say the same," Daisy replied. "I suppose it's a good thing we don't actually like each other."

"That would complicate matters."

"We cannot afford complications."

Theo raised his glass in a toast to Daisy alone. "To not liking one another."

"To not getting married," she added.

"To happily-ever-after . . . with other people."

"Cheers to that."

They clinked their glasses together and took a sip. But his eyes never left hers. And not for the first time that evening did they share a pointed, heated glance. But this one lingered. This one did not let go.

Later, near the coat room

THEO THOUGHT HE would grow old and die, waiting for that eternal, infernal dinner to conclude. Now the end was nearly in sight and he had plans to meet his friends at the Casino Theater for a show and some entertainment after. He could not wait to get away from the pressures and prying eyes.

He was emerging from the coat room and there she was. Daisy. They found some sort of truce over dinner, by virtue of both loathing their circumstances. That they were co-conspirators in this farce was the saving grace.

"Are you going to tell me what that was all about?" she asked. As if they were friends now.

"You'll have to be more specific."

"You. Your father. All that tension about working for Prescott Steel."

Oh, she had noticed. Splendid. And only somewhat mortifying. It was one thing to be a failure in his father's eyes and even worse when someone else noticed it.

"It was exactly what you think it is, Daisy. He wishes me to work there. I do not."

"I gathered as much. What will you do instead?"

"Who says I will do anything? I'm just some idle, entitled heir. Who says I have to do anything other than *wait*?"

"That's one gruesome way of looking at it," Daisy said. She slightly adjusted her wrap. "You're also a wealthy, well-connected man with a degree from Harvard. Seems to me like you could do whatever you wanted. There's nothing stopping you but . . . you."

Great. Now he was getting an inspirational and motivational talk from Daisy Swan, on top of everything else this evening. If she was so smart and sure of herself, maybe she could figure it out for him. After all, he was just a pretty face.

"There is also the fact that whatever I do must meet my father's approval."

To which Daisy only asked, "Why?"

It was a question he didn't have an answer for.

Chapter Eight

Mrs. Evelina Swan will stop at nothing to throw
the wedding of the season. It is confirmed
that she has ordered a million roses to be
delivered to Manhattan for the wedding.
—*The New York Post*

Mrs. Gould's Ballroom
Fifth Avenue

*P*retty. All around Daisy, everything was pretty.
Mrs. Gould's ballroom was a study in beautiful, luxurious things—crystal chandeliers, gold
everything, portraits of beautiful people hung on
crimson walls, gleaming parquet floors—and full
of beautifully dressed people. Pretty girls in pale
blush silks and satins laughed and smiled as they
whirled around the dance floor in the arms of society's finest gentlemen.

Daisy felt very out of place. She always did.

No amount of pleading migraines or typhoid
or something equally dire would get Daisy out

of appearing at Mrs. Gould's ball this evening. After all, they had been expressly invited by the hostess herself, and one did not refuse Mrs. Gould's invitations.

So Daisy wore her best dress.

And then there was Theo, sharply dressed in his evening attire of black wool straight-cut trousers, a black tailcoat with peaked silk lapels that highlighted the taper of his shoulders to his waist, a crisp white shirt to contrast. His blond hair gleamed; his blue eyes drank in the scene. His attentions landed on her.

She was glad she wore her best dress, made of a pale gold silk and tulle affair that complemented her complexion and had the benefit of making her feel like a warrior. She could, perhaps, hold her own in this dress.

"Fifty-five days," Daisy murmured so only Theo could hear. They were standing off to the side of the ballroom, abandoned together. He glanced at her quizzically. She explained.

"Fifty-five days. The number of days before the third Sunday in October, which is the date my mother has selected for our wedding."

"Oh, dear God."

"My sentiments exactly," Daisy replied.

"It seems like a lifetime away and yet I also feel an urgent pressure to call it off."

"It pains me to agree with you. And yet I do."

"Someone ought to tell your mother that we

are merely pretending and have no intention of actually marrying each other. Otherwise, I fear she will keep arranging us together at various social events until we are . . . together."

"I wholeheartedly endorse you for such an endeavor," Daisy said. "If I could vote, I would vote for you to do it."

"Nothing puts fear in a man's heart like delivering bad news to a woman."

"Coward."

"Call it self-preservation."

"I suppose I shall jilt you at the altar, then," Daisy mused. "Much less confrontational, though it will hardly do our reputations any favors."

It would not. For a millionaire playboy to be ditched by a plain spinster would have eyebrows raised all over town. The speculation as to why would be rampant. They would be discussed, endlessly. If they weren't doing this to preserve their reputations for other reasons, what were they doing it for?

"Do you intend to let things progress that far?" Theo asked, plucking a glass of champagne from a passing attendant and handing it to her. He took one for himself, as well. As if this conversation was hard for him to have otherwise.

"Do you have another plan?" Daisy asked, highly suspecting that she already knew the answer.

"Not at the moment. But fear not, my lady. I shall find a way to rescue us from this dreadful predicament," he said with only a touch of sarcasm. She was not consoled.

He lifted his glass to hers in a toast.

Their eyes met over the rims of their champagne glasses. His blue eyes, fringed with impossibly long lashes; hers just an odd brownish-greenish swamp color that the family portrait painter once lamented as an impossible color to mix, and not in a good way.

And just like that, all at once, Daisy got that feeling she always got at balls, especially when she had to stand next to her mother or one of her sisters. The feeling of being judged as a dreadful frump even though she wore excellent dresses and had her hair styled well. It was all too easy to imagine people looking at her, and the company she kept, and thinking how *different* she looked. Such beauty and then . . . her.

With Theo, especially, Daisy was certain everyone was staring at them like a mathematical equation that did not add up; like two and two equaling three.

This feeling always made her want to flee to a space where Daisy felt safe and free and the best version of herself—the ladies' club, the classroom, the laboratory, or her bedroom. Anywhere but here, with him, in front of all those prying eyes and wagging tongues.

When Theo said, "We should probably try flirting with each other," she choked on a sip of champagne.

"I beg your pardon?"

"Since everyone is watching us, we might as well put on a show."

Well, so much for the hope that she had imagined people staring.

"Well, now that has my pulse racing, Theo."

"I know. Flirting with each other will be a tough job, but we must endure."

"And what do you know of tough jobs?"

For the briefest of instants, something like dismay flickered over his features, but then his usual arrogant expression was firmly in place.

"The lady wounds. And here I thought my proposal was sparing you from becoming a spinster."

"Carry on like that and I daresay I shall swoon."

"If you don't mind," Theo drawled. "That would do wonders for my reputation."

"Why are you so keen on maintaining the reputation of a ladies' man anyway? You are already wealthy, pretty, and popular. I'm sure some beautiful nitwit female will still have you after I jilt you. What do you even care what others think of you?"

He evaded her question. "Why *don't* you care what people think of you?"

She replied with a shrug. "Who says I don't?"

"You do a mighty fine job of seeming like you don't care in the slightest what people say about you. In fact, you act like you're bored by all of us. Above us."

"Perhaps it's because for most of my life I've been called Ugly Duck Daisy by nearly everyone I've encountered."

"That again? It was just some flippant remark."

"Yes, that again. That flippant remark taught me that people don't care to know me before they judge me. And so I decided long ago not to let my confidence rely on their opinions. I have friends who truly care for me. And that is all that matters."

"Well, aren't you just the luckiest girl in New York."

AND SO THEO and Daisy embarked on a tour of the ballroom, arm in arm, with a carefully maintained space between their two fashionably attired bodies.

This insurmountable distance between him and Daisy—like the magnetic force of two repelling magnets—only now made Theo realize how women tended to drape themselves on him as if presenting an offering at the altar to some pagan god. He did always savor the subtle, suggestive, and affectionate touch of a woman—something that he realized now he stood to lose if he embarked on a marriage of mutual loathing.

He did have some notion of fidelity to his future wife—playboy and flirt he may be, he wasn't a *cad*. Theo even had a mad idea of liking and being liked by his future wife. He wasn't one to force affections and he did crave a deep sense of genuine connection. All reasons why the idea of marriage to her was so intolerable.

Because it was her and him and they hated each other. She could never forgive him for what happened when they were thirteen, for one thing.

By mutual agreement, they strolled along the perimeter of the ballroom at a sedate but somewhat determined pace designed to avoid conversations. The Four Hundred couldn't help but be curious about one of the least likely pairings in recent memory, and everyone wanted to probe and discuss. Conversations had to be avoided as both he and Daisy hardly had kind words to say.

Such a pace also allowed them to overhear choice snippets of conversations as they passed.

"What does he see in her?"

Theo glanced at the *her* in question. A subtle lift of her chin higher told him that she had heard that and would not be dignifying it with a response. It was an unfortunate fact that there was nothing Theo could say to reasonably comfort her. He hardly even knew her. What he did know was not exactly the stuff of raptures and poetry. Their hands had been forced and there was no denying it.

But still, he felt this urge to comfort her.

Even as she held her head high like he could keep his comforting to himself, thank you very much.

They continued to stroll. Slowly.

People continued to talk. Loudly.

"She's not very pretty."

Oh, God, why did people say the worst things at an unnecessarily loud volume?

There was no way that Daisy hadn't heard that but, damn, she was putting on a good show of feigning deafness. Except for those spots of color on her cheeks. It was a blush of anger, of embarrassment. And if he was to say he thought she was pretty, she'd just call him a liar. Helpless. He felt helpless. He, who always had a witty retort, was unsure of what to say in this situation. It called for something heartfelt, and Theo didn't know if he was even capable of that.

"And she's . . . old."

He and Daisy were the same age. *The same age.*

At this point in the ballroom they had unintentionally become involved in the crush of people making their way into supper and so their progress came to a standstill. As such, they were stuck in place and forced to overhear even more idle chatter.

"She does have a beautiful complexion."

Theo glanced over and confirmed that, yes, this was a true fact. Daisy's complexion could be described in one word and that word was *flawless*. Or perhaps *luminous*. It was definitely beautiful.

"I would pay good money for skin like hers."

Too bad one could not buy it, he thought. The vanity of women—and some men—knew no bounds. But one would somehow have to bottle and sell her inherently beautiful complexion and that seemed impossible. Beyond his comprehension.

"Yes, but that's really all she has to recommend her. Not only is she old, and ugly, but I've heard she's quite shrewish. It's an arranged match, of course. Poor Theo. If only he'd asked me first!"

Here, the ladies sighed.

Here, Theo groaned.

He had never felt so awkward. Anxious. Enraged at other people and the awful things they said where anyone might overhear them. And these were the sorts of women with whom he usually flirted and waltzed and paid social calls upon. The kind of women he'd considered spending his life with.

Nor had he ever felt so exquisitely sensitive to the emotional state of Miss Daisy Swan. It was impossible not to, given the situation. He was aware and he cared and he didn't know what to do about it but he wanted to do something.

Daisy wasn't old, and she wasn't exactly pretty. She wasn't ugly, either. In fact, she was rather smartly attired and well put together on most occasions that he saw her—that rainy day encounter in Central Park notwithstanding.

If he was really being honest, she wasn't shrewish, either, though she was smart, opinionated, and fearless about expressing herself. Perhaps *shrew* was simply a way to say she stood up for herself in conversation.

These were all revelations to Theo. He had never stopped to consider them before, but standing next to her had forced him to listen and interpret the world from her point of view. What he learned made him feel a slow-dawning shame.

For these were also things he had said on previous occasions. He was struck with the sudden urge to apologize to her now, but he suspected that would only make things worse. She was a smart girl who already thought the worst of him. Nothing he could say would change that.

He realized, then, that this was the maddeningly wonderful thing about Daisy: he did not have to pretend. Not like he did with other women and his friends, or with his father.

But, oh, dear God, these ladies were still talking and still oblivious to the fact that he and Daisy were close enough to hear their every awful word. He considered making their presence known and putting these two young ladies on the spot, but that would likely make an awkward moment downright humiliating for all involved.

"*I mean, it's clear what she sees in him. He's so dreamy.*"

"They must not have met you," Daisy said. Finally, she said something. "Otherwise they would know better. Unless by 'dreamy' they mean to say that you are so boring you'll put a girl right to sleep."

Theo was so relieved he could have kissed her. Her snark was a profound relief that saved the moment from being even more uncomfortable.

Yet he had not managed the same for her. In fact, he downright ached when he empathized with her in this moment. He was also amazed. Because she had overheard all those awful things and didn't look fazed in the slightest. Like she was unbothered by *feelings*. Theo knew better. He, too, had presented such a front on occasion, even though a storm of emotion raged within him.

"Daisy . . ."

"Don't, Theo." She rested her hand on his arm. "It's nothing I haven't heard a thousand times before. There's nothing you can say that wouldn't be some platitude. We both know I'm smarter than that."

She did not need him to validate her, or to soothe her presumably wounded feelings or damaged ego. After all, she had heard it a thousand times before, so her heart must be hardened to it. Right? He did not think so. For the first time he thought of Daisy as a woman—a girl—with a heart and feelings that could be wounded even if she was acting like she hadn't a care in the world. Just like at thirteen, just like this evening.

"She's very lucky to have snared him. I mean, who else would marry her?"

Really, that was too much.

"Good evening, ladies." He flashed them a smile. "I couldn't help but overhear your conversation."

The two young ladies reddened considerably. Was it wrong if he took some satisfaction in their discomfort? They certainly deserved a little.

Daisy's grip tightened on his arm. "Theo . . . This really isn't necessary."

"Do you mean to congratulate me on my choice of bride?"

Of course that was *exactly* what they meant! How did he even know? Gosh, he was so intelligent and handsome and wasn't Miss Daisy Swan the luckiest woman in New York? Everyone thought so.

Everyone except Daisy Swan herself.

"I don't need you to be my hero," she said sharply as she turned and stormed off. He was hot on her heels. Because he was starting to care about her in addition to how they appeared to everyone else.

"Someone has to do it," he said. He finally felt useful. He could make amends by standing up for her. It would help their reputations; it would give him a sense of purpose. "Here I am, at your service."

"Find something else to do other than being my white knight, Theo. Contrary to the opinion of everyone in this ballroom, I'm no damsel in distress."

Chapter Nine

Given that the marriage between Theodore Prescott the Third and Daisy Swan is understood to be an arranged match by their parents, one does wonder how it will go the moment when the groom kisses the bride.
—*The New York Post*

*A*fter years of diligent practice, Daisy had perfected the art of pretending not to care what people said. Daisy had learned that she could also absorb a fair amount of snide remarks about herself before she either had to retreat—or risk showing everyone just how sharp-tongued and shrewish she could be.

But with Theo, she was attracting attention. A *lot* of attention.

Attending a ball with him was like stepping out with a lion on a leash.

People noticed.

People discussed.

But tonight she could no longer absorb the comments she'd been overhearing all night—all her life, really—and she especially did not have the capacity to handle Theo acting all heroic all of a sudden, twelve years too late.

A swift exit from the ballroom was an absolute necessity.

So she made one.

"Daisy—wait!"

"I do apologize," she said with all the grace she could muster, which was very little. "I simply have an urgent need to find some other entertainment. Sticking a hot poker in my eye, for example."

"Sounds delightful. May I join you?"

"You don't need to follow me. I don't need you to be my hero. This show of gallantry and concern is really unnecessary."

"Well, it's not like I have anything better to do," he replied, and she was somewhat soothed by this truth.

Theo could swoop her into his arms and kiss her passionately in the middle of a crowded ballroom and people would still wonder who had dared him to do such a thing.

The prospect of kissing him was not as unappealing as she had expected.

Nevertheless, Daisy moved quickly out of the ballroom and into the hallway, walking until the din of the party faded and she reached the private rooms. She yanked open one heavy wooden door and found their host's blessedly empty study and went in.

Theo followed.

He left the door slightly ajar, a tacit acknowledgment that he had no dishonorable intentions and that she was free to leave whenever she wished.

And so they were alone in the dimly lit room with some light spilling in from the corridor, and with the din of the ball nothing but a memory.

They were alone.

They were away from prying eyes and the cutting comments about her, which she'd had enough of for one evening, thank you very much.

They were alone and there was no need to maintain any ruse.

"Daisy, I don't know what to say, other than that I'm sorry."

"It's not your fault. You didn't say any of those things." He remained silent, a confession of sorts, and she understood. "You didn't say any of those things within earshot," she corrected. "Tonight."

"I am so sorry. It is unkind for anyone to say such things in any circumstances. And with you, it's also just plain wrong. For one thing, if you are old then so am I."

Daisy couldn't care less about being considered old, not when she was counting the minutes until she was officially On the Shelf and an Unredeemable Spinster. But she wasn't so hurt or stuck up that she couldn't recognize his offering of peace.

Funny that, coming from him.

But she wasn't so hardened that she didn't appreciate the overture. Even if she didn't know what to do with it. In fact, it left her speechless.

They stood there in the dim light, not talking. It was as if, by mutual agreement, neither of them had any fight left and so they were left with an unspoken but understood truce. She was grateful for that, for she needed a little more time alone before she could go back and face the world.

"You do have beautiful skin," Theo said softly.

"You don't need to compliment me in an effort to soothe any hurt feelings you may think I have. My confidence does not rely on the good opinion of society. Thank God."

She had genuine friends, she had a talent for chemistry, and she had an ambition that sustained her. She would be fine. But her confidence was not unshakable and her feelings were not invulnerable.

The things she'd overheard tonight weren't really about her age or her looks or her manner. They were about a girl like her being seen with a man like him. It was because she, the Ugly Duckling of high society, had dared to stray from her little corner and step out and claim some prime territory for herself that their claws had come out.

This stupid engagement would not be as easy as she'd thought it would be. It might not even work in her favor, as she had hoped it might— that Theo's status in society and hers as his betrothed would help her product launch be successful. Maybe it wouldn't help at all. Then what was this all for?

She was thinking about going downtown right now to place an announcement in the newspaper declaring the end of the match, when he spoke.

"I'm not saying it because it's necessary," Theo said. "I'm saying it because it's a true thing that I noticed and I couldn't think of anything else to say. And I wanted to say something nice to you."

"Well, then, thank you."

"You're welcome," Theo said. She shifted her gaze toward the door. He would leave now, of course. They had made some sort of peace. They had spent the better portion of an hour not killing each other in the ballroom. Certainly that had to be enough to calm the gossips.

And yet, he remained. With her. In the near-dark, otherwise empty room.

In fact, he strolled closer to her.

"Now, tell me. Why can't you accept a compliment?"

She laughed. "From the man who called me Ugly Duck?"

"I *am* sorry about that."

"Fifty-five days before our supposed wedding and you are now sorry."

"Better late than never?"

"I might have appreciated your apology more, should it have occurred on Valentine's Day of 1889, when I received a gruesome note addressed to *My Ugly Valentine.* Did you know that I was called that name so often that I even answered to it upon a few utterly humiliating occasions?"

He had the decency to pale.

Anguish looked good on him.

Damn him.

"I am very, very sorry, Daisy. You have to understand that at the time, I was a thirteen-year-old boy, trying to impress my friends. It's no excuse, I know."

To think some young boy had possibly altered the course of her life. Just to impress his stupid friends.

She shrugged. "It's a catchy name. You have a talent. But your friends are idiots."

"That doesn't excuse anything. Daisy, I had no idea . . . If I had . . ."

"You would have done it all the same. Because you were a thirteen-year-old boy with no thoughts beyond impressing his friends at any cost. Even then, you had a precious reputation to maintain. Why do you care so much?"

He had nothing to say to that.

Not with words anyway.

Theo reached out for her now. His hand closed around her upper arm, the space left bare between her elbow-length satin gloves and the short sleeves of her evening gown. His touch was gentle, but it was not without intention.

She had never really been touched by a man with intentions before. Daisy found herself immobilized by some strange, potent force between them that was not repellent.

Theodore Prescott the Adored was touching her. They were alone. In the dark. It was clear what he wanted. But what did *she* want? This was a situation for which she had never expected and thus never prepared. She considered leaving through that open door but decided to stay. Maybe she was curious. Maybe she ought to give all the other girls in the ballroom something to really be jealous about.

When he spoke, his voice was soft and heavy.

"You drive me mad, you know. And not in a good, romantic way."

"Tell me what else I do to you in a bad, unromantic way." She made her voice go low and smooth, like her father's expensive whiskey. "Tell me what I do that gets your heart pounding. Your temper flaring. Your heat rising . . ."

"Oh, Daisy . . ."

And then he kissed her.

He kissed her.

Theodore Prescott the Third closed his beautiful blue eyes and pressed his widely admired mouth to hers and the world as Daisy had known it no longer made sense.

It was Theo. And her.

And they despised each other and yet . . .

He kissed her.

And it was . . .

Fine.

As a novice to this whole kissing business, it wasn't *quite* how she had imagined it. Her toes did not curl; her lungs and heart did not forget how to perform their functions. Her pulse was as steady as ever.

She knew these things were supposed to devastate her sense of equilibrium, wreak havoc on her breathing and her heart's ability to pump blood. She knew the world was supposed to irrevocably change. She knew she was supposed to feel a surge of feeling so powerful, so intense, so overwhelming, that she would emerge from this kiss a new woman.

Daisy read novels, she eavesdropped on other women's conversations, and so she knew what she was supposed to feel during a first kiss with a handsome rogue, and it wasn't this.

She said his name, *Theo*, or tried to. The word was mumbled against his mouth, pressing against hers, nudging her to part her lips. When she did, to mention his name, *Theo*, his tongue swooped in to deepen the kiss.

This okay kiss.

This ho-hum clashing of lips and mouths and tongues.

Very well, it was almost quite nearly bad.

She pushed him away.

"Theo, stop."

To his credit, he pulled back immediately. His sense of entitlement at least had some limits.

"You're right," he murmured, caressing her cheek. "I left the door open. What if someone comes in here and catches us? Then we really would *have* to marry or our precious reputations will be thoroughly ruined."

She was not willing to risk a lifetime of underwhelming kisses, thanks to an impulsive kiss and an open door.

"I should go," she said.

"You're right. We ought to return to the ballroom and continue our charm offensive."

She would rather fling herself off the Brooklyn Bridge. Fortunately, she didn't have to choose between the two.

"I would like to go home, actually."

"I'll escort you."

He was probably only considering appearances. But he did look genuinely concerned. She thought, for the first time, that he was more than just pretty. But one so-so kiss and some sympathy did not easily override a decade's worth of angst that he'd caused.

"I'd like to go alone."

His gaze drifted from her eyes to her lips.

"Is it because of what everyone said? Because you shouldn't take it to heart—"

"No, it's not that. Nothing said tonight was anything I hadn't heard—or been made to understand—before."

She watched as he bit his lip as if trying to restrain himself, before giving in and asking the question on his mind.

"Is it because I kissed you?"

She could lie. She could plead a headache or fatigue. But it was her and him and when had they ever spared the other's feelings? She had a reputation as a shrewish, plainspoken spinster so why stop now?

"Yes. Precisely." She paused. "When you kissed me, I found myself . . . whelmed."

He furrowed his brow, having no care at all about wrinkles. Drat the man.

"Whelmed? I'm not familiar with the word. What with my second-rate education. From Harvard. Perhaps you mean anticlimactic."

"Anticlimactic would imply that I have been anticipating kissing you," she said softly. Before tonight the thought had not even occurred to her. Because it was her. And him. And them. Still, she found herself tensing because she had refused him, and insulted him while they were alone, and she didn't know how he would take it.

"The lady wounds," he said softly. She exhaled.

"It's a polite way of saying I was underwhelmed by your kiss and should like to conclude our evening."

Daisy winced at her own frankness, but she really was tired now and did feel a headache coming on. She braced herself waiting for his retort that an ugly, old shrew like her wouldn't know a good kiss if it stuck its tongue in her mouth. There was nothing worse or downright dangerous than a man with a wounded ego.

But Theo surprised her with his soft-spoken reply as he stepped aside to let her leave: "The lady slays."

THEO COULD HAVE returned to the ballroom and struck up a flirtation with Esme, or Margaret, or Viola, or any of the young ladies whose company he enjoyed at parties. They'd all grown up together, come out together, and now took the city and social whirl by storm together. Theo could have handed any of those women a glass of champagne and agreed in hushed tones and seductive murmurs what a ghastly spectacle his fiancée had made. He could elicit their sympathies publicly, and privately lament the hold his father had over him.

Because he was nothing but a wealthy, well-connected man with a first-rate education, as Daisy had so astutely observed the other night. His options were all at once vast and limited to what would meet his father's approval.

Which was of the utmost importance.

Theo recalled Daisy's shrug and question of *why*?

He did not have an answer for her.

But damn, if that girl didn't have a way of speaking the truth and making him call into question . . . *everything*. Theo was in no state to socialize. Not with so much beating around in his brain.

Instead, Theo left the party without a second thought or a backward glance.

Instead, his boots hit the Fifth Avenue sidewalk, slick from a recent rain, and he started to walk.

Theo had some idea of making his way down to The Tenderloin, that infamous stretch of street where gentlemen could be assured to find some amusement or entertainment and where he might spend a pleasant hour with Violet or Gwendolyn or one of the other girls he liked at Madame Rosa's establishment. He could silence all these thoughts and questions, soothe his flummoxed state of mind with wine and women who didn't find his kisses merely whelming.

Or did they?

With women in positions such as theirs, would he ever truly know?

Disconcerting thought, that.

Damned unsettling to realize that maybe you weren't the man you thought you were. Worse yet, that you didn't know the man who you wanted to be.

Most terrifying of all: he needed a woman like Daisy to reveal him as he really was.

Theo kept walking.

One could do worse than a walk down Fifth Avenue in New York City when one needed to sort out one's entire existence. Even if all the new buildings—each one taller than the next—were constructed of Prescott Steel. As if he needed a reminder of how his father loomed large in this town and loomed large over him, especially.

Much as Theo appreciated what steel had done for the city skyline, he knew in his heart that he had no interest in that business. Not even to earn his father's attention and approval. Yet he wasn't ready to give up on it, either.

If only he cared less.

If only there were some other way . . .

Theo let his gaze drift lower, to the business names and brand slogans painted on the sides of the buildings and hanging over storefronts that lined the streets. There were signs and banners promoting patent medicines, millinery, uphol-stery, sailcloth and whalebone, antiques, dresses and boots, and all manner of things anyone could need to make their lives feel complete. Anything anyone could ever want was for sale. And even things people didn't even know they wanted. Steel may be the skeleton of this city, but commerce was its engine.

If only there was something else he could do . . .

Theo kept walking, letting his direction be determined by the flow of traffic. He had some idea of where he wanted to go and he let the city push and pull him in that general direction. Eventually, Theo stood before Madame Rosa's establishment, one of dozens along this stretch of Twenty-Third Street. The lights were blazing bright; the sound of a piano and a drunken sing-along spilled out onto the street. It was just one of the haunts that he and his fellow Rogues of Millionaire Row were known to frequent.

Here, at Madame Rosa's, he would be assured entrance.

But whether because of himself or his father's money, he could not say for certain.

For the first time, Theo wanted to be certain.

Right now the only thing he was sure of was that Daisy Swan was the only person in New York who dared to be forthright with him, and that was what he needed in order to move forward. To find something that would enable him to stand on his own.

And to do *that* they would need to clear the air between them after that kiss. He had kissed her for all the wrong reasons. He would find her later for an honest chat. And who only knew what he would do after that?

Chapter Ten

Mrs. Evelina Swan has been spotted touring
the Fifth Avenue Hotel as the site of a possible
wedding reception venue. One must conclude
that wedding planning is in full force.
—*The New York Post*

Barnard College

It was two days after the disastrous kiss and
mere weeks before the alleged wedding, and
Theodore Prescott the Third was venturing
where no man had gone before. Probably.

Barnard College had recently opened its gates
to welcome women into the ranks of higher education. He was not remotely surprised when,
upon calling on Daisy at home, he was informed
that she was at school. Specifically, the laboratory.
He went to find her there. They needed to talk.

He found her at work on some project involving beakers and bowls and low flames. He hadn't
a clue what any of it was, or if it was explosive,

but he didn't care. Theo just leaned against the door frame and watched the surprisingly wonderful sight of Daisy Swan, clad simply in a gray skirt and shirtwaist, at work.

This was obviously a place where she felt at home, right in the world, even. Her movements as she poured, measured, transferred, and mixed were smooth and controlled. She knew what she was doing and she was lost in concentration. It was a good look on her. Gaze focused, lips parted slightly.

She hadn't seen him yet; he could still leave. If they never spoke again, other than to communicate the end of their engagement by letter, it wouldn't be strange in the slightest. But he had this hankering now for more. He still hadn't quite figured out the *more* yet, but he knew that making a woman feel overwhelmed from his kiss—and not just whelmed—was part of it. They had to talk about it. Clear the air. Move on with their lives.

He knocked on the door frame.

She looked up, perplexed.

"I hope you're not brewing some poison to be rid of me," he said with a nod toward the beakers before her.

"A marvelous idea. Why hadn't I thought of that?" Daisy quipped. "What are you doing here, Theo? How did you even find me? Are you even allowed here? This is a college for women, you know."

"Good afternoon to you, as well. Your mother told me where you were. In fact, she hoped I would come and distract you."

"Of course she did," Daisy said dryly.

Theo pushed off the door frame and strode into the room, approaching the bench where she worked. He was curious about what she was doing. *Was* it poisonous?

"Can't a man pay a visit to his fiancée?"

"If the couple in question is you and me, the answer is no. There is no point. No reason. No purpose."

He leaned in. "But there is."

"Hmmm." She spooned a mixture of gloop—for want of a better, more scientific term—into a plain old jar that had obviously been repurposed.

"Our kiss," he said. "We need to talk about our kiss."

"Oh, that."

"Yes, that. I kissed you."

"Yes, I do seem to recall that happening."

"You said it was underwhelming."

There, he had done it. The impossible. He had broached a conversation that had the great potential to shred his ego and sense of self-worth to ribbons. He'd even gone all the way uptown to do it. He had questions and wanted answers, even if he feared what she would say. And it was Daisy, who never missed an opportunity to cut him down to size. He could count on her for the truth. And then he would know how to kiss her to leave her breathless and wanting more.

"I did find it underwhelming."

"I'm hoping you'll tell me why."

"I was hoping to avoid this conversation."

"I'm not exactly keen to have it, either. I'm not in the habit of honest, heartfelt conversations. I haven't exactly had practice, given how busy I've been living my life of idle dissipation. But I'd like to be good at this one thing. For my reputation . . ."

"Your precious reputation."

"And women's pleasure. Don't they deserve a good kiss? Listen, Daisy. I just want to clear the air and come to an understanding about this. Then we'll go our separate ways and never speak again."

"Hand me a jar, will you?"

He handed her a jar, while casting a critical eye at it. "So tell me, Daisy, why was the kiss underwhelming?"

"Do you really want to know?"

"I have come all this way, haven't I? All this way in the northern reaches of the city. I have even come across town. You know what a trial that is. I have infiltrated the gates of a ladies-only college."

"All this way is merely uptown on public

transport. It is easy, safe, and reliable enough that a woman can do it alone in daylight without irreparably harming her reputation. As long as she wears sufficiently lethal hatpins in her hat. Which I do, of course."

"Well, it's not as if it was just next door to my club. That would be convenient."

"Yes, if your membership hadn't been revoked."

"Suspended," he corrected. His father had somewhat cut him off; a warning as to what his life would be if he broke off his engagement. "Let's not mention it."

"Fine. You have come all this way to my laboratory. To talk about kissing."

He couldn't resist giving her a rakish grin. "Unless you'd rather just kiss and make up?"

She gave a huff of vexation. "This is the *laboratory*. It is where I have lessons. I perform experiments and I work on important things. This is not where I kiss men to whom I am faking an engagement."

"What are you working on anyway?"

Daisy glanced up at him, wary. He saw the hesitation in her hazel eyes. Was she waiting for him to tease her for this, too? He cursed his thirteen-year-old self.

"Complexion balm," she said. It was not what he'd expected. He didn't understand it. But his instinct was to understand it, not mock it.

"It must have been a trial to convince your mother to let you study at college, to say nothing of the sciences," he remarked.

"It was. Because what would a society wife need to know of chemistry?" Daisy said dryly, repeating her mother's argument.

"Yet you are *here*," Theo persisted, becoming animated now. "You have gone to battle and *won*. And now you are dedicating your time and brain to making *complexion balm*. You are devoting yourself to the study of something possibly useless and definitely frivolous."

"Says a man." Daisy dabbed one manicured fingertip into the cream. Yes, this consistency was finally perfect. Silky, smooth, and cool to the touch with just a hint of resistance. "Men never worry about their appearances quite like women do. They never have to. Yet women are expected to fight this battle against perception and the clock without any tools or secret weapons. I intend to change that."

"Speak for yourself," Theo said. "Some men care about their appearance."

"You're special in that regard," Daisy replied. Then she held out a sample. "Since you do admittedly care, would you like to try some? After all, you have come all this way uptown. Crosstown, even."

"Why not?"

She applied the littlest amount to the smooth

skin of his clean-shaven cheek. It was shockingly cool at first contact and it warmed under her touch as she smoothed it in with a circular motion of her fingertips. It took only the lightest touch.

"I had to experiment to find the right consistency," she explained. "Something that blends easily and blends in well, yet still holds its shape."

"It smells like . . ."

"Primrose and bergamot. My earlier attempts didn't have the most enticing scent, according to my testers."

"Your testers?"

"Just some friends," she added hastily. "So I have added my own blend of distilled fragrance oils. It's a custom blend. I wear it as my perfume. You may have noticed it."

"I have," he said. "So now I smell like flowers. Like a woman. Like you."

"You smell faintly like Daisy's Complexion Balm."

"And what are your plans for Daisy's Complexion Balm?"

"I'm going to sell it. I'm going to make a fortune selling it."

He first thought, *Ha!* And then he thought, *How clever.* And then he thought, *It's impossible.* For a multitude of reasons it was impossible. Women weren't exactly in the habit of using the stuff, so they certainly didn't buy it, so no stores would stock it. Those were just the initial obstacles. But he took one look at Daisy—proud and braced for teasing—and he bit back the words because he wanted to do better. Be better.

Instead, he started thinking about why it was impossible and how they could fix it. So he said, "Not with that name you're not."

"What's wrong with it? The name says what it is."

"Exactly. There's no magic in it. No mystery. No romance. No seduction," he said, leaning in close and dropping his voice to be more romantic, more seductive. To show her.

"So?"

"Such a name leaves me whelmed, Daisy." She had the decency to blush. "And by that I mean it's underwhelming."

"It only needs to work, which it does," she said. "And quite well, I might add. My friends saw improved complexions within a month."

"Sure. I bet it does." Theo dabbed a little more on his other cheek as he considered the product. The texture and fragrance were alluring. If she succeeded in getting a woman to try it, she'd have a chance. Especially if it worked as well as she claimed it did. Given her glowing complexion, he was certain it did. "But no one will know that because it won't sell with a name like that."

"Fine," she huffed. "I'll think of something else."

"What is your sales plan?"

"I have some friends who plan to buy it. Then they'll tell their friends and . . . word of mouth. That is my sales plan."

"Not with this name. Not with this jar."

"But I need this to sell. Spectacularly," she told Theo in no uncertain terms.

"Why?"

"So that we don't have to get married."

Oh, he understood now. She had plans, she'd said. And this was it. If she could earn her own fortune—or just *enough*—then she could afford to tell him, her mother, and all of society the wedding was off. She would ride off into the sunset alone, with a fortune and independence of her own making.

Theo was suddenly struck with an almost violent pang of jealousy. Because all he wanted in this world was their wedding to be called off and something to do all day.

Theo took another look at that jar. It was so plain, and old, and used. He had a vision of what it could be instead.

And he thought maybe her purpose could be his, too. He saw exactly what to do to make it at least better. He also could not really fail at an industry that didn't even exist yet. His father would hate it but if they were spectacularly successful maybe that would make it all right in the eyes of Prescott Senior. Given what Theo stood to gain (everything he wanted) and what he stood to lose (nothing), it was worth a try.

For her. For him. For them and their freedom.

"We can make this a success," he replied. He stood up straight, tall, ready. "To do that, we will need a new name, Daisy. We'll need new packaging. A label that entices. We'll need to make it romantic, seductive, and irresistible."

"We? *We?*" she retorted. "Last I checked this was *mine.*"

"Anything to get us out of this unwanted marriage, right?"

"So you're saying I just need to take this ugly thing and make it pretty?"

Theo smiled, feeling for the first time like he knew exactly what to do. "I'm saying I might be just the man you need after all."

AT SOME POINT the earth had taken a wrong turn, spun off its axis, and was imminently likely to collide with Mars. That was the only reason Daisy could think of to explain what was happening to her perfectly ordered existence.

Theodore Prescott the Worst was carrying her books and escorting her through the gates of her college and talking about escorting her home as if they were friends. A couple. Or business partners.

Just like that, he had inserted himself into her life. He had thoughts and opinions about her secret passion project and was already speaking as if he was her partner in this endeavor.

Was she supposed to just *welcome* him? Daisy bristled at the notion. This was *hers*. And she was supposed to share it with him because he needed something to do all day?

Terribly vexing, that. Maddening, truly.

He was so self-important. And entitled. And what a know-it-all!

Except that she had to admit that he was also right—though it pained her tremendously to admit it. Pained her like surgery without ether. The product was good but it wasn't pretty or seductive or enticing. This is what the Ladies of Liberty had been trying to tell her, and her plan had been to hope they didn't really mean it. To hope that her product was so efficacious that no one minded how it looked. Because Daisy didn't have any other ideas. Her brain whirred to life at the thought of chemical compounds and the like. She didn't have an eye for art or beauty or sales.

She had to admit that Theo knew art and beauty and sales. One look at him in his preferred habitat—a ballroom—revealed that he knew a thing or two about presentation, seduction, and creating a sensation. From the clothes he wore, to the women he surrounded himself with, to the way he carried himself, he knew how to stage a scene people wanted to be a part of.

She could use his help.

Especially if she never wanted to see him again.

The only reason Daisy hadn't flat out told him *no* already was that he hadn't laughed. Of all the people in Manhattan, he was the one who hadn't laughed. Funny, that. Everyone else had thought her dreams were silly and impossible and didn't hesitate to tell her so. But Theo immediately saw the possibilities for making it better and making it successful. They both had a reason to do anything to make it work.

Maybe, just maybe, she would give him a chance.

Or maybe not.

"We were talking about kissing," he said, once they were ensconced in his carriage; he had offered to drive her home through the park. She accepted because they had things to discuss. But not *this*.

"We were also talking about you and me and . . . complexion balm," she said, wincing. The words sounded ridiculous aloud.

"But back to the kissing," Theo said and she groaned and rolled her eyes. "I want to clear the air between us."

"Fine."

"I kissed you."

"Yes, you did. Your mouth collided with mine," she said. "We have been mortal enemies for more than a decade and then you kissed me, suddenly. For no particular reason."

"And you didn't like it."

Daisy glanced over at him. He kept his eyes focused on the road, thank goodness. This was far too perilous a conversation to have while driving through Broadway traffic. The alternative was to launch herself from a moving carriage, a prospect that did not enthrall at the moment. But she considered it.

Theo continued, "I am trying to ascertain if it was me, or you, or us together."

Daisy shrugged. "What does it matter? It was something you did on the spur of the moment for no reason I can think of, other than perhaps you felt pity for me after that soul-crushing turn about the ballroom. Seeing as how we will hardly need to socialize together again, I hope, you won't be made to feel pity for me and thus you won't feel compelled to kiss me. In short, I can't imagine we would do it again."

"Right, then." He coughed as if trying to clear words that were stuck in his throat. She snuck a gaze in his direction. Eyes, fixed on the road. Hands, gripping the reins. This was *hard* for him, she realized. But he was trying anyway.

She did not want her heart to soften to him. But her heart did it anyway.

"Oh. You imagined doing it again," she said

as understanding dawned. She felt a flush of warmth steal across her skin as she realized that Theodore Prescott the Third had not only kissed her once but had some notion of kissing her again. She felt . . . wanted. Desired. Maybe for the first time; she hadn't really stopped to consider it before.

Lest she get ideas, Theo continued, "There is also my reputation to consider. You know how much I care about my reputation. I can't have word going around that my kisses are only whelming. So I need you to tell me why it left you whelmed so I can do better for the next woman I kiss."

Daisy snuck a glance at him; did he really mean that or was he obsessing over his pride again? Or was there another reason? What did go on in the head and heart of Theodore Prescott the Third anyway?

"Well, I can't speak for all women, only for me. And your kiss was too . . . much. Too fast. Too deep. Too much and too soon."

"That was unrestrained passion. The thrill of the moment."

"I might find some restrained passion more seductive," Daisy said. "While I'm admittedly a novice, I do know what sparks desire and what doesn't. Also, Theo, we don't *like* each other. The kiss felt like . . . a pity kiss. While I appreciate the sentiment, I don't need it."

Theo was silent. Daisy tried not to feel bad for

saying so much. But he had asked. And he had to know that she was never one to hold her tongue. And he was still sitting calmly beside her, listening and not launching himself out of the carriage into oncoming traffic.

So she said even more. She spoke from the heart. "When a man kisses me, I want it to mean something. Desire for me. All of me, body and soul. And I want to feel the same way. That's all."

That was everything though.

The carriage rolled to a stop before her family's home. Neither she nor Theo moved to alight.

"Thank you, Daisy, for enduring an awkward conversation with me."

"It wasn't exactly my pleasure but . . . you're welcome."

"We have done it again. A civil exchange."

"Pity no one is around to see it."

She was looking at Theo, looking at her. He was so handsome. But for the first time she found herself *attracted* to him and it was because of the way he was looking at her, as if he really saw her as a whole person whom he admired and not a collection of features and a silly nickname. There was something like kindness in his blue eyes. And appreciation. And all that made her reconsider him. And her.

This was a terrifying, troubling feeling.

"We'll never speak of kissing again," he said and she was relieved. "And now that we might be business partners, it would be rather unseemly for us to be kissing."

Business partners. Her. Him. She'd believe it when she saw it.

"We don't have much time to do the impossible," Daisy said. "Are you certain you're up for it?"

To which Theo replied, "I'll call on you tomorrow."

Chapter Eleven

An orchestra has been engaged for the wedding
   ceremony and celebration of Miss Daisy
   Swan and Theodore Prescott the Third.
          —*The New York Post*

The next day
854 Fifth Avenue

*I*t was a Thursday that Theo finally woke up
with something to do. Something other than
idle dissipation or tennis or social calls, that is.
He was going to help make a young woman's
dreams come true. No small thing, that. In doing so, he might just make amends for the past
damage he had unwittingly inflicted all those
years ago. He might even find his life's work.
That was asking a lot of a face cream or complexion balm or whatever one called it. And
himself.

   And yet here he was, knocking on the door
of the Swans' town house, dressed in one of his
finer suits.

Mrs. Evelina Swan was all too eager to show Theo to the parlor, send a servant for a tray, and make excuses as to why she would be otherwise occupied and could not, alas, properly chaperone them. That was matchmaking mamas for you. It suited their purposes admirably. Daisy had been right that pretending to be together would afford them the freedom to pursue other things.

Daisy soon appeared, wearing a smart blue serge dress with her hair styled elegantly. She cut a smart, stylish figure, even if it was just the two of them for a business meeting masquerading as a social call. Or had she always presented herself thusly and he'd never really noticed? It was entirely possible.

"You're here," Daisy said by way of greeting.

"Hello to you, too. I said I would be, didn't I?"

Her mother swiftly made herself scarce on the other side of the drawing-room doors.

"I suppose I am still shocked that we are doing . . . this," Daisy said.

"If there's one thing I've learned from my father, it's the value of one's word. So here I am. Which means today we are going to do precisely as we agreed yesterday."

Even if he wasn't sure he could do it. Theo had stayed up late, sipping whiskey and thinking about possible names and ways to advertise it, and what was required in a sales plan anyway? He considered seeking his father to ask, but that would lead to all sorts of questions and Theo wasn't ready to risk his father's laughter.

Theo very badly wanted this to work, so here he was.

Daisy reached into the pocket of her gown—it was all the rage among a certain set of ladies to wear gowns with pockets, made exclusively by the House of Adeline—and handed him a little, unmarked jar.

The complexion balm.

Some white, creamy stuff in a nondescript glass container with no label whatsoever. Theo knew this, as it was, would never entice a woman who cared about beauty to pick it up or try it or rave about it to her friends. It needed a more attractive package. It needed a name. It needed to make a promise. It needed *style*.

He dared to think it needed him.

"Tell me about this," Theo said with the hope that her words would inspire some spark of brilliance on his part.

"It's based on my grandmother's recipe," Daisy explained. "She grew up in some remote corner of Eastern Europe, where winters were harsh, so I suppose it was created to protect her skin from those elements. It was one of the few things she brought to America when she immigrated here."

"Immigrants bring all kinds of treasures to America."

"Oh, absolutely," Daisy agreed. "But while her

formula was effective—my mother, sisters, and I all used it—it had its problems. The base ingredient spoiled easily and so fresh batches had to be made constantly—and who has time for that in this day and age? Certainly not working women, or middle-class women. Society ladies simply wouldn't."

"Even if a woman had the time, she might enjoy something ready-made," Theo said. "Something prepared just for her."

"The original recipe also didn't have the best scent."

Theo opened the lid and took a deep breath.

"It smells good now."

"It's my perfume."

"So I noticed."

Oh, he had noticed. Her fragrance was softly applied, uniquely hers, and he could still catch the hint of it on the jacket he wore to the ball the other night. Her perfume wasn't intense or overwhelming, but strong and subtle and it snuck up on you.

Like her.

Theo lifted his gaze to Daisy. She didn't look away.

It was the strangest thing. All of a sudden he didn't want to be anywhere else in the world than here, with her, at this moment. Except closer, perhaps. Suddenly, he wanted to kiss her just for the sake of kissing her.

The other night it had been to prove something. Or because he felt sorry for her. Whatever the reason, it had been wrong. But now he just wanted to get lost with her. She was right about that, too; he hadn't kissed her for the right reasons and she had felt it. Next time . . .

There would be no next time.

And this was a business meeting.

"I fixed all those problems with my training in chemistry," she said, bringing him back to the conversation. "I spent hours of trial and error to refine the process so the scent and consistency are . . . enticing."

Theo knew an opportunity when he held it in the palm of his hand. This complexion balm—of all the things in the world—was his big chance to make something and to prove something.

And Daisy was watching.

He felt something like anxiety over his performance. After all, he had inserted himself into her business. He had leaned into her and said, *I'm the man you need.* He had made promises and now he had to deliver. On the spot. No pressure.

Could he take this ugly little jar of scented gloop and make it so irresistible and enticing that women would want it desperately? Could the women of Manhattan go so mad for it that they started a sensation? That they earned a fortune and their freedom from each other?

Theo started to pace. It always worked for his

father, it seemed. Maybe pacing would get his brain sparking. At the very least, it might make him look like he was trying in Daisy's eyes.

Suddenly, he cared what he looked like in Daisy's eyes.

"Secret family recipe . . ." Theo repeated. *Focus, man.*

"I didn't say it was secret."

"It is now," he said. "That sounds so much more intriguing. Secret family recipe meets the latest science. For a luminous complexion."

"Luminous?"

He turned to face her. Looked into her eyes.

"This is the secret to your complexion, is it not?"

"Yes."

"Luminous," he repeated firmly. "Like a Pre-Raphaelite painting or a portrait in the old style. Your complexion is enviable. A marvel. The eighth wonder of the world."

To which she replied, "Thank you."

Theo took another step closer to her and dropped his voice.

"Tell me, Daisy, is your skin as soft as it looks?"

"You tell me, Theo."

An invitation. That was an invitation to touch her. Nothing to get excited about. And yet . . . Suddenly, Theo's heart started beating with the anticipation of touching *Daisy Swan*. He had probably declared her the last woman on earth that he'd want to romance and yet there was no denying that she was the only woman he was interested in caressing. And kissing.

It was a small step to close the distance between them. Theo reached out, brushing his knuckles along her cheek.

So. Damn. Soft.

He took a step closer and thought about cradling her cheek in his hand and holding her still so he could lower his mouth to hers for a kiss. He wanted, badly, to kiss her. Just because he wanted to.

His heart was already thundering when she stepped closer and turned her face up to his. As if she knew what he was thinking. As if she had the same idea. This was an invitation and his body was responding accordingly.

His nerves hummed with anticipation, which surprised him.

"Enticing," he murmured.

And just when he couldn't stand the distance and started to lower his head to hers, Daisy stepped back and turned away.

"It's just complexion balm. I put it on before bed and—"

"Let it work its magic overnight," he finished. "And then you wake up like this. Flawless."

"I've got plenty of problems, but my complexion is not one."

He stepped back, needing air and space to

think about the task at hand, not the girl. Kissing the girl. Touching the girl. Wanting the girl. He told himself it was *Daisy*. Only the most maddening and intriguing woman he'd met. And he was here for *business*.

"So, Daisy, you've got a story. You've got magic . . ." There was something here. He could feel it. Sense it. All he needed to do was catch it. Hold it. Bottle it. Sell it. He so badly wanted to do right by her, by this, by himself. His father would hate that when his son finally developed an interest in business, it was for "women's stuff." Theo knew this alone would not get him the approval he yearned for. But if he could make it so, so, so stunningly and spectacularly successful then maybe he would earn his father's grudging respect.

"It's not magic, it's science."

"There you go. We'll put that on the label."

"I should have thought of that."

"But first . . . the name."

Theo stepped away from Daisy of the enticing skin and alluring scent and promises of kisses. He needed to think. For that, he took a turn about the room, a large spacious affair stuffed with fine furniture, marble-topped tables laden with silver stuff, walls heavy with the weight of portraits and paintings. Large windows overlooked Central Park and the city.

It was a glorious view.

What had started as just a favor for a girl swiftly became his own personal quest. He wanted to dream up something catchy, something seductive, something that would sell. For her sake. For his own. He wanted to be good at something. To have a purpose. To look back on this day later tonight or years from now and think, *I did something that made a difference.*

And so he paced. And racked his pretty, Harvard-educated brain.

Magic. Overnight. Enticing. Science.

Something that would take the town by storm. Something the city had never seen. Something he could see on a woman's dressing table in her Fifth Avenue bedroom or up on a billboard high above the city streets. Something one didn't realize one had been missing from their life. Something that made promises—and kept them.

Soft, silky, smooth. Here for a moment of pleasure before vanishing forever. Like a dream.

Theo paced. Drummed his fingers on a tabletop. Rearranged some knickknacks on the mantel. Daisy was watching him. Her eyes never left him. He feared that she expected him to fail at this, even if she didn't want him to. How long had he been here anyway? Hours?

He glanced up at the clock.

And then in an instant it came to him.

"I've got it."

"You've got it?"

"The Midnight Miracle Cream. *Feels like a dream.*"

"Oh." It was a soft-spoken *oh* and he couldn't tell if she thought it was good, terrible, or execrable. If he had to explain it, then it was all ruined. It either worked or it didn't. A connection between two people was either there or it wasn't. And then she sighed. *"Oooh."*

His heart did undignified flip-floppy things that it had never, ever done before. He felt a surge of something—pride, maybe? Satisfaction? Joy?

Daisy's lips quirked into a smile, and then she broke into a grin. "You've got it, Theo!"

DAISY KNEW THEO was onto something when she found herself practically leaping into his arms. But she was vibrating with the possibilities of such a name, and the thrill of being present the moment someone experienced a spark of genius. Before she knew it, Daisy was off the settee and wrapping her arms around him.

It felt so right and very good until she remembered it was him, and her, and they hated each other.

How embarrassing!

But it so happened that Theodore Prescott the Third was not just a pretty face, a Harvard diploma, and regular, salacious appearances in the gossip columns. All his rubbish playboy practice to woo, seduce, and entice women had now just been used in her favor. His talents for teasing and name-calling had been finally focused on creating something *good*. He took her basic product and found the pretty, the style, the spark. He took her science and added magic.

She found herself wooed. Seduced. Enticed.

By *Theo*.

It was an afternoon miracle.

She had to admit, he felt like a dream. All fine cashmere wool and lean, firm muscles. He was hot, too; she felt her temperature spike standing here in his arms, waiting for the inevitable.

Daisy was waiting for his mouth to crash down on hers.

The memory of their first kiss had faded. She hadn't particularly enjoyed that consolation kiss, driven by his pity, yet now she felt herself wanting to try again. Because for the first time she felt something like magic, and a genuine connection, and she wanted to get closer to the feeling and make it last and last.

And she was in his arms, for goodness' sake!

She was still waiting for his lips to collide with hers.

But he did not kiss her.

Theo just looked at her. Really looked at her.

She was used to dismissive glances or men making an effort not to meet her eye, lest she think they might be interested. Sometimes Daisy debated what was worse: being looked at dismissively or not being regarded at all. This level of looking and seeing was something she wasn't prepared for.

Her instinct was to worry about what he saw—the nose a little too large, the eyes a little too close, the mouth that wasn't a fashionable little rosebud. It occurred to her that he was looking at her up close and intimately *and he wasn't going away.*

He saw her, and his arms held her just the same. The distance between them was minimal.

Daisy took the opportunity to look at him instead of dwelling on her own anxieties. What she saw took her breath away. The way his blue eyes were transfixed—there was really no other word for it—upon her. The way his dark lashes lowered as his gaze dropped to her mouth, like he was wondering if her lips were as soft as they looked. It wasn't his features that made him attractive; it was the way he looked at her, reverentially and with questions and desire that started that slow burn in her belly.

"Yes . . ." she whispered.

His lips parted. Hers, too.

Theodore Prescott the Third, her nemesis, her enemy, the bane of her existence for over a decade, was about to kiss her. And she wanted him to.

Finally, she felt the lightest, briefest caress of his lips upon hers.

It felt like a dream.

Like it was so ethereal that it didn't seem real. She wanted to reach out and hold on to it, this precious, dreamy thing, but it was all air and fantasy and spun sugar. Like a dream this kiss was light and fleeting, over before it really began, and left her confused.

Before his kiss had been too much, too soon.

Now here she was like Goldilocks; one kiss was too little, one too much. One too fast, one too slow. One was rude in its presumptions, one was far too polite.

She wanted to thread her fingers through his blond hair. Was it as soft as it seemed? Grab fistfuls of his finely tailored jacket and wrinkle it. What was wrong with her? Where had this passion come from?

She did not recognize herself or this feeling of urgency and desire bubbling up within. Yet there was no denying she wanted to explore it, to know it, to get intimate with it.

Did he not feel this, too? Did he not want to seize this moment when two longtime sworn enemies dropped their swords, closed their eyes, and surrendered to each other?

This was a kiss that inspired more questions than answers. And this was a kiss that came to an end. A slow, bittersweet parting. She even felt herself stumbling toward him as he pulled away.

How embarrassing.

"I'm sorry, Daisy. As business partners we should not . . . do that."

The hot rush of desire she'd been feeling cooled instantly. He was right, and she would have to admit it. Daisy smoothed her skirts and agreed with him. For the sake of their new business and not getting married and everything she'd ever wanted.

"Yes, you're right," she said. "Especially if we are trying not to get married. Kissing in a drawing room is really an unnecessary risk."

"I promise I won't let it happen again."

"That would be for the best," Daisy said. But she wasn't sure she meant it. She definitely didn't know what to make of that feeling.

Chapter Twelve

> While many in Manhattan are curious about
> the wedding plans for the forthcoming
> Swan-Prescott match, all anyone really
> wants to know about is the dress.
> —*The New York Post*

The House of Adeline

*D*aisy may still have had the taste of him on her lips, but she had absolutely no intention of marrying Theodore Prescott the Third and yet here she was, being fitted for a wedding dress. And not just any wedding dress, but one that would leave no question in anyone's mind that a spinster wallflower like Daisy deserved the likes of Theodore Prescott the Universally Adored.

"It should be the pinnacle of fashion," Evelina Swan told Adeline Black, who was presently *the* dressmaker for Manhattan's elite, soon to be the duchess of Kingston, and eternally a woman who did not need to be told about fashion.

It should not be anything, Daisy thought. *It should not even exist.*

Just because they had shared a kiss or two and now, apparently, a business venture, didn't mean she actually wanted to marry him. They had despised each other for more than a decade and had only managed some sort of truce in the past few weeks. This new, fragile something between them was too new and fragile to be the basis of a lifetime together.

And now they might not even have to say "I do." In the space of one afternoon, Theo had taken the tragically named Daisy's Complexion Balm and reimagined it as *The Midnight Miracle Cream: Feels like a dream!* She could readily admit that if she had a chance of success, it was in part because of him. And she really, truly felt like they did have a chance of success.

So she really did not need this dress.

"I have a vision of a wedding dress like Consuelo Vanderbilt's—but fancier, and more expensive," her mother said.

No, Daisy thought. *Just no.*

Adeline tilted her head as if she was actually considering it and murmured, "Hmmm."

"I think satin and lace," her mother said.

I think a smart traveling suit, Daisy thought. *For when I flee the country. Alone. Rather than don a monstrosity of a gown and marry a man I don't love.*

"I have recently obtained some lace that

had been handmade by three sisters—identical triplets—in a nunnery in Belgium," Adeline said. "They used silver thread that had been locked in a castle for a hundred years but somehow miraculously preserved. It was hand delivered by a lady-in-waiting to the queen."

"I suppose that will do," her mother sighed.

Daisy wanted to scream into an upholstered pillow.

This was getting out of hand.

This was officially too much.

Thank God she had an ally in this farce.

Daisy and the dressmaker exchanged a look. This was not their first time collaborating on a gown. The House of Adeline had supplied all of Daisy's most fashionable frocks. Unbeknownst to Mrs. Swan, they were both members of the Ladies of Liberty Club. Daisy knew she could count on Adeline to take her side. It was the saving grace of this nightmare of a dress fitting.

"And what do you think, Miss Swan?" Adeline inquired.

"Why don't we go with something simple?" Daisy replied breezily. "Something very modest, as well. Definitely a veil. Instead of satin, let's consider bombazine. And instead of white, let's make everything black."

"Daisy! Black is for mourning! You are describing a mourning dress!"

"Exactly. I shall be in mourning for the death

of freedom. The death of my hopes and dreams of spinsterhood or at least a marriage for love. It will be the death of innocence and hope and—"

"How can you not fall in love with Theo?" her mother asked incredulously. "He's wealthy, well connected, and so . . . pretty." Mrs. Swan turned to Adeline and said, "Her fiancé is incredibly good-looking. She'll need a gown that holds its own when she stands beside him."

"I see," Adeline said.

Daisy looked away, but caught her reflection in the mirror. The nose a trifle too big, the eyes a little too close set, the mouth that was nothing to write poems about. Her hair, which couldn't decide if it was blond or brown. She wasn't pretty. An extravagant gown wouldn't hide or distract from that fact. She would only look like a woman trying too hard to be something she was not, which Daisy steadfastly refused to do.

"Mrs. Swan, why don't you take a look at our fabric selections while enjoying some refreshments?" Adeline offered as she ushered her out of the fitting area. "Please do look for just the right satin in a shade that you think is suitable. I'll confer with Miss Swan on her measurements. Whether a wedding gown or a mourning dress, it must fit perfectly!"

This was a relief to all parties involved. The

moment her mother was out of earshot, Daisy turned to Adeline and said, "There will be no wedding. Obviously."

"Obviously."

"If you couldn't make the dress in time, it would not be a catastrophe," Daisy said, as an idea occurred to her. She brightened considerably. "In fact, we couldn't possibly go through with the wedding if something happened to the dress."

"One could not possibly get married in any old dress," Adeline agreed. Perhaps one could, but not if one was going to marry the most eligible bachelor in Manhattan in an extravagant wedding organized by Mrs. Evelina Swan.

"We'll have to ruin it somehow. At the last minute," Daisy said, thinking quickly.

"What did you have in mind?" Adeline smiled mischievously.

"Fire. Flood. Ink stains. It could be stolen, lost, or never made in the first place. I'm not particular."

Adeline's smothered chuckle turned into a lovely, full-bellied laugh. Daisy couldn't help but join in.

"What will your fiancé say to all this?" Adeline asked.

"He is wholly supportive of my plans. Or he will be, when I inform him of them."

"That's something special to have a fiancé who is supportive of one's plans. It's a wonderful thing to have a co-conspirator."

"Yes, I suppose it is." Daisy found herself agreeing. Thus far, Theo had been a good sport about this fake engagement business, which made the whole thing a little more bearable.

"It's not every day one finds a man who shares the same dreams. And one who will support you in yours," Adeline said. And she didn't even know the half of it; that Theo was the only one so far who had wholeheartedly embraced her dreams of creating and selling her own preparations. That was above and beyond a shared dream of not wishing to wed each other. This was, she might concede, something special.

"I certainly hadn't in the past twenty-five years," Daisy said. "But now . . ."

"But there are more things to consider in a partner of course," Adeline continued. "Like passion. Kissing. Making love. These are important considerations, too."

To this, Daisy only said, "Hmm." Why did everyone want to talk to her about kissing lately?

"From that blush on your cheeks and the dreamy look in your eyes I'm guessing you have . . . considered it."

"Perhaps," Daisy admitted, and to her mortification, her cheeks felt awfully hot. Because ever since that kiss with Theo in the drawing room—

the one that wasn't enough—she had been considering kissing him. A lot. More. Pity, then, that he'd been busy on errands and hadn't come to call and so there really hadn't been an opportunity to see if they might just maybe perhaps kiss again.

"Are you sure you want to call off the wedding?"

"Completely. Utterly. Absolutely."

"What shall I do about the dress?"

That was the question. The dress that Mrs. Swan was envisioning—all that satin, that fancy lace, and probably some pearls, too—would be an extraordinary expense. One the Swan family might not even be able to afford. The dress would be a work of art and it would require hours and hours and hours of delicate work by Adeline's team of highly skilled seamstresses. Minutes, hours, days, weeks of their lives dedicated to a gorgeous gown that would never be worn.

What a waste.

And yet . . . there was the small complicating factor of the way Theo had kissed her once, twice, and she wanted more. There was also the complicating factor of their burgeoning business, which, if it worked, would give her the life she always wanted: mistress of her own fate, a creative outlet that assured she could afford her own independence. She couldn't risk all that for just a few kisses.

Besides, they had raised a glass to not getting married.

And so, Daisy was not prepared to don an extravagantly and exquisitely crafted gown and walk down the aisle in front of all of New York Society when she wasn't sure that she wanted him to be waiting at the altar.

With confidence, Daisy said, "There will be no dress."

Chapter Thirteen

The couple of the hour has hardly been
seen at society events recently. One
wonders what they are up to instead.
—*The New York Post*

27 Union Square

*T*he newspapers reported that the Rogues
of Millionaire Row were up to no good again.
They were in Newport—or, more precisely, on a
yacht—with a bevy of tycoons, an assortment of
actresses, and a seemingly endless quantity of
champagne. Theo was not with them.

He had spent the week in the city.

Working. Yes, *working.*

But it hadn't felt like his previous experiences
with work, when he'd been sent to shadow a factory manager and ruined his best pair of boots or
when he'd been given a desk at his father's office
and told to make himself useful. Which he failed
to do.

But when it came to surveying the options of glass and crystal jars for the Midnight Miracle Cream, or designing and producing a label, the hours had passed pleasantly and he had something to show for his efforts at the end of the day. This was a satisfaction like he'd never known.

That wasn't the only task that had kept him busy from dawn till dusk.

He had something else to show Daisy and he'd never, ever anticipated something as much as he did this. It had consumed his every waking hour. It had tested his connections, his education, and his commitment to this mad venture. He was deeply proud of his work and had every expectation that Daisy would be *thrilled*.

It was vitally important to him that Daisy be thrilled.

"Close your eyes," he told her. The carriage had dropped them at one end of the bustling city square, just steps away from the Ladies' Mile. He just needed her to close her eyes the last few steps until their destination.

"That requires an amount of trust I am not sure that I am prepared to extend to you," Daisy replied.

"And here I thought we were friends now," Theo remarked.

"A stunning, unexpected turn of events."

"Do you want the good news or the bad news first?" Theo asked.

"Bad. Of course. Immediately."

"I have not had success getting the department stores to stock the Midnight Miracle Cream." That was the task that had not been satisfying and had been downright demoralizing. The department store managers took his meeting—the name Theodore Prescott did tend to open doors in this town—but they were not convinced by his sales pitch about proper, respectable women stepping out in public to purchase such intimate items, most usually associated with actresses and "actresses." He added, "They are not confident that the sort of clientele they cater to will take kindly to the kind of product we're selling."

Daisy pressed her lips into a line. She was obviously disappointed. But she needn't be—Theo had figured it all out. That was what he was so excited to show her.

"And the good news?"

"Close your eyes." Arm in arm, he guided her halfway down the block. Past the shops and boarding houses. Alongside the horses, carriages, and pedestrians walking along the sidewalk in a rush. He brought them to a stop in front of one particular storefront.

"Open your eyes, Daisy."

He watched her face as her lashes lifted up, as her gaze settled on the large, lavender sign above the windowed storefront. His heart was pounding. He realized he was nervous because this mattered—and not just to get out of the wedding, either. He wanted his work to be remarkable and for his business partner to find it agreeable.

"I thought we could open our own shop. What do you think?"

"Doctor Swan?" The name on the sign was *Dr. Swan's Apothecary*.

"I thought a bigger name for the business was in order, in the event that you create other products. The *doctor* adds a touch of respectability. Madame Swan's sounded too much like a brothel, I thought." Daisy's expression didn't betray her thoughts or feelings. He asked nervously, "Do you like it?"

"It looks . . . expensive, Theo. I've been saving my allowance for ages to prepare the initial batch of the Midnight Miracle Cream. I have enough for that, but I certainly don't have enough for such an impressive sign. And a whole store to go with it."

"Don't worry about that. A friend's father cut me a deal. And I took out a loan."

"Oh."

It was not a good *oh.* It was an *oh* that fell flat and died fast.

"Let me show you the inside."

The floors were gleaming hardwood; the chandeliers were crystal and shiny brass. The walls were lined with mirrors and glass shelves to display the products. In the center of the room there was a large carved wooden counter with a gray marble top. Stacked upon it were piles of Dr. Swan's Midnight Miracle Cream in their new cut-glass jars meant to look like crystal. The labels were printed on a soft lavender paper that reminded him of Daisy: cool, but sweet. Feminine, but not cloyingly so.

He had spent the better part of the week getting the shop and the product in order. To find just the right look that conveyed sensation, not scandal. Beautiful, but accessible.

The only thing that kept Theo from thoroughly taking pride in his task was the knowledge that this was not the purpose or professional work that his father had envisioned for him. In fact, his father would probably disown him if he discovered that *this* was what had kept his son busy and . . . happy.

They were Prescott Steel! Strong, hard, and long-lasting. It was the stuff of massive, phallic skyscrapers and dangerous weapons—manly, masculine stuff.

Glass was delicate, prone to shattering. It was pretty. And it was for ladies.

But now Theo only had eyes for Daisy, who did a slow turnaround, taking it all in. She picked up a jar and examined it from all angles. She opened the lid and breathed in. Yes, it was her genius product just in a new package.

"Oh . . ."

This *oh* had a little more life in it.

"We'll need to hire some salesgirls," he said. "People who can explain the product and help sell it."

"I can handle that. I have a connection," she said without a second thought.

"Of course."

"This is all so . . . beautiful, Theo. It's so *luxurious* for such an industrious product."

"I thought that since we were doing something people consider tawdry, we should make the space radiate beauty and quality."

"That's a good idea. You certainly managed it."

"Wait, there is more to show you." This was the part he was especially keen to show her. It was his atonement, perhaps, for calling her Ugly Duck Daisy so long ago. It was his way of recognizing her talents, of encouraging her beyond just words. It was a genuine compliment, in physical form. And as he saw it, this was her ticket to freedom from him.

Theo took her hand and led her through an unmarked door to a private room brightly lit by large windows and those new electric lights. The center of the room was dominated by a large laboratory table with a black soapstone counter.

This was one soft, breathless "Oooooh."

"I don't know what equipment you'll need, and I wouldn't presume to guess. Given that this is your area of expertise, I have a supplier standing by for whatever you wish to order. You have space here to make the product and do experiments and create more. I thought that since you're graduating soon, you will need laboratory space . . ."

"Oh, Theo." She turned to him and her eyes were bright with—gah, were those *tears*? That was not the reaction he'd been aspiring to. He didn't want to make her cry. "Theo, this is remarkable. And so thoughtful. And possibly the kindest, most wonderful thing anyone has ever done for me."

Not just a pretty face after all.

She liked it. Theo breathed a sigh of relief and leaned against the wall and watched as she walked around, traced her fingers along the soapstone tabletop, noted the open shelves waiting for her equipment, and peeked out the window (the view wasn't much; this was the ground floor of a Manhattan building, after all).

"I hope you don't mind," he said. "You're not the only one with your heart set on independence from your family."

"You want to get out from under your father's thumb, don't you?"

"I know this isn't what he had in mind for me—anything other than Prescott Steel would be a disappointment—but I hope that if we're successful enough he'll be somewhat impressed. Maybe he'll even approve."

"Why does it matter so much that he does?"

"Why wouldn't it? Don't you want your mother's approval?"

"It would be nice. But I know she loves me regardless so . . ." His face must have betrayed him and Daisy kindly refrained from finishing the sentence or pursuing the matter further. Because that was the thing; he didn't know that his father loved him unconditionally. He didn't want to talk about it. He just wanted to make this work.

Instead, she turned and wandered around the store slowly and he was glad she let the matter drop. She seemed to like everything, but hers was not the joyful display he'd been hoping for.

"What's wrong, Daisy? You seem . . . whelmed."

"It's so much. So fast," Daisy explained. "For so long, it was all mine and now it's . . . not. I never imagined sharing it. But already it's as much yours as it is mine."

"I didn't realize—"

"What you have done here is magnificent, Theo. I never would have packaged it so prettily or had the courage to open a shop so soon. Your taste is exquisite and if it works, it will be because of your contributions. But it's all happening so fast."

"We don't have much time," he said gently. "Your mother has sent out invitations to the wedding."

"It's really happening. Unless . . ."

"I'll tell you what, Daisy. Let's make a deal. Once we repay the loan, seventy percent of Dr. Swan is yours. All the profits, the ownership, all that. We'll have lawyers draw up paperwork. But for now, I give you my word as a gentleman."

It was an offer his father never, ever would have made. Prescott the Second would have offered her a hundred dollars for the recipe and left her out in the cold. Theo could already hear the old man hitting the roof if he ever learned that Theo had relinquished so much, so early in the game, and to a woman. Maybe he didn't want his approval that much, at any cost. Because already he didn't want to be the sort of man who stole a woman's lifework and livelihood just because he could.

But Theo had come to realize that he wanted something more than just money. A purpose. And maybe even Daisy's happiness.

Definitely worth it for that spark in her eye as she walked toward him to stand just in front of him.

"You have a deal. But I don't want your word as a gentleman."

"Oh? What do you want?"

"A kiss."

Sealed with a kiss. Of course. Theo was pretty sure that this was not how business was usually done. But given the way Daisy was looking at him, he was also pretty sure he didn't care. Because Daisy was looking at him like she wanted all of him for him—his head, his heart, him—not just his pretty mouth. Or his father's last name or fortune.

"Close your eyes, Daisy."

This time she did. Their lips met, softly at first. He had some idea of keeping his distance, of keeping things light and not getting too serious, of keeping this a perfunctory kiss to mark a business arrangement.

This was no perfunctory kiss. No. Not at all. Because once his lips touched hers, once her lips parted, and once he tasted her, he knew he wanted to kiss her for hours for no reason other than pleasure.

His hands skimmed from her shoulders, lower, to her waist and with a gentle pressure on the small of her back he urged her closer. Because if they were going to break the rules and kiss, then they really ought to kiss.

Savor it.

Sink into it.

Theo caressed her cheeks with her soft, feels-like-a-dream skin in his palms, cradled her head and drank her in. He followed her lead on how fast or slow or deep or just nibbled on her lower lip and when she mewled with pleasure he knew it was worth it—all of it. Putting himself on the line, laying himself bare, and taking the risk of laughter or awkward conversations or worse.

She grabbed on to the lapels of his jacket, holding on to him and holding him close. The fabric would be worse for wear, but whatever. Because this was a slow burn of a kiss in the middle of the afternoon with the woman he least expected. And there was nowhere else he'd rather be. And so they kissed for hours or minutes or both.

He definitely lost track of time.

Until she suddenly pulled back.

"What time is it?"

Somewhat dazed, he pulled out his pocket watch. "Two o'clock."

"I have someplace to be. I'll be late!"

"What? Where? I'll take you." Theo watched as she took a jar or two of their Midnight Miracle Cream and tucked it into her satchel.

On her way out, she gave him a smile and said, "I would tell you but I have been sworn to secrecy."

Chapter Fourteen

Opening today: Dr. Swan's Apothecary,
purveyor of ladies' toilet preparations,
the likes of which we have been assured
have never been seen before.
—*The New York Post*

One week later
854 Fifth Avenue

*H*ow Daisy was supposed to survive breakfast
with her mother on a day like today, Daisy did
not know. It was the day that Dr. Swan's Apothecary was due to celebrate its grand opening. It
was also the day that an advertisement for said
event would be appearing in the ladies' pages of
The New York World. Which was all to say that
today was the day that determined Daisy's fate.

She had saved her pin money for ages to finance
the first batch of the Midnight Miracle Cream, including the expensive jars Theo had selected and
the fair wages of the women she'd hired to help
her produce it and sell it. Theo had taken out a

not-insignificant loan to finance the shop; Daisy almost fainted when he told her.

This day would either make them or break them. They would have an idea whether they could afford to skip the wedding, or whether they'd have to go through with it because they owed money to people all over town.

A horrible thought, that. Marriage to a man whom she did not love—and whom she shared some knee-weakening, toe-curling, breathtaking, heart-pounding kisses. Marriage to a man who definitely understood her—he built her a laboratory of her own, a better gift to her she could not imagine.

But it was still Theo. The man who had the greatest capacity to hurt her and had done so before.

So it was not just any other day, or any breakfast with her mother. Her father, of course, having been down at Wall Street for hours already, doing whatever one did on Wall Street.

To say Daisy was nervous was a massive understatement.

And now her mother wanted to have a talk.

"Daisy, we need to talk," her mother said.

"Hmm." Daisy sipped her tea and did her very best not to tear through the newspaper looking for their advertisement. *Perhaps it's all a dream*, she thought. Perhaps she had imagined Theo, the shop, the wedding, everything. But once she saw the ad, she would know it was real.

"Daisy," her mother persisted. "We need to talk about your future."

"I do believe we've had this conversation, Mother."

"Yes, Daisy, but hmm . . ."

Daisy set down her tea and looked up.

"Mother, you are making a sound that indicates you are having thoughts."

At this point Daisy finally saw the advertisement. It was right there, on the paper her mother had been reading. Daisy didn't need to look any closer to know what it said; Theo had submitted the text with her approval.

Dr. Swan's Midnight Miracle Complexion Cream

Positively made from a recipe used for years by society beauties, newly enhanced by science. Never before manufactured for sale. For the New Woman who wishes for a luminous complexion. $1.50

Grand Opening Today at 27 Union Square

"I just find it curious that there is an advertisement for a new complexion balm produced by one Dr. Swan, who is opening a new store this very day."

"My felicitations," Daisy murmured, her heart picking up the pace.

"It's such a coincidence that someone with the same name as you should be launching a product you have been chattering about. Do you find that curious? I find that curious."

No. Not at all. Not even remotely.

Daisy just shrugged. She didn't quite trust herself with words. She may have been on the far side of twenty-five years old, but when her mother looked at her like that, she was thirteen all over again.

"It says the store is opening today," her mother said, pointing right to the page.

"Does it?"

Daisy did her best to sound like this was new information when, in fact, she had lain awake for most of the night obsessing about it.

"I don't suppose you'll be there. If only to scope out the competition," her mother said. "Seeing as how someone else has taken your idea and your name and opened a shop with it."

"I have a meeting of the Charitable Ladies' Auxiliary Club," Daisy said. It was not technically untrue.

"I'm so glad to hear it. Because it would be dreadful if people thought this was something you were involved in. Can you just imagine if people thought Jack Swan's daughter was engaged in trade? They might worry about our finances, and how the brokerage firm is faring. The last thing we need is skittish investors, particularly when things are already so precarious. I'm sure I don't need to say how vital one's good reputation is and at least the illusion of success."

Her mother sipped her tea and resumed reading the newspaper.

She did not need to say more.

Later that morning
27 Union Square

ON WEDNESDAYS, THE Ladies of Liberty embarked on adventures. There were always protests to join, demonstrations to make, or volunteer efforts to undertake.

A woman's work was never done.

On this Wednesday in particular they gathered for the grand opening of Dr. Swan's Apothecary to celebrate one of their own and to present a show of respectable, ladylike force to support this daring, lady-led venture.

After all, they could not allow one of their own to marry a man she didn't love due to a lack of alternatives. And if the solution was as simple as going shopping, then it had to be done.

But the Ladies of Liberty did not just show up en masse. They had a simple plan, stylishly executed. At precisely eleven o'clock in the morning a small group of well-attired, respectable women entered the store. This was not a particularly remarkable event for a shop just steps off the famed

Ladies' Mile, especially one that had placed an advertisement in the newspaper that morning.

But it was a daring new shop.

And one could not risk that the only patrons were there to gawk or gossip. Indeed, quite a few women did wander in, though they seemed not to have the courage, means, or desire to make a purchase and walk out with it. For that, one required a certain type of customer. Fashionable ladies accustomed to setting trends and respectable women who would make this new thing appear safe and acceptable.

Fortunately, another group of those women arrived at precisely fifteen minutes after eleven. Harriet had organized a strategic onslaught of lady shoppers to show in no uncertain terms that this was a product with high demand among respectable ladies. They arrived at their appointed time, engaged with the salesgirls, and made their purchases, daringly exiting the shop with their packages wrapped in Dr. Swan's signature lavender paper. But not without raving about the Midnight Miracle Cream.

"I've been using this cream for a month now and I swear I look years younger," Miss Parks said and nearby a woman who had been tentatively considering it proceeded to make her purchase.

"I honestly don't know how we have lived for so long without this magical stuff," Miss Lumley said.

"It's not magic, it's science," Daisy explained to a small group of women. "We have all simply lived with dry skin or poor complexions. Well, I refuse to settle and I use the Midnight Miracle Cream."

A few more women took one look at Daisy's complexion and made up their minds to buy.

Another batch of Ladies of Liberty descended upon the shop, a few lady reporters among them, all of whom had columns in the various city newspapers. Other women who were curious after seeing the advertisement arrived to see plenty of women inside, and thus it seemed perfectly acceptable for them to come in, as well.

By midafternoon the shop was bustling and Daisy's cheeks were flushed with the promise of success. She wished Theo could come out and feel the energy in the air, but they had both agreed that it would be best if he remained in the laboratory and refrained from mingling on the floor. It was one thing for women to start making public purchases of items for their private grooming; it was quite another to do so in the presence of a man, and an infamous playboy to boot.

And then one woman's high voice cut through the chatter.

"It's the devil's own brew!"

Silence fell swiftly.

"My fellow womankind, do not fall for this

appeal to your pride and vanity! It's the work of the devil, it is," she carried on. She was a woman of indeterminate middle age, dressed in unrelenting black. Daisy tried to reach her but struggled against the tide of customers having second thoughts and moving toward the door.

The woman in black carried on. "When I saw the notice in the newspaper this morning I knew it was my solemn duty to come warn the young ladies who would fall prey to this devious Dr. Swan person. Some man, probably, who wants to seduce you all. First, it's just some complexion balm, next it's cosmetics—your lip paints, your rouges—and then it's straight to the flophouse."

"That's not true!" Daisy cried. But *oh, damn*, she was not supposed to draw unnecessary attention to herself, lest someone here make the connection between Daisy Swan and Dr. Swan. She definitely wasn't supposed to get involved in a scene.

Neither was Theo. But there he was, strolling onto the floor, cool as you please. Oh, he just had to play the hero, didn't he? Daisy feared it was going to backfire spectacularly.

"Ma'am, good afternoon. If you please—" He linked arms with her in an effort to escort her out.

"I do *not* please, thank you very much. Unhand me, young man!"

"As you wish." Theo relinquished his hold on her immediately. But still, he tried to console her.

"My good woman, just because your complexion has no need of the balm does not mean that other women—"

"Spare me your flattery, pretty boy." The irate woman turned to address the crowd at large. "This rogue and flattery just proves my point! Decent women have no business with *cosmetics* like this."

She just had to use the dreaded *c*-word. Daisy closed her eyes and groaned. They had deliberately marketed it as a balm or a preparation; definitely not a cosmetic, which would cause all the respectable women to flee. Even mention of the word *cosmetics* had some ladies moving toward the door to leave.

"It's a patent medicine. A balm," Daisy protested feebly.

"What will your fathers and husbands think when they learn you have all been purchasing intimate items in the company of a man?"

"Ooh, this is terrible," Daisy groaned.

"It is not ideal," Harriet agreed. "I'll handle everything at the shop. I think this is a good opportunity for you and Theo to make yourselves scarce."

They didn't need to be told twice.

Chapter Fifteen

While Mrs. Swan rushes around Manhattan single-handedly planning the wedding of the year, one wonders how the romance between the bride and groom has been progressing.
—*The New York Post*

Later that afternoon

$\mathcal{A}$ few hours later, with the shop shuttered for the day, Theo and Daisy climbed into his waiting carriage, idling outside and slowing traffic that was already slowed down due to the steady drizzle of rain. They climbed in and Theo just said, "Uptown," to the driver because his mind was reeling from the events of the day.

"Except for that one irate woman—" he started.

"Let's never speak of it again," Daisy said as she leaned back against the velvet cushions and closed her eyes. At Harriet's urging they had separately made their way to the back of the shop to lie low, which they did while Harriet expertly escorted the woman in black out of the shop and consoled the others. Thanks to her brilliant plan, new waves of women kept entering every fifteen minutes, like clockwork.

"Let's celebrate our success instead," Theo said, and Daisy's eyes brightened.

A celebration was certainly in order. Because in spite of that one irate woman, most women had been pleasantly curious and eager to try it. The sales had been exceptional. The young ladies hired to work in the laboratory—some of Daisy's fellow chemistry students and some other bright women who struggled to find other respectable work—would definitely need to arrive early tomorrow and begin preparing another batch of the Midnight Miracle Cream.

If the newspaper reports and word of mouth were favorable, it seemed they had a good chance of success.

The carriage lurched forward and then just as it was gathering pace it slowed again. And stopped. And started.

So it was to be one of those journeys, plagued by a seething mass of humanity and vehicles all slowed to a sedate pace and confounded by wet weather. Usually, Theo would be annoyed but today he didn't mind. They were alone in the carriage—the driver stationed outside, up front— and they would have to make the best of it.

"How do you propose we celebrate, Theo?"

Theo had some ideas.

From the heated look in Daisy's eyes, he knew that she was of the same mind.

There was an energy between them that was almost palpable. It was nothing less than giddiness over their success—not that, as a man, he would ever describe himself as feeling giddy aloud. There was the exhilaration one felt after taking a risk and winning and he felt it now.

And then there was this potent feeling between them. Something magnetic. Electric.

Something had to be done about it.

Theo's lips first touched hers at Nineteenth Street.

Or hers touched his? It seemed so natural that they should mutually crash into each other's arms, sink into a frantic kiss like time was running out even though the journey uptown would take an eternity at this pace.

This kiss was hard and fast, tooth clinking against tooth. Heads turning the same way at the same time, awkward. Noses colliding. Their choreography was a mess but the passion and pleasure was real. And that made all the difference.

All they could do was laugh softly through it and try it again.

At Twenty-Third Street they found their rhythm.

She parted her lips, and the kiss deepened. Lips against lips. Tongues tangling, tasting. Nibbling, sucking, teasing all around the main thing, the main thrust. Hands grasping. Breath gasping. It was him. And her. Imperfect and wonderful, all at once.

He'd never been so aroused by just a kiss. It was going to wreck him, this kiss. Because Theo was giving it everything.

Her fingers twined through his hair as he nipped her bottom lip.

"God, Theo, I had no idea."

He managed a mumbled *mmm* and found that his new mission in life was to explore kissing Daisy in places other than her lips. The soft flesh of her earlobe, for example. Oh, she liked that. The soft hollow of her throat. The spot where her neck curved to her shoulder. Oh, she *really* liked that. And even a little lower and lower . . .

Eventually, he looked up and saw they were at Thirty-Fourth Street.

Time. They had time.

And privacy. Steam and heat and water conspired to fog up the windows. Daisy could probably explain the science of it to him if her mouth wasn't busy with activities other than talking.

He let his hands start to roam over her body. That was how he discovered that Daisy had been hiding something from him. There was no doubt about it—she had been hiding a marvelous figure. Curves and flares and long, slender legs. Breasts that fit perfectly in his hands, and that were perfectly responsive to the slow and steady back and forth caress of his thumb, even across the fabric of her dress.

The pleasure of it drew a slow hiss of a *yes* from her lips.

Buttons. These little things were in the way of what they both wanted. His hands on her bare skin. Theo flicked them open, one by one. Her skin, God, was smooth and soft, like silk under his touch. It felt like a dream. A dream he never wanted to wake from.

At Thirty-Ninth Street he claimed the dusky pink center of her breast with his mouth. He teased with his tongue, the heat of his mouth, the cool rush of air from his lips just to see what drove her wild.

Yes, she whispered, an exhale as she twined her fingertips in his hair and let him know with her touch that he should keep doing exactly that. Now he knew a little more about what Daisy liked.

Theo did things with his mouth and tongue and hands that had her writhing beneath his touch. He felt a surge of satisfaction and arousal. He'd never, ever been this hard before. He was desperate for her. Not any woman, but her.

Yes, she whispered again and again.

He was thinking about *more* and *more*.

Theo cast one heavy-lidded glance out the carriage window. They were at Forty-Fourth Street now. Rain was lashing at the windows.

The traffic was easing up but still moving at a glacial pace.

Time. They still had time.

And he had ideas.

"Daisy . . ." he murmured, pressing his lips against hers. He reached for her hand, her waist, her. Then he reached for her skirts, dragging the heavy layers of finely spun wool skirts and delicate lace and cotton petticoats up and away, letting his hands graze across her silk stockings and slender legs.

And then his touch went higher.

"I like your idea of celebrating," she murmured and her lips formed the sweetest tempting smile.

"Just you wait."

He started with the sweetest, subtle touch on the delicate, sensitive, secret spot between her legs. Light as a feather. Gentle, as befitting a lady. And he felt something shift in her. This wasn't working. Something wasn't right. That hot fire of desire started to fade away . . . That something electric between them started to dim . . .

Theo could fumble all around her, trying this or that to revive the spark or . . . he could just *ask*. Presumably, a woman knew her own body and what it wanted.

"Show me how you like it," he murmured.

And she did.

Oh, she did.

Her dark gaze met his as she closed her hand

around his. She guided his fingers to exactly the spot she liked, demonstrated exactly the amount of pressure that made her moan and close her eyes. A soft gasp of pleasure escaped her lips as she showed him exactly where and how she liked to be touched. And there it was again, that spark between them that crackled into a fire.

Her cheeks were pink, almost feverish. Her lips parted, reddened from his kiss, and she was close, so close.

"How do you know this?" he asked in a whisper.

She gave a soft laugh. "How do you think?"

"I think I'll be imagining that later."

But for now he was content to revel in the here and now. Her hips started to rock and he moved with her and that drew a low moan from her lips.

Her soft, sweet lips beckoned and he was helpless to resist. Theo kissed her. But not before stealing a glance at her. Eyes closed. Flushed cheeks. Lips red from his kiss and parted. A glimpse of a woman losing herself to pleasure; a glimpse of true beauty.

THE CITY ROARED outside the carriage, but Daisy barely noticed. Her dress was undone. Her hair was probably a wreck. But who could care about that at a moment like this, when Theodore Prescott the Adored had worked her up into this state of frenzy with his kiss, his touch, his naked desire to pleasure her.

She forgot that she hated him.

That until recently, they had been enemies.

That their first kiss was merely whelming.

Because this kiss—this everything—was something above and beyond anything she had ever imagined as she touched herself at night, learning what she liked.

Now Theo knew.

Now Daisy knew that he knew.

Daisy gripped the handles on the carriage door, holding on for dear life as this intense pressure built within her from her core and spread out through her limbs. Heat suffused her. She was nearly at the breaking point.

So much for being enemies.

So much for hating him.

He kept touching and teasing and kissing her.

So much for being business partners.

And he did something designed to push her over the edge.

He dropped to his knees. Right there on the carriage floor. She gasped and then smiled as she realized what he was about to do. Theodore Prescott the Adored on his knees, for her. There was a rustle of fabric as he pushed her skirts aside. She let her legs fall open and she discovered the exquisite pleasure of being kissed on the inside of her knees, her thighs, and higher and higher still . . .

This was outrageous behavior to engage in anywhere, let alone in the backseat of a carriage while stuck in traffic. She gave a little laugh of shock, delight, wonder. His strong hands gripped her thighs. He wanted this as much as she. Then Theo pressed his mouth to her sex and she didn't laugh; oh, no, she gasped.

Yes . . .

She let her head fall back. What *a day* it had been. This was the perfect way to celebrate, to relax, to let go and just revel in pleasure.

Oh, yes . . .

She closed her eyes and gave in to the feeling. The warmth of his mouth. The danger of his touch. The fire of her wanting.

Yes . . .

The heat raging within her. This dress. Too much. She wanted it off. She gripped a handful of fabric. The pressure inside her was building and building and building until there was no room left for her lungs to expand. Breathing. She could not catch a breath.

Her heart slammed in her chest.

And then just like that the orgasm rocked through her and she wasn't exactly quiet about it.

A few blocks later the carriage rolled to a stop.

It took her a moment to realize that they had

arrived at her destination—home—and she was in no condition to leave the carriage. Her hair tumbled around her shoulders. Her dress was unbuttoned, her breasts bared to the air. Her breath was still uneven and her heart was still tripping to an erratic beat.

And the infamous Theodore Prescott the Third was looking right at home between her thighs. His blue eyes were heavy-lidded and his own lips were reddened and full from all the pleasure they'd pressed upon every exposed inch of her skin, and then some. His hair—those pretty blond curls—was a tussled mess. His suit was terribly rumpled.

He was gorgeous.

Heart-achingly gorgeous.

A girl could get used to this.

A girl probably shouldn't though.

"This doesn't change anything," she said as her fingers trembled with her buttons and he sat back and pulled her skirts down.

"Everything is exactly the same," he said, voice rough.

It was a lie because everything had changed.

A short while later

DAISY SHUT THE door to her bedchamber, fell back against it with a thud, and slid down to the floor. She offered up a silent prayer of everlasting

gratitude that she made it into her room undetected. Her mind was so overrun with thoughts
and feelings and memories it just gave up and
went blank. She had to sit down.

Wait—she already was sitting.

So that was how well functioning her brain
was at the moment. And to think, she was a
smart girl. Theo had just been *that good.* She was
lucky that breathing was an involuntary action
because she was so distracted by what had just
happened that she could think of little else.

Her legs had given up on her completely.

Her heart was still bopping around like an
erratic and unchoreographed display of fire-
works.

If she was not mistaken, the golden boy of the
Four Hundred, the object of many girls' fancy,
and her longtime enemy, Theodore Prescott the
One and Only, had just made love to her in a carriage. With his mouth. All the way uptown.

She reached for a pillow to scream into it.

It hadn't been her first experience with pleasure, but it had been her first time sharing it with
another person and it happened to be the very
last person on earth who she had ever expected
to indulge with.

Now he was also her business partner?

There could be no mistake; they were in business together. They had a shop. They had employ-
ees. And best of all, they had customers. A whole

store full of customers who raved and purchased and not all of them were Ladies of Liberty. Together she and Theo had created something new and exciting and possibly life-changing.

Business. Just business.

Face cream. She was thinking about face cream.

She was so *not* thinking about face cream.

Daisy clutched the pillow to her chest and . . . smiled.

Oh, she smiled like she had never smiled before. Like her cheeks hurt from so much joy. Because suddenly her whole world had cracked wide open. Today had been an undeniable success both professionally and personally. And that success went straight to her brain and told her in no uncertain terms that the possibilities were infinite. Endless. No dream was too big. There was no prize she couldn't reach for and seize.

She felt pretty. And giddy. And possibly feverish.

Daisy put her hand to her cheek and found it hot to the touch.

Daisy dragged herself up and over to her dressing table. She plunked down on the tufted seat and took a good look at herself in the mirror. She wanted a glimpse of herself as joyous, and well-pleasured, and outrageously optimistic for her future. And so she lifted her gaze to Daisy in the mirror.

For the first time she thought, *I am pretty*.

And then she looked longer and thought, *No, I am beautiful.*

Nothing about her features had changed. Nose: still a trifle too large. Eyes: still a little too close together. Mouth: still not an alluring rosebud of a mouth. Her buttons were unevenly done—once again she thanked God that she hadn't encountered anyone on the journey from the carriage to her bedroom. Her hair looked exactly like a man had dragged his fingers through it as he cradled her head and kissed her deeply. Which was exactly what had happened.

But . . .

Her eyes had a brightness, a sparkle.

Her lips were fuller, redder.

Her cheeks were pink with the sweet flush of pleasure.

Nothing had really changed but everything had changed. She had succeeded at something she'd long dreamed of succeeding at. A man had made love to her, had brought her to dizzying heights of pleasure. While Daisy had daydreamed about one or the other she had never expected to actually experience them both together, on the same afternoon.

Both success and pleasure gave her a glow.

There was no denying it: she felt beautiful. She looked beautiful. She felt like she could take the world by storm.

What if I could feel like this all the time?

Perhaps not the messy hair, but the wide eyes, the pink cheeks, the just-made-love-to glow? She wouldn't mind *looking* like this all the time. She wouldn't mind people looking at her, wondering what put this sparkle in her eyes or this flush on her cheeks. She wouldn't be bothered if people thought she had just been kissed.

What if any woman could look like this whenever she wished?

Her brain slowly but surely resumed its basic function of thinking actual thoughts. Her brain presented the obvious answer first: kiss Theo all the time. But this would be logistically impossible for all sorts of reasons: technical, practical, and emotional.

What if any woman could look like this whenever she wished, and a man wasn't necessary for it?

A second thought was more promising though: What if she could make, say, a powder to give a glow of blush across a woman's cheeks? What if a lip tint could make a girl's mouth seem just-kissed? What product could she make— using her training in chemistry—to make eyes seem brighter? Perhaps with her training she could improve the formulations that people had been using. And perhaps with the help of Theo, Harriet, and the Ladies of Liberty, she could make them seem respectable. With her shop, she could certainly make them accessible to her customers of the Midnight Miracle Cream.

This was no longer just about wanting to escape a marriage or earn enough money for her freedom. Daisy felt so beautiful for the first time, and she wanted any woman to be able to feel this way. If she wanted. The only question was: Did she dare?

Chapter Sixteen

It's not every day that one of the darling sons
of Manhattan's elite is involved in a skirmish
among women in a new shop selling ladies'
toilet preparations. When it does happen, it's
on a Wednesday and the playboy in question
is none other than Theodore Prescott the
Third. Dear Reader, I shall explain . . .
—*The New York World*

The offices of Prescott Steel

$\mathcal{T}$heo and Daisy made the newspapers the following day—and not just a write-up of the store
opening in the ladies' section, either. They made
the gossip columns. Because what reporter could
resist writing up the story of the Millionaire Rogue
inserting himself into a skirmish over the morality
of complexion balm amongst a throng of women?

None of the lady reporters who had been present, that much was clear.

It was their big chance to get a byline beyond the women's pages and they took full advantage. There was Theodore Prescott the Third "attempting to charm an old crone lecturing a fashionable set of ladies about the evils of cosmetics at the otherwise successful grand opening of Dr. Swan's Apothecary." Another reporter wrote that "Theodore attempted to broker peace amongst an anxious crowd of women forced to confront the morality of their shopping."

It wasn't terrible. Not at all. To mention the shop name and fashionable women in the same line was better publicity than the half-page advertisement he had taken out. To be written about in all the papers thusly would spark conversation, arouse women's curiosity, and perhaps inspire them to visit the shop. That was all he could do: get them into the shop and give them the opportunity to say yes.

The mentions in the newspapers were only remotely terrible if one was trying *not* to draw the attention of Theodore Prescott the Second.

Theo wasn't ready for that—not yet.

His father summoned him.

Theodore Prescott the Second, through one of his secretaries, let Theodore Prescott the Third know that the hour of one o'clock on Thursday was held for their conversation at the offices of Prescott Steel.

Theo entertained the outrageous thought of not going.

After all, he had business of his own to attend to.

Theo knew what to expect and yet he harbored hope.

Perhaps this time, it would be different.

And so here he was, in his father's suffocatingly opulent office, suffering through his aura of disapproval. Theo had taken a chance on coming today because the write-up hadn't been entirely terrible. If there was the slightest chance that Prescott Senior would be glad that his son had finally found an occupation, Theo wanted to be there for it. He made a silent vow to himself: if his father asked the questions that would make Theo feel like he could share the news, he would.

This could be the day. The moment he'd always wanted.

But first, The Stare.

A selection of newspaper clippings were in an array on his desk. One as busy and important as Prescott the Second didn't browse the newspapers himself, for that took time, and time was money. He had people to do that. They clipped the relevant and interesting articles and presented them in order of importance. Theo had long been aware of this and knew that getting into the newspaper was the best way of getting his father's attention.

Prescott Senior launched right into it. "Would

you care to tell me why you were engaged in a 'skirmish' at a ladies' cosmetics store?"

"Not particularly." Because to do so would begin to unravel the barely concealed fact of Daisy's involvement. They had discussed it and decided for the moment that it was best if they kept it quiet. People would certainly figure it out and talk about it, which would be fine. But Theo and Daisy wouldn't, say, put an ad in the newspaper about it just yet.

"Do you think I called you here for such a vague, impertinent answer?"

Theo waited a beat before answering. "Not particularly."

"I find it curious that you were at a store that shares a name with your fiancée. Do you?"

Theo bit back a grin as he replied. "Not particularly."

At which point his father leveled him with The Stare.

At which point Theo discovered it didn't have quite the same hold on him.

The reason: not just something else but someone else. An outstanding first day of sales and the promise of more. His own sense of self-worth. And Daisy.

Just tell them we're engaged, she said.

We'll go our separate ways, she said.

She was gloriously, wonderfully wrong. They were friends and lovers and business partners.

And when he phrased it like that . . . Theo's breath hitched in his throat as he finally, truly noticed how his feelings for her had changed. They were . . . intense and complicated and not what they used to be. They were definitely maybe not *just* business partners. Or *just* friends. This was something he didn't have a quick name for, or a pithy label. Just a feeling. In his heart.

"I cannot imagine what you were even doing there. My son, in a ladies' cosmetics shop!" Prescott Senior said, oblivious to the emotional turmoil his son was experiencing. "I do not want to imagine what you were even doing there."

Theo thought *if only* . . . he could tell his father the truth: that he'd gone into business and wasn't making a total hash of it. But in his father's book, business was the urging of iron and steel; it was construction; it was poorly paid hard labor (others' of course). Business was ruthless, dirty, and a man's work.

Business was not clever text, glass jars, and lavender paper. It was not Daisy's hours of dedicated study and experimentation to find just the right formula to make a woman feel beautiful. It was not something for women or the people who cared to cater to them.

Yet for the first time, Theo had money he'd earned in his suit pocket. It was his share of their sales. He had earned it.

And he felt he couldn't tell his father that.

This struck him as terribly sad.

Theo also knew that he couldn't confide in his father about other things . . . For example, oh, just off the top of his head, that he was possibly falling for a girl he'd always ignored and disliked when he'd bothered to think of her at all. Now he couldn't get her out of his mind and wasn't sure he needed to.

Theo wanted, badly, to ask for advice. But his father didn't discuss matters of the heart, and his friends were equally ill-equipped to offer guidance or commiseration. Business advice, maybe. But not lady business.

Today Prescott Senior was only concerned with appearances.

"How am I supposed to explain this to people when they inquire? Because they will inquire. First the Saratoga Scandal and now this. A *skirmish*, Theo. Not even a brawl or a fight. Something more dignified."

"You would have preferred that I brawled in a store full of women?"

"I would have preferred that you not be in a store selling ladies' cosmetics at all. There are no good conclusions to draw."

Theo shrugged and said, "Tell them I was buying it for my fiancée."

It was a rather inspired answer if he thought so himself. It would make it seem glamorous, aspirational, and acceptable all at once, if word got round that two members of the Four Hundred found the Midnight Miracle Cream a suitable gift to exchange.

That was not the conclusion his father arrived at.

"So the courtship is progressing."

Theo found himself saying, "Not particularly." Again.

Because it was starting to feel like he and Daisy were none of anyone else's business.

Especially if to say yes, it was progressing, meant a declaration that his father had been right. That their parents had done a good thing by meddling so monumentally in their lives. He was certain Daisy would agree that it was impossible they should admit their parents were right.

To say no meant to deny the something brewing between him and Daisy and it wasn't just Dr. Swan's Midnight Miracle Cream. He wasn't ready to talk about it, or declare his feelings, but he couldn't deny that she was no longer the last girl in Manhattan he'd consider marrying.

Fortunately, his father was not one to wait for another person to contribute to the conversation.

"Your courtship ought to be progressing, given that Mrs. Swan is busy planning the wedding. I have received requests for a guest list. There are seven hundred names on it."

A real wedding was in the works for a fake engagement.

That was something of a predicament.

"Is that all?" Theo asked. He would have to talk to Daisy. About their predicament. But that would then require him to analyze and discuss his feelings for her. There it was again: that hitch in his throat and pressure in his chest. It was so much, too much.

"You'll join the company after the wedding, of course," his father carried on either oblivious or unconcerned with Theo's increasingly anxious state. He kept talking about roles, responsibilities, growing families, and all other manner of panic-inducing topics.

As if it wasn't all pretend.

Which Theo could not say.

There was no end to it—first the engagement, then the wedding, then *after* the wedding. There was no end to his father's meddling and machinations in his effort to shape Theo into a miniature version of himself. Theo had long suspected this, and it was only now that he could parse the difference between being a replica and being himself, a man both he and his father could be proud of. For his father, there was no distinction.

Finally, his father asked, "Does that work for you?"

There was only one reply. "Not particularly."

Chapter Seventeen

Mrs. Evelina Swan has been confiding in her friends about her daughter's dress for her upcoming wedding. One expects that for a wedding this anticipated, the gown will be stunning and require no less than hundreds of hours of work by a dedicated team of seamstresses working round the clock. One hopes they are already at work on it, for the wedding itself is fast approaching.
—*The New York Post*

The Triangle Shirtwaist Factory
Washington Place, New York

*I*t was a Wednesday, which meant the Ladies of Liberty were up to either good or no good, depending upon whom one was asking. On this precise morning, they were gathered outside a factory near Washington Square Park.

On a normal day young ladies of limited means and opportunities would be inside behind locked doors and closed windows sewing and sewing and sewing. From dawn until dusk they would sew. Stitch after stitch after stitch.

For this they would receive a pittance.

Today, however, the ladies were all outside.

Today the ladies were on strike.

"What are we protesting today?" Daisy asked Harriet as she joined the throngs of women on the sidewalk.

It seemed there was *always* something to protest these days.

"The insufficient wages and deplorable working conditions of the city's seamstresses," Harriet explained.

"Adeline brought the matter to our attention," Ava added. While Adeline was the dressmaker for the most fashionable women in Manhattan—and about to become a duchess—she hadn't forgotten the girls she'd grown up with, especially those who worked in the factories. She now used her position to help theirs.

Similarly, Daisy was using her new business to create decent positions for young women, either as chemists or shopgirls. She did not require them to work long hours and she did her best to pay them a fair wage.

"Did you know the seamstresses work ten hours a day?" Miss Archer asked. "And they are not even permitted to visit the necessary if necessary!"

"They also lock the doors so no one can sneak out for a break or leave early. How barbaric."

Daisy picked up a sign and joined the hundreds of young women in shirtwaists, skirts, and smartly tailored jackets embellished with bits of lace and ribbon, likely whatever castoffs they could afford. They wore brooches—made of paste, of course—and feathered hats. One even noted the occasional fur among the Ladies of Liberty who had joined them.

A protest, it seemed, was an occasion to dress up for. Daisy noted how their well-dressed appearances leant an air of credibility and respectability to the strike. How could one be opposed to these fine ladies having a place to hang their hats, fair wages, and time to spend with their families?

A few dozen women held signs and banners and together they all made a statement with their mere presence in front of the factory. Daisy was proud to be among them.

"How goes the wedding planning?" Ava inquired. "I hold out hope that I'll receive an invitation."

"Or are you planning the cancellation of the wedding?" Harriet asked, eyes bright at the possibility. "Shall we help plan your escape?"

"You know, I haven't even thought about it recently."

This stopped both Ava and Harriet in their

tracks. Ava's smile revealed that she found this to be a most welcome turn of events. Not thinking about standing up the groom was definitely a step on the way to happily-ever-after.

Harriet, however, was less thrilled. Her eyes narrowed as she asked, "You haven't thought about how to end the engagement to the man you despise?"

"I might not despise him anymore?" Daisy said.

"Is that a statement or a question?"

"You kissed him, didn't you!" Ava said with unconcealed glee.

Daisy opened her mouth to protest with a "just once!" or "it didn't really mean anything" or "it was just a kiss." But none of those things were true and she didn't lie to her friends.

"I don't even want to know," Harriet replied, shaking her head. Which was good because Daisy did not want to explain.

Her friends would ask questions about when and how was it and what did it mean and did this change her plans for the wedding. In the process of answering, Daisy would be forced to reckon with her thoughts and feelings about Theo and kisses and what it meant for their future plans. This was not what she'd ever imagined, and everything lately had been such a whirlwind she hadn't had a moment to consider it.

Also, it had to be noted that thinking about

it or talking about it was not high on her list of things to do. It ranked somewhat above a trip to the surgeon but below taking a final exam she hadn't studied for.

Besides, she had other things on her mind.

"The reason I have not been planning an escape from my engagement is because I've been busy with something else." Indeed, Daisy had neglected her studies, her wedding planning, and even Theo to spend hours and hours at the laboratory experimenting with ingredients and processes until she hit upon something that would work. "Something scandalous. Sensational. Something pretty."

"Well, do tell."

"I'm going to make cosmetics," Daisy declared proudly. And loudly. Harriet, Ava, and a few nearby clubwomen around her slowed their steps and gave their full attention.

"Cosmetics? Like lip paints and powders?"

"Exactly like that."

"The complexion balm is one thing, but cosmetics . . . ?"

Once again, Daisy had hoped for enthusiasm. Hoped that Dr. Swan's Apothecary had helped make it all seem a little more acceptable. It quickly became clear that was too much to ask for.

Perhaps polite interest? Blank faces told her even that was also too much to ask for. Respectable women did not wear cosmetics. They presented their bare faces—as God had made them—to the world to signal their virtue.

To do otherwise was to risk unwanted assumptions and attentions.

To be labeled one of *those* women.

Daisy *knew* this. Every woman was brought up knowing this.

But she also knew that she *felt* prettier when she applied paint to her lips and some color to her eyes and a rouge to her cheeks. When she felt prettier, she felt like maybe she could stand beside Theo—or any of these smart-looking women—in a crowd without a sense of inadequacy. More than just holding her own, she felt like she could take on the world.

She'd had success with the Midnight Miracle Cream—sales were brisk, and she had been able to bring on more women to help her with it. She and Theo were making money. This, too, made her feel like she could take on the world. She thought she'd be content with enough. It turns out she wasn't.

That was the feeling she wanted to give to other women who wished for it. She wanted them to demand *more*.

"That's a scandal waiting to happen, Daisy," Ava said. "What if it poorly affects sales of Midnight Miracle Cream?"

Daisy didn't have an answer to that.

"You'd be lucky if it's a scandal. I daresay you won't even be able to sell it," Harriet said frankly.

"You will, but I doubt that you will find a sufficient audience," Miss Archer said, putting it very delicately. "A woman has nothing but her reputation in this world."

It was a sad but true fact. They all acknowledged it.

"It's an audacious scheme, I know," Daisy said with a sigh. "But I really believe I'm onto something. If you'll just try it and see. And see how it makes you feel."

"There are real problems in the world, Daisy," Harriet pointed out gently. She gestured to the women gathered to support the girls on strike. "These girls work ten-hour days, six days a week, and barely earn enough to survive. They cannot afford to be concerned with a little lip paint."

Daisy bit her tongue. The problem, as she saw it, was not the lip paint. Or even the priority of feeling pretty. She raised her sign.

They should all be able to afford a little adornment, if they wanted it. They should have the liberty and money to pursue their dreams without relying on a respectable reputation and a man to achieve them. They should have a little color to brighten their days, if they wished for it.

"Daisy, I'm worried that if you pursue this, you'll find yourself married because of it. You cannot afford a scandal that will jeopardize your current sales. You cannot afford to cause a scandal that will require you to wed just to survive. The last thing any of us wishes for you is a marriage you don't embrace with your whole heart."

Daisy pressed her lips—her unfashionable, unremarkable lips—into a firm line.

She kept marching. This time she stomped her feet. There was *so* much to protest these days.

"Have you considered faking your own death?" Harriet asked. Daisy laughed.

"It's not on the top of my to-do list, no."

"What are you planning in order to get out of the wedding?"

"Success selling cosmetics."

"I think you should consider faking your own death. It'll be easier."

There was also the small, somewhat consequential matter of if she still *wanted* to get out of the wedding. There was the intimacy she shared with Theo. God, yes, that. What woman wouldn't want such pleasure in her life? She could do worse than a man who was eager to discover what pleased her—and her alone—and then deliver.

But they had agreed in no uncertain terms that they would never say *I do*.

Did she dare risk their burgeoning success and imminent freedom on lip paint?

Maybe there was a way she could have her lip paint, her reputation, and true love, too.

No, she would not be faking her own death.

Yes, she would risk everything.

No, she still had no idea what to do about the looming, alleged, anticipated wedding that was quite possibly going to take place in just thirty days.

Chapter Eighteen

The women of Manhattan all look a little more radiant, all of a sudden. We are told it's all due to Dr. Swan's Midnight Miracle Cream, which has been flying off the shelves.
—*The New York Post*

Later
27 Union Square

$\mathscr{I}$t was a week after their exquisite, all-the-way-uptown kiss and just a few weeks before the alleged wedding, and Theodore Prescott the Third was venturing where no man had gone before. Probably.

The laboratory in the back of Dr. Swan's Apothecary was bustling with women at work, with starched white aprons over their shirtwaists and dark skirts as they worked to produce more of the Midnight Miracle Cream. It had been flying off the shelves, especially once they introduced discreet packaging for carrying it home, so no one needed to know that a woman sought help in caring for her complexion or got ideas that a woman didn't wake up perfect.

Theo paused in the doorway to take in the scene. Though she was dressed like all the others, one particular woman caught his attention and held it. Daisy. She was hard at work at something . . . pink.

He strolled over and leaned on the counter next to her.

"What is Manhattan's most famous secret chemist working on now?"

"Famous *and* secret?" Daisy laughed. "How impressive that I should manage to be both those things at the same time."

"Famous because Dr. Swan's Midnight Miracle Cream has taken the town by storm. Sales are increasing by the day. I have already been able to repay the loan. And secret because still, no one knows that it's all the work of a high-society girl and her fake fiancé."

"You repaid the loan already?" That got Daisy's attention. "That surpasses my expectations. But the *real* sign of success is that I saw a jar on my mother's bedside table. We are both pretending not to know that I am involved, which I have decided to take as tacit approval and a sign of success."

It went without saying that Theo had not seen a jar of the Midnight Miracle Cream on his father's bedside table. And *that* improbable event seemed more likely to happen than Theo telling his father he'd gone into the ladies' toiletries business and receiving his father's approval for it.

Theo also ought to be ecstatic that they were experiencing this runaway success. It meant that everything was going according to plan. It meant they would not have to marry. It also meant that they had no excuse for their engagement. Which would be *fine* if Theo wasn't starting to have complicated feelings about that. It was no longer the most dire fate he could imagine.

"Anyway, I am working on something new," Daisy said. "Lip paint. Perhaps a rouge, as well. But I am having all sorts of problems with the formulations, to say nothing of finding the right shades of pink . . ." She went on, explaining the science behind it all, but Theo could only repeat her words. *Lip paint. Rouge. Cosmetics.*

They had only just launched their business and now she was chasing a new challenge. One that seemed more impossible than the impossible one they had already embarked on. One that was keeping him busy from dawn till dusk learning the ropes of production and sales and promotion. It was exhilarating.

But now she wanted to embark on more. He didn't know what to make of it. He needed a minute to think and she was already off on a new topic when he finally tuned in to what she was saying.

"You kissed me, Theo. Really, truly, deeply kissed me."

"Yes." He had some idea of doing it again. The sooner the better.

"Afterward, I looked in the mirror and saw my lips were full and red. My cheeks had the most becoming flush. My eyes were brighter. I looked *beautiful*, Theo, for the first time ever."

"You are beautiful," he said quietly. But she continued as if he hadn't spoken. Because it was him and her and he said that and he was surprised to find he truly meant it.

"I wondered. What if a woman could look and feel like she's always just been kissed? Like she has love on her side. Like she can take on the world."

"There is a much easier solution, you know," Theo murmured.

If they'd been alone, he would have kissed her.

As it was, there were half a dozen women present to act as chaperones, or, should he try anything ungentlemanly, a vigilante mob.

"But one can't be kissing or just kissed all the time," Daisy said. "*We* cannot be kissing all the time. And I should like to look and feel this way when you are not around."

"Who says I won't be around?" Theo dared to ask.

He was starting to like her. Desire her. She had a catalog of her perceived flaws at the ready.

Yet the more Theo looked at her and learned her, the more beautiful she became to him. To him, hers was a face of challenge and opportunity, pleasure and adventure. Who wouldn't find that beautiful?

She was the one who gave him the opportunity to do something. To take the privileges he'd been born with—wealth, connections, status, an eye for beauty, and an understanding of fashionable women—and put them to good use. Theo liked the man he was becoming because of her and her ideas, schemes, and ambitions.

But these were truths that got stuck somewhere between his heart and his mouth. Because it was him. And Daisy. And they were, until recently, enemies.

"You. Me. Our scheme."

"Your mother has sent invitations. My father has been tasked with a monstrous champagne order. Which of course he's having his secretary handle. My point is, it seems like there will be a wedding. Everyone is proceeding as if there will be a wedding."

"I won't marry you because our scheme has run amok and I expect you wouldn't marry me for that reason, either. We'll figure something out. In the meantime, I need you to take me to the theater."

"Why?"

"Because greasepaint. And lip paint. And rouge.

It's not unusual for actors and actresses to wear it, especially with the new gaslit theaters. I need to understand how it works, how it performs, how I can possibly improve it."

"Daisy, I can't take you backstage at the theater. If we are seen or glimpsed or if someone so much as makes a fleeting glance in our direction while we are there, your reputation will be ruined."

"And yours will be just fine," she retorted. "It is so unjust."

"I'm sorry that's the way of the world."

"When did you become such a stickler for propriety? Here I thought you were one of those Millionaire Rogues. One of those dissipated playboys who had Manhattan as your playground. One of those idle bachelors who was forgiven everything because you are rich and a man. Since when does *that* man shy away from a quick jaunt backstage with a girl?"

"I am as horrified as you by my sudden concern with propriety, but the fact remains that your reputation—"

"What if I don't care about my reputation?"

"You might not. But other women do. And one of the easiest ways for a woman to raise questions about her virtue, to use an old-fashioned double standard, is for her to wear lip paint. Rouge. Whatever cosmetics you concoct. If you are going to convince enough women to start wearing cosmetics that you'll have a profitable business,

your reputation will have to be unimpeachable."
He paused and added, "Speaking as your business partner."

Her expression darkened. "I was annoyed when you were just a pretty face but now—"

"Now that I am talking sense and reason, I am even more frustrating?"

"Precisely." She scowled at him. "As my business partner I would think you would be amenable to a little risk in order to grow our business. To invent something new, to start a whole new industry. To show everybody who underestimated or dismissed us that we are daring and successful."

Drat, she was right and he did not want to admit it. This new ambition of his flared. Because if they, say, could make a million or if they could, say, inspire competitors, then he might be successful enough to risk telling his father and maybe, just maybe, earn the old man's grudging approval.

There was also one other little matter that he had to bring up.

"If we go to the theater, if we go and consort with actors and actresses, then we run a real risk of needing to marry. For our reputations. For the sake of our business. Are you willing to risk it?"

Chapter Nineteen

The greatest performance happening in
New York right now is taking place at Jack
Swan's brokerage firm. One has never before
witnessed such unprecedented returns.
—*The New York Post*

Tuesday evening
The Empire Theater

*I*t was just a night at the theater, Daisy told
herself as she dressed in a very new, very stylish gown from the House of Adeline. But this
was not a dress for *just* a night at the theater. The
midnight blue taffeta was made to fit every curve
of Daisy's body. The flourishes were minimal;
burnished brass buttons, unfashionably small
sleeves that suited Daisy's face and frame more
than giant puffs of the current style, and tufts of
tulle around the waist and bustle to draw the eye
and conceal the designer's signature pockets.

Daisy applied a whisper of lip paint to her
lips—a new formula she was testing—and slid

the tube into her pocket, along with some spare money, so that she would not be beholden to Theo tonight, and a key to the house in case she wished to creep in at a late hour unnoticed.

Convenient things, pockets.

There was no hope of slipping *out* of the house unnoticed—not as a young woman of means, with a mother like hers—and so their faux engagement was spectacularly convenient as Theo came to call and collect her for their evening out.

"Oh, hello, Theo. How lovely to see you." Mrs. Evelina Swan was in fine, fawning form. Her delight in seeing her marital scheme making progress to the altar was barely concealed.

By barely, one meant not at all.

Daisy almost felt guilty for deceiving her mother and taking this supposed triumph from her. Then she remembered that her mother had no qualms about forcing her daughter to marry against her wishes and found her conscience remarkably soothed.

But then, as some sort of torture, Daisy had to stand aside and watch as Theo and her mother— two pretty people—acted all pretty toward each other.

"Good evening, Mrs. Swan." Ever the charmer, Theo gave her a roguish smile and kissed her extended hand. A bit much in Daisy's opinion but 1) no one asked her and 2) her mother was lapping it up. "I swear you look younger every time I see you."

"Oh, Theo, you know just what a woman wants to hear." Her mother batted her eyelashes. Good God. He was potentially her future son-in-law.

"We don't want to be late," Daisy said. With all the nuance and romance of a pipe bursting at a construction site.

Because her mother.

Was flirting.

With her pretend fiancé.

"Where are you two young things off to?" her mother asked.

"We have tickets to see *It Had to Be Her*," Theo answered.

"I haven't heard anything about that performance."

They had deliberately selected an unfashionable, unpopular production to see in order to minimize the risk that they might be spotted.

Regardless, the only aspect of the theater that interested her mother was what one wore to it. And with that in mind, she cast an appraising eye at her daughter. It wasn't something Daisy hadn't endured a thousand times before. This time she felt different. Tonight she had a purpose beyond just enduring the evening. So she straightened tall and showed off this fabulous frock to its best effect.

Theo's palm resting at the small of her back didn't hurt, either.

"How fun. Daisy, you look . . ."

"Beautiful," Theo declared. There was no hiding the appreciation in his eyes. She could almost believe he meant it, too. She knew he desired her; after that heated carriage ride there was no pretending otherwise. But she hadn't thought he might also think her beautiful, even standing in the drawing room next to her mother, who was once named eighth out of the ten most beautiful women in Manhattan. It didn't matter, but it did mean that something had changed. She didn't know what to make of it.

Her mother, however, took this compliment as not just a compliment but a sign that her plans would soon be successful. They would have a devil of a time getting out of the wedding now.

"Don't encourage her," Daisy muttered as she took his arm and they took their leave. Her maid, Sally, would join them in the carriage and they would meet Harriet at the theater, who would act as their chaperone.

Her mother thought they were off to the theater as some sort of thing that couples did to enjoy each other's company and ensure that everyone else knew it. She would have fainted if she'd known their real plans. Any mother would.

The show was merely an excuse.

At the conclusion of the performance, Daisy and Theo bid good-night to Harriet, exited with the crowds, and then promptly swung around to the back of the theater and clung to the shadows as they searched for the back door.

"I never imagined I'd be skulking around back alleys with you," Theo remarked.

"I think we've done a lot of things together we never imagined," she quipped.

All he did was reach out and hold her hand.

Just like that the moment was suffused with romance. There, in some dirty back alley with just the glow of streetlights and the thrill of danger and the promise of adventure.

Just like that without any words, he said, *I feel the same.*

And, *I'm glad.*

And, "We should get going."

"Right."

The reason they were attending a less popular play at a theater that Theo didn't usually frequent was because they determined it would be better for everyone if they didn't run into his friends who were prone to being idiots and gossips, and this mission had to be stealthy. Word could not get out that Daisy Swan was cavorting backstage. Word could not get out that they were embarking on schemes like this together.

It was also because of Eunice.

"Tell me again who Eunice is?" Theo asked.

Eunice was a member of the Ladies of Liberty Club. She was a playwright and representative of actors and actresses and lived an exquisitely Bohemian existence. A woman like Daisy should have no business knowing a woman like Eunice. So she simply answered, "A friend."

He rapped at the back door to the theater.

Theo knocked again and the door finally swung open to reveal a rather tall woman wearing gentleman's attire.

"Ah, there you are," Eunice said. "I was getting nervous. Delicate, sheltered flowers such as yourselves skulking around the stage door is a recipe for disaster."

Theo cleared his throat. It was a very strong, manly clearing of his throat, which served to remind Daisy to provide introductions.

"Theo, this is my friend Eunice."

"And who do we have here?"

Daisy introduced him. "This is Theodore Prescott the Third."

"The fiancé."

"Allegedly," Daisy replied.

"Rumor has it," he added.

"People are saying," Daisy said.

"And how are you two acquainted?" Theo asked politely.

"If we told you, we'd have to kill you." It was not clear if Eunice was joking. She was not known as the joking type. But then she propped open the door and motioned for them to follow her in.

And so began their backstage adventures. For, ahem, research.

Research indeed. Daisy was here for a reason, one reason only, and it wasn't to watch scantily clad actresses throw themselves at her fiancé. Her alleged, rumored, but definitely pretend fiancé.

But—*oh, look!*—Theo had scarcely made an appearance when he was encircled by a throng of nubile young women with the perfectly formed, symmetrically arranged features that a girl like Daisy could only dream about. Without any overt effort being made to cut her out of the circle, Daisy found herself standing off to the side, watching, with only Eunice to keep her company.

Theo did not look disappointed by this turn of events. This made her feel . . . things.

Greasepaint.

She was here to learn about greasepaint.

"I had not expected everyone to be so . . ." Daisy's brain flailed around, trying to find a proper word but in the end she could only say, "Naked."

"They're not naked, Daisy," Eunice pointed out. "They've got their shifts on. Marianne is even wearing a robe."

"Well, then," Daisy huffed. "If Marianne is wearing a robe."

She had no reason to feel . . . something that might have been either jealousy or possessiveness. Because they were here for business, but it looked an awful lot like Theo was here for pleasure. She knew they were in a fake engagement but all of a sudden she was confronted with the reality of it: he had no obligation to be faithful to her. And she wanted him to be? What did that even *mean*?

Eunice leaned against the wall and gave Daisy a once-over. "Hadn't pegged you for the prude matron type, to be honest."

Daisy just sighed. "I hadn't, either, until I caught sight of all these pretty, young, nearly naked women flitting around my fiancé."

"Your alleged fiancé."

"Right."

"Rumored fiancé."

"Right."

"You told us that you don't even like him."

"I take your point, thank you."

"Well, go on, then." Eunice gave her a gentle shrug. "Go get him. Or go do what you came here to do. If you and I wanted to chitchat about boys and girls and birds and bees we could do that at our club meetings."

"Right."

Daisy squared her shoulders. Thank God she was wearing this House of Adeline dress. She took some comfort from the lip paint she had reapplied (again, she really had to work on that). But it was worth the effort, she thought. By making her mouth seem larger she would swear it made her nose seem smaller. She felt almost pretty. She definitely felt more confident.

Confident enough to approach Theodore Prescott the Flirt with some idea of staking her claim. As his business partner, of course. And his fiancée, even if it was a sham. No other reason at all, of course. Or so she told herself.

"Daisy! Let me introduce you." He introduced her to Marianne of the robe, Claudette in a blush-colored chemise, Cordelia in a blue silk tea gown. "And this is my fiancée, Miss Daisy Swan."

That word *fiancée* wasn't enough to dim the heated, craving glances of women who liked what they saw—Theo—and hoped for more. They wanted his attentions, his kisses, the contents of his purse, jewels, and prominence by association and . . . kisses. The way they regarded Daisy indicated that they didn't think a fiancée was any sort of obstacle at all. And why should they? Everyone knew their engagement was a forced match. Daisy and Theo hadn't exactly presented themselves as an adoring couple in love.

So she tried not to take it personally.

"It is so thrilling to see the backstage area," Daisy remarked. "But you, Theo, must also be accustomed to all this."

By *this* she meant the actresses. The fawning.

The beautiful bare flesh on offer. The beauty she could not compete with. Especially not with lip paint that didn't last.

"This is not my first time at the theater, no."

"How delicately phrased."

One particular woman, late to the small party that had gathered, strolled over and draped her long, bare, waifish arm around Theo's neck. Interesting. What Daisy found more interesting were his slow reflexes when it came to removing said arm. Her confidence started to waver.

"Well, if it isn't my favorite Rogue of Millionaire Row," she cooed. "I've missed you, Theo."

"Esmerelda, hello. May I present my fiancée."

"I thought that was just a rumor," Esmerelda said with a laugh.

"Allegedly," Daisy muttered.

"People are saying," Theo quipped.

Still. That arm though. Right there. She felt a flare of jealousy so hot and fierce it scared her. That meant . . . she did not want to consider what that meant. Not now. It was such an effort to get here, so risky to be here, that she couldn't waste her opportunity to learn.

"I'm actually just here to learn about the greasepaint," Daisy said. "If you don't mind pointing me in the direction of someone I could speak to about that? Possibly even someone fully clothed? Theo, why don't you remain here? You look like you're having a splendid time."

The actresses found this curious.

"Theo, you have brought your fiancée backstage with the likes of us—"

"And she wants to go off and learn about greasepaint."

"While you leave him here with us."

"And you're not at all threatened." They peered at her. Daisy thought it was best to let them think that. There was not enough lip paint in the world for Daisy to feel like she could compete with these women. Not *yet* anyway. Most of all, she hated that she felt in competition with them.

Even in the clamor and glamour of the backstage it wasn't difficult to discern what she was feeling, though it was hard to admit. She did feel the hot flares of jealousy and possessiveness as she watched other women touch her alleged, rumored, utterly fake fiancé.

Mine, she thought.

That she should feel possessive left her quite *confused* because this was Theodore Prescott the Worst, whom she had diligently avoided for a decade, and now she was on the verge of enragement because Cordelia was leaning against him and stroking his cheek.

And because Theo had his arm around Esmerelda. And really, those could *not* be their real names.

"Greasepaint," Daisy said. "I am here to learn

about greasepaint. He's merely here for decoration. Enjoy."

THEO WATCHED AS Daisy stalked off to Eunice, who led her to a different corner of the backstage area and introduced her to a man stationed next to a mirror. Before it, a rickety old chair. Around it, the debris of backstage.

By all appearances they seemed to be chatting amiably. One by one, they examined the contents of various jars and different brushes. And so began Daisy's great education in the use of paints and brushes for theatrical purposes. Theo had a hankering to join them. It would be interesting to hear the conversation. Perhaps he'd even gain some insights that would help in the naming of whatever she would invent next as a result of this reconnaissance.

But no. He had been dismissed. *Stay here and be pretty*, she had said, in so many words. While she attended to matters of business and science and brilliance. As if he were frivolous. Ornamental. *Decoration*. Or present merely to provide a distraction. This was why he felt annoyance. Yes, that was exactly the feeling. Annoyance.

"Greasepaint?" Marianne asked. She lifted one brow skeptically. She glanced over at Daisy.

"Greasepaint," Theo confirmed. What a terribly named product. Someone ought to have consulted him about that.

Daisy had explained it to him during the carriage ride to the theater. Greasepaint was an essential tool in any performer's toolkit. Bright lights were being newly installed in various theaters and providing a strong light for the players on stage. This necessitated some visual support for the actors' and actresses' faces, in the form of greasepaint and other such cosmetics.

In Daisy's opinion, it logically followed that as more and more of the world electrified and thus lit up to expose every flaw, more and more women would want a way to put their best face forward. That is where she, and her amazing new products—yet to be perfected—would come in.

Theatrical greasepaint would be an excellent starting point for her product development: what was used, how it worked, what it was made of, how it might be removed.

"Who is that with my fiancée?"

"His name is Max."

"You don't have to worry about them."

Theo wasn't worried about them. He simply wanted to be there with her. Max brought out a selection of pots and brushes and began to demonstrate the application on Daisy, covering up her exquisite complexion and doing God only knew what to the rest of her.

He wanted a closer look.

He wanted to learn it all, with her.

But no, he was supposed to stay here and look pretty and provide a distraction so she could do the real work to make their enterprise a success so she could eventually leave him. Theo was somewhat shocked to find that he did not care for that at all. Not any of it. Not the part where he did not contribute to the venture and not even the part where she eventually left him.

Theo set about disentangling himself from the actresses—as fun and lovely as they were, it was Daisy who called to him tonight with a siren song he did not make any effort to resist—and made his way toward Daisy.

She had that look about her that he loved: cheeks flushed with excitement, eyes bright with ideas and inspiration. Daisy Swan was out of place and in her element all at once. This is where he wanted to be—by her side in moments like these.

"You have this sparkle in your eyes and a flush on your cheeks that is entrancing," he said.

"I'm so glad," she said dryly.

Upon a second look, it became clear that appearances deceived. That flush in her cheeks and sparkle in her eyes wasn't excitement; it was anger. It was hard to read in these dim back-stage lights and with her face made up for the stage. The truth of her was concealed under all those layers of paint and color.

"Did you get what you needed?"

"I could ask the same of you," she replied coolly without even looking at him.

Theo revised his assessment. It wasn't just anger; it was pure molten rage. Which was ridiculous and unfair, seeing as how she had told him to stand around in the company of a bevy of beautiful women when he had *wanted* to be with her. It was almost as if she was jealous. Possessive. Which was ridiculous because it was Daisy. And him.

They hated each other.

Except they didn't. Not anymore.

His heart began to pound. Things had changed. He had to acknowledge it.

"Daisy, that was just me standing there and looking pretty and generally distracting everyone from your true purpose here. It didn't mean anything."

"You succeeded spectacularly. You could earn good money for that if it was something people paid for."

"Something to aspire to," he quipped. But *shit*. Daisy was madder than mad and he didn't want her to be. Because he was beginning to accept what he had suspected: that there was *something* between them that wasn't just business. He wanted her to see it, too.

"Daisy, wait—" He reached out for her.

"I'm ready to go home. I have all I need here," she told him. "It was a very illuminating evening.

But you can stay. You seem . . . unfinished. Dare I even say unsatisfied?"

Theo ignored that. "Obviously, I will escort you home."

"Obviously? What was obvious to me was that you delighted in the company of all these other women."

"Daisy . . ."

"I suppose it can't be helped since you are so easy on the eyes. How could a girl not fling herself at such a fine specimen of man as yourself?" She was definitely angry. But it was absurd that she be angry at him now, for his appearance.

Unless she is mad about something else . . .

Unless she cared about appearances and what other people thought, despite what she had told him. She would be embarrassed if word got out in the papers that her loathed and fake fiancé was seen cavorting with other women.

But Daisy doesn't care what other people think.

Theo's heart started to pound as he considered his next question, phrasing it with as much delicacy as he could muster. "Daisy, is it a remote possibility that you might be feeling angry because other women flirted with me? Are you perhaps experiencing a feeling that other people would identify as jealousy?"

"No. Yes. Perhaps." She gave an annoyed huff. "I will certainly stay up all night festering about it and then I shall yell at you tomorrow about it."

There was no need for her to stay up tossing and turning and trying to figure out what she was feeling. Because Theo knew. His heart pounded harder now. Faster now. Like a schoolgirl kicking up her heels, giddy, because she pulled the last petal on a daisy and it landed on "he likes me." Good God. He didn't even know that he could feel that way. But there it was. Heart-pounding stuff.

She liked him.

More than liked him. Enough to be caught up in the throes of jealousy. Enough to feel possessive. Theo knew that if Daisy liked him it wasn't for the usual reasons women did—his pretty face, his last name, his family fortune, or the chance to be his bride. She was not impressed by any of those things. Yet she still liked him. The connection between them was something real and strong and palpable.

He felt it now.

He liked her back.

Theo didn't know when or how or where it happened but at some point his feelings changed and the last girl in Manhattan that he'd ever imagined wanting was suddenly the only woman he wanted to be with.

There was only one thing to do with this fragile state of things: not wreck it.

He treaded carefully.

"Daisy, I think you might have feelings for me."

"What did we say about you thinking? I'm the brains in this operation and I say—"

"Shhh. Fear not. I won't tell a soul. But look at your cheeks. You're blushing. Let's call that color *Secret Passion Pink*."

"Save that for later. I am too furious with you right now. If my cheeks are pink, it is because I am hot with rage. Or the multiple shades of powder that Max applied. I'm definitely too angry to decide."

He couldn't tell real blush from fake but he was beginning to know her. Theo reached out for her hand and she let him take it, no resistance. That was how he knew. From his head to his heart. But how to *say* that to the woman he'd only ever sparred with or spoke to about matters of business?

It was hard for Theo to talk about these feelings, this turn of emotional events that he really ought to have seen coming. And it was hard for her, too. This was uncharted territory for them both. And so much was at stake now. That was either a reason to evade and escape . . . or a reason to delicately confront it. Theo chose the path that scared him more.

"Daisy, I think you might be furious because I hurt you tonight. Unintentionally, but still. You could only hurt if you cared. You could only be jealous if you wanted me for yourself."

"Did they teach you this at Harvard?"

"Drop your guard, Daisy. It's me."

"Exactly. It's you. And it's me. We are longtime enemies."

"We're not two children at odds anymore. We're not even two people faking an engagement. I don't know what we are."

"We're business partners," she replied flatly.

"What if we want to be more?" he dared to ask.

"I can't believe it."

"Let's test it, shall we? For science?" He quirked one brow. Cool as you please. Even though his heart was thundering in his chest.

Daisy kept him on tenterhooks for a moment before she gave a sigh and said, "Well, for science."

They both knew science had nothing to do with it.

Theo tugged her close to him and she took one, two halting steps into his arms. Darkness and shadows surrounded them and the sound of everyone chattering backstage was now a distant din. He felt her skirts, her breasts, her arms brush against him. Though he'd had women touching him all night, this was the first time all evening he'd been aroused.

Theo pressed a kiss on her neck. Where he knew she liked it.

She turned her head, her mouth finding his.

This was not the first time he had kissed a girl backstage, after hours, but it was the first time that it meant something. It was the first time his heart and soul were in it. The first time he had something to lose. The first time he was scared and excited all at once.

They were rushing headlong toward the point of no return. The point at which they might as well just marry. Then he pulled back, gave her a devilish smile, and asked, "Or do you just want me to stand here and look pretty?"

It so happened that Daisy did not want him to stand there and look pretty. Not at all. She wanted him to pull her into his arms and ravish her in the most base, elemental way. There was no denying it: she had been feeling jealous. Possessive. Hot with equal parts anger and desire.

She had been watching him all night out of the corner of her eye and so she saw the way the actresses draped their bodies over his, the way they touched his arm flirtatiously, or gave him smiles full of wicked promises. She saw how he didn't move or return their affections. It gave her hope. It made her think *maybe*. And that somehow made it feel worse.

It took every inch of her self-control not to fling her notebook aside, stomp over, and demonstrate that he was hers. But that would have consequences. Life-altering consequences.

It was truly terrifying to think of how close she came to doing just that.

Jealousy. Oh, yes, she felt it, a hot storm stealing over her.

Daisy thought by now it was a feeling she had long grown out of and cast aside because she had accepted certain things about the way the world worked. Girls like Daisy did not have a chance with boys like Theo. So there was no point in getting all emotional about any of it.

Except she did seem to have a chance with Theo—a man who encouraged her, challenged her, helped her, and pleasured her. By some strange twist of fate and circumstances, she did. More than a chance, even. And the threat of losing her chance made her jealous. Possessive.

For the first time she was a woman with something to lose.

Her heart. Her composure. Her innocence.

In the dark dinginess of the backstage, Daisy felt things she'd never really felt before: craving, wanting, liking, arousal, all of which made her feel like she could take the risk of a lifetime and win.

Theo's hands skimmed slowly over her. Her breasts. Her hips. Her belly.

Her breath hitched.

Then, she dared. He had gotten to explore her in the carriage that day. But tonight she was going to take her turn to know him, to claim him. She spread her palms across the taut muscles of his chest. *Mine.*

Theo had a lean, lanky frame but it was a mistake to think of him as skinny. That was muscle she felt—hard, firm, and strong. His arms. His chest. His flat abdomen. She splayed her fingers along the waistband of his trousers, nervous but desirous.

They were backstage, for Lord's sake.

There were people *just over there.*

Apparently, none of that mattered. It was dark and they were here, together. Theo claimed her mouth for a kiss and tugged her against him. She could feel how hard he was for her and that soothed her vanity and stoked her desire.

There was also the undeniable fact that he had his choice of beautiful women here and now, yet she was the one in his arms. The one who had made him so hard.

There was also the fact that they had gotten good at kissing.

Really good.

Overwhelmingly good.

So good that there was a mass exodus of sensible thoughts from her brain. If this went further it would be harder—perhaps impossible—to break their engagement. Something to consider . . . later.

She never really thought of marriage at all—not to him, or any man. Why start now?

Theo kissed her back. She had some thought of her lipstick having long worn off and perhaps she could invent one that would last and last and last but . . .

Later. She would think about that later.

And that was how it happened. This man who had discovered through trial and error how to please her kissed all thoughts from her head. She practically waved them goodbye, except her hands were busy feeling him. Holding him hot and hard against her. The fine materials of his suit jacket and shirt. His heated skin underneath.

This. Felt. So. Good.

"We can't stay here," she murmured. "We might be discovered."

"That would be terrible," he murmured his agreement. "Someone might see how much I want you. I know you can feel it."

"*Yes,*" she gasped.

"Someone might see the way I am overcome with passion for you."

"*Yes,*" she sighed. He turned their bodies so her back was up against the wall. His hands boxed her in. His arousal was pressing against the vee of her thighs and she silently cursed all the layers between them.

"So much so that I am on the verge of taking you, backstage. Not very gentlemanly of me."

"Yes. No. Perhaps." She was mumbling. She didn't know what she was saying. He was kissing that exquisitely sensitive part of her neck and nothing else mattered.

"Not very ladylike of you."

"Not in the slightest."

Good God, it felt good to not be very ladylike. Why had no one ever told her?

"Anyone could see us being so . . . intimate," he continued, his voice a low devastating hum vibrating across her skin. "They could see you and me. Together."

She sank against him and said, "Let's get out of here."

Chapter Twenty

It seems that Mrs. Swan is already thinking
ahead to the honeymoon. She has purchased
first-class tickets on one of the premier
ships for the couple to sail to Europe.
—*The New York Post*

After midnight
854 Fifth Avenue

*T*here were few precious places where a young
couple in lust might steal away for a few hours
to ruin themselves for all others without ruining
their reputations in the process. It was quickly
decided, between a rush of frantic kisses, that
they would endeavor to sneak into her bedroom.

In the history of the world, Theo would not be
the first romantic hero to sneak into a woman's
bedroom.

Given the circumstances, her mother would
probably be *delighted* to catch them.

The carriage ride was brief. The time was
passed with kisses.

The whole journey was fraught with significance.

Daisy was going to make love to her longtime enemy tonight. Except he didn't feel like her enemy anymore.

Theo was then—and now—the man who had hurt her the most and who could hurt her irreparably. She *knew* this. Any woman of sense knew the risk that Daisy was about to take and yet it seemed that cloistering her heart and soul and body away for all time simply wasn't an option. She had no illusions that this would change their plans to not marry.

She was always going to remain unwed. That had been her plan and she was so close to reaching On the Shelf status and, with it, her freedom. Thanks to their business, she would be assured her independence. It was everything she ever wanted.

But she also wanted the experience that tonight promised to be. The shiver up and down her spine, merely from the anticipation of his bare skin touching hers. The relentless rush of blood coursing through her veins as her heart pounded, imagining what would soon transpire. This feeling of the warmth of his mouth upon hers.

For better or for worse, Daisy desired him. She liked him. And she trusted him.

As if the gods and goddesses were smiling

on them, it was mercifully easy to steal into the Swan residence and up to her bedroom undetected.

The light in her bedroom was low, giving a soft, barely there glow to the room. If ever there was lighting to flatter Daisy, this was it. She felt no shame, no second thoughts, no reservations, for what was about to happen.

"So this is your bedroom," Theo said softly as he gazed around. The bed, of course. The windows overlooking the park, delicate curtains fluttering almost imperceptibly in the breeze. A desk, covered with her chemistry supplies and notes. A vanity table cluttered with cosmetics and a jar of Dr. Swan's Midnight Miracle Cream.

Theodore Prescott the Third was in her bedroom!

It didn't seem real.

Theo closed the distance between them, his footfalls quiet on the plush carpet. He cradled her face in his hands and looked deeply into her eyes. Then his gaze slowly drifted to her mouth.

She had expected a kiss, but with one determined motion of his thumb, Theo wiped the paint from her lips.

"You don't need this, Daisy."

He found a cloth and cool water on the vanity table and proceeded to wash away all evidence of the evening: the greasepaint and rouge that covered her skin, the shadow and liner around her eyes, the red paint upon her lips. She had been made up for the stage, in bright lights and an audience of thousands.

But here she was with an audience of one, who wanted nothing between them.

You don't need this, Daisy.

Telling her she was beautiful would have struck her as a platitude; a thing one said in these circumstances. But telling her she didn't need that covering, that armor, that mask, that disguise . . . that made her feel beautiful and cherished, just as she was.

"Theo?"

"Yes?"

"Kiss me already."

THEO HAD BEEN in women's bedrooms before, but he had not been in Daisy's. Of course. Obviously. Indeed. But here he was, stripped down to nothing but his wanting, and reaching for her in the dark. None of his experiences had prepared him for this yearning—wanting to act on his intense desire, desperately wanting to get lost inside her, definitely wanting to please her.

Theo pulled her into his arms. The last girl in Manhattan he expected. The only one he wanted.

Kiss me already, she'd said.

"Whatever the lady wishes," he murmured.

So he did. Mouths claiming mouths. Tasting, teasing, taking, and giving. They had gotten good at this. Really, *really* good. Her taste and touch sent a bolt of pleasure rocketing through him and his cock hardened. Their clothes were removed and tossed aside. Taffeta dresses and wool trousers. Linen shirts and shifts. Until there was nothing left but just her and just him and this slow, burning passion between them.

They tumbled to the bed and she whispered his name.

The lady wished for a repeat of the events that transpired in the carriage that day. She fell back on the bed, a soft laugh from her lips, legs falling open for him, pulling him with her. He obliged.

He used his hands, his mouth, his everything, and took his time to bring her closer and closer to the brink until she was gripping his blond curls in her fists and crying out in pleasure.

And then the lady had other ideas.

"I want to please you," she said softly. "The way you please me."

This was not an invitation that Theo had to think twice about. Her eyes roamed over his naked flesh hungrily. Her soft hand closed around his cock. A soft hiss escaped his lips.

He clasped her hand in his and squeezed.

He'd already been hard for her but this . . . this was a level of arousal he'd never before experienced. Because it was her. And him. Together. It was as exquisite as it was unexpected. Then he guided her hand up and down showing her how he liked to be touched. How much pressure was just enough to send him spiraling toward the edge of oblivion.

Her hand. His cock. Her. She did this to him: a state of arousal so hot and intense that if he survived he'd be a changed man. Because it was her. And him. In an ever-more-complicated knot that would be impossible to untangle.

Or something like that.

It was hard to think when Daisy was clenching her little fists around his cock and stroking and making him feel things. He found her lips for a kiss, lavished his attentions on her breasts, and his fingers found her clit so he could drive her mad, too. His orgasm was a ferocious storm building up to an intensity that he'd be helpless to stop soon. Soon. Soon.

Unless . . .

"Wait," he gasped. "Stop."

STOP. HE'D SAID *stop*. How could he want to stop at a time like this? Daisy had been entranced watching every stroke of her hand affect him: eyes darkened, then closed. Lips parted, breathing hard. Chest rising and falling. The length of him growing hotter and harder under her touch. *She* had brought him to this state. And all the while he'd been teasing her, too, stroking her sex, exploring her bare skin with his hot mouth. She was right there with him, on the verge, ready to really truly give in to all these feelings.

And then he'd said *stop*.

He'd been kissing her and stroking her, too, bringing her with him on this mad escapade.

And then he'd said *stop*.

Of course she stopped.

"I want you, Daisy," he rasped.

"I want you, too, in case you hadn't noticed."

"I want you to be ready."

"I'm ready, Theo. I want this—"

"No. As ready as I am. Ready to let go and lose control." He murmured these things as he left a trail of kisses down her belly. "Ready to forget everything but you. And me. Us." He kissed her, there, until a low moan escaped her lips. Then he was off the bed, fumbling with his clothing, searching for something. A moment later, she saw that he'd pulled a rubber sheath from his jacket pocket.

His heated gaze connected with hers.

It was a chance to say no.

To call it a night and send him home.

Her answer was a softly whispered *yes*. Her feelings for him were complicated and tomorrow was another matter entirely but right now, tonight, she wanted this connection with Theo.

He rolled on the sheath and then moved above her, pressing his arousal against her pelvis. He dropped a kiss on her lips. The ones that had always been unfashionably thin. Funny how that didn't matter in the slightest now. How she looked didn't matter at all, only how she felt. And she felt ready. Oh, so ready.

Skin met skin.

"Just you. Just me. Just us. Just tonight," she murmured.

Theo hovered above her, kissing her, stroking her sex in a way designed to drive her wild. He remembered how she liked it and damn if that didn't intensify her pleasure all the more. She writhed against his hand, eager—maybe even desperate—for more.

"You're so ready for me," he murmured.

She laughed softly. "Tell me something I don't already know."

"I'm so ready for you."

She reached down and stroked his hard cock once more. "That's your worst-kept secret."

There was nothing to do but smile in the dark and sink fingers into hair and get lost in a kiss as Theo eased into her inch by tantalizing inch until it wasn't clear where she ended and he began.

He thrust in and out, slow at first as they fumbled to find their rhythm. They kissed and laughed and figured each other out. She leaned into him, the warmth of his weight on her. There was the taste of him, like champagne and promises. The slight friction of the smooth expanse of his chest as it rocked against her breasts. The slick sheen of sweat on his back that she felt under her fingertips.

And then finally they clicked and found their rhythm. He thrust in, hard, and she was wet, so wet. So hot and wanting. Her heart was thundering. There were gasps and moans—hers or his, she didn't know. She felt him on the verge of climax. His breaths came harder and faster now, roaring in her ear while his cock throbbed inside her. And just like that he thrust hard and his shout of pleasure was muffled by her hair, the pillow. He collapsed on her for one sweet, sweaty moment before he rolled over, still gasping, and said, "Now let's take care of you."

And he did.

And it was a greater pleasure than she'd ever imagined.

Chapter Twenty-One

The Prescott-Swan wedding and reception will feature a million roses, at tremendous expense. To think, for this wedding one could have just ordered the bride's namesake flower, the daisy.
—*The New York Post*

The next night
The Patriarch's Ball

*T*here was no question that they would both be in attendance at the annual Patriarch's Ball. It would in essence be just another party—the usual champagne, small talk, and parade of fashionable people. Yet it didn't feel like just another party. Because Theo was going to see Daisy for the first time since last night.

Since everything changed.

They had bared their bodies to each other. And even more significant, they had admitted, in their roundabout way, that they had *feelings* for each other. Theo had been turning the matter over and over in his head all day and had drawn no conclusions about what it all meant for him, her, them. Their wedding.

He couldn't do that without talking to Daisy. He moved through the ballroom, looking for her, and when their eyes met across the crowd she excused herself from her conversation—she was speaking with some of the more political society ladies whom he was surprised to see here—and made her way toward him.

They stood off to the side of the ballroom, where one might stand against the wall and attempt a private conversation while a party raged on around them.

"Hello, Theo."

"Hello, Daisy. Is that a blush you've created in the laboratory or are you thinking about last night?"

"I couldn't very well admit to either, now, could I?"

"About that . . ." he said just as she blurted out, "Theo, we need to talk."

"Yes, we do."

"The wedding . . ." she started.

They had every reason to go through with the wedding. They had been intimate in the way that usually sent one to the altar sooner rather than later. They had a shared business interest. Plus, invitations had been sent, and nearly a million dollars in roses were to be brought in to Manhattan.

But there was also the not-insignificant matter of love.

A word that he wasn't ready to say. It was too much and too soon. They had only just admitted to liking each other. He didn't want to move too fast. Go too deep. Didn't want to confuse unrestrained passion and the thrill of the moment with *love*.

All around them people chattered and laughed and danced to the orchestra. But a long, awkward silence settled between them. The kind that became even more acutely long and painfully awkward with each second that no one spoke. The kind that made it downright impossible to say anything serious or meaningful.

"We do have options . . ." Theo said, to be deliberately vague and to allow her to lead the direction of the conversation toward "I've made a list and I think option six on my list of ways to get out of the wedding is the most practical" or maybe "We might as well just go through with it."

But when she paused and waited expectantly for him to speak, he had to say *something*. "The announcement in the newspaper. We could go down to the *New York World* building tomorrow."

"We could leave now and write the announcement tonight," she said.

Neither of them made the slightest move to leave.

If they left now and went off together, alone,

they would not write a word. Which ought to have told him everything he needed to know. Perhaps they didn't need to cancel the wedding just yet. Perhaps they could take more time to assess the situation.

"If we are going to pursue that scheme, then we have a little more time," Theo suggested. "We might even want to wait until closer to the date. For maximum impact."

"Yes, excellent! If we wait until closer to the date of the wedding to cry off, there will be less time for our parents to pressure us into reconsidering," she said. This was sensible. *Or did she want more time with him?* "It wouldn't really assure anything though. If we are truly serious about this, Theo, we have to do something permanent."

"What did you have in mind?"

"One of us could fake our death."

He choked on a sip of champagne. "One *could* do that."

"Or one of us could elope with someone else. It would have to be you though," she said and that made his heart clench in a somewhat painful way. He did not want anyone else. "After all, I have grand plans to be a spinster."

"Yes, the stuff of many a woman's dreams and fantasies."

"Don't laugh. It's always been mine," she said. She took a sip of champagne. The woman did know her own mind.

"There's no one else I want to marry, Daisy," he said. And it was the most he could bring himself to say in this crowded ballroom with everyone hovering around them, possibly eavesdropping.

"Perhaps I shall run off with a husband of my own invention. May I present Ned, my beloved fictional spouse?" She gestured to some empty space and air beside her. "Isn't he handsome?"

"If you're going to have a fictional spouse, at least give him a better name. Roderick Steele, for example."

"That is better, Theo." She smiled. "Whatever would I do without your talents for naming things?"

Well, for one thing, she might not have been tormented by that awful nickname he'd inadvertently given her a dozen years earlier. He decided it was best not to mention it. Not when they had come so far past it.

"You would rather wed a pretend man than me," he said dryly. And if he had any questions about how she felt about him, they were answered. Marriage should be a choice. He believed that. And she chose no.

"Don't take it personally, Theo. I would have all the benefits of marriage without having to actually marry. Honestly, now that I consider it, I don't know why more women don't try it."

He took another sip of champagne.

Just pretend to be engaged, she had said.

It will be easy, she had said.

But now it was complicated. Hearts and happily-ever-after-on-the-line level of complicated. Because he was starting to think *maybe* and she was running in the other direction, so to speak.

"And what of the matter of our business concerns?"

"I hardly see how my fake husband will complicate that."

"We both know you are not going to have a fake husband, Daisy. It will be more effort than it is worth and we have more important things to devote ourselves to. Soon you'll have perfected the cosmetics and I'll be busy packaging and selling them. Maybe it's best if we stay in town and focus on our work."

And that was how he convinced Daisy Swan not to invent a fictitious husband to get rid of him.

"If we are considering our business concerns, then it's probably best if we don't cause a scandal," she said slowly. Carefully. He hung on her every word. "It goes without saying that calling off the wedding would certainly be a scandal."

"It might actually be good if you were married. If *we* were married," he ventured, giving every appearance of a bored society bachelor. But in truth his heart was thundering in his chest, under the coal black satin lapels of his evening jacket. "We're embarking on a scandalous proposition for womankind. A little respectability might go a long way into making cosmetics sellable. Nothing is more respectable than a married woman."

"Much as I'm loath to admit it, you do have a point, Theo." She sighed. "But that's still just a marriage of convenience, even if it's one we choose."

She didn't need to say that wasn't *enough*. Not for a woman who had ideas about love and freedom and wasn't afraid of spinsterhood. And, frankly, he did, too. While neither of them would dare mention the word *love*, one had to consider the matter of lust.

Which one could not help but consider after the champagne they had just been drinking. Not that Theo needed the excuse. The memory of her soft skin and the warmth of her body entwined with his hadn't exactly faded from his memory; it had only been last night. He'd been thinking about it all day.

This fraught and tense conversation didn't diminish his desire; if anything, it made him want to kiss her and forget everything. To get lost in her and to think of nothing but how she felt beneath him, legs wrapped around his back, her moans of pleasure in his ear. To convince her to think about maybe forever.

He leaned in close to her and murmured, "There is another reason for us to go through with it, Daisy."

"Is there?" she replied coyly.

"I know you're a modern woman, Daisy, but . . ." But people tended to marry after they made love. Especially if they were women. Yet Theo didn't want her by default. It was like winning tennis on a technicality. One was still victorious, but it was a hollow victory. No, he wanted to remind her that they had already joined together in the ways that really mattered. "We might want to do it again. And again."

"To marry because of what we did one night is just another obligation," she said. "It's not a good enough reason. I told you, Theo. I never want to marry at all, and if I do, then it shall be for love and if I change my heart and mind and marriage becomes what I want most in the world, you'll be the first to know."

Chapter Twenty-Two

The House of Adeline will be creating the
wedding dress for Miss Swan. The department
store Dalton's will be providing her trousseau,
which will be crafted of fine linen, embroidery,
and real lace and will include numerous corsets,
chemises, hand-embroidered handkerchiefs,
and more. No expense has been spared.
—*The New York Times*

Two days later
The House of Adeline

*I*f Daisy wanted to keep up appearances, then
she was required to attend a fitting for her wedding gown even if she had told the dressmaker
not to make anything. She hardly had the time
given everything happening with Dr. Swan, but
visiting her friend Adeline would be far more
pleasant than explaining to her mother why it
wasn't necessary to go to a fitting mere weeks
before the big day.

Her mother was shouldering the burden of

planning the wedding alone with no help from Daisy, who had been occupied with other more interesting things—mixing colors, making lip paint, plotting a new commercial empire. Given that Daisy hadn't been involved in even the choice of groom, she thought she could not be expected to care about the reception menu.

There might not even be a wedding.

Ever since their sham engagement began, she and Theo had plotted a half-dozen ways to call it off. Why, she even had a list somewhere on her desk. Her feelings for Theo had changed and undergone a dramatic transformation; she no longer despised him. She actually even liked him. She definitely liked the intimacies they shared and had some idea of stealing off with him to do it again. And she really liked that together, they had made her daydream real, their business a success.

But she was so close to getting everything she ever wanted: the freedom of spinsterhood and the means to enjoy it. Especially if she could convince Theo to jilt her; then she really wouldn't be plagued by pressure to marry. Besides, could she really turn back from her plans now?

But occasionally in the darkest and quietest hours of the night, she gave in to the most scandalous thoughts of all: *actually* marrying him. It was no longer the worst possible fate she could ever imagine. Perhaps not even in the top ten most horrible ways to spend the rest of her life.

But really—was one night of making love supposed to just *undo* the past twelve years? It couldn't possibly.

Any person of sense knew that a conversation was in order. Yet actually broaching this subject with him was downright terrifying. After all, Theodore Prescott the Third had once altered the course of her existence with just a few throwaway words. Ugly Duck indeed. Was she really going to risk that happening again? He was already in a position to hurt her terribly and irreparably.

She knew he was capable of it; he'd done it before.

And now the stakes were higher.

Which was why she thought maybe they might just . . . get swept along with all the wedding plans and let the cards fall where they may.

The clock was ticking on the big day.

There was an increasing sense of urgency.

Something would have to be done about her. And him. Together.

And the dress.

Something definitely had to be done about the dress.

Daisy arrived at the House of Adeline and was welcomed by Rose and Rachel, Adeline's two longtime friends and fellow seamstresses. They showed Daisy to a private chamber, hidden by thick velvet curtains.

It was not empty.

There was a gown draped and pinned to a fabric mannequin. It was just a muslin version, made of cheap fabric to confirm the drape, the seams, the cut, the measurements before one made a real commitment with expensive satin, that extraordinary lace.

Nevertheless, it was clear that this was a gorgeous gown.

The kind of gown that took your breath away.

The kind of gown that made you feel so righteously beautiful and confident in your own body that you could conquer even the most daunting challenge. Maybe even marriage in front of no fewer than seven hundred members of Manhattan high society.

Things started to feel very, very real all of a sudden.

Between the lovemaking, their business, and now the dress, there was a distinct possibility that the wedding would *actually* happen. There was a distinct possibility that this dress alone had her considering it.

Before Daisy could suffer some attack of the nerves, Adeline appeared with a slightly apologetic smile.

"I hope you'll forgive me but I made a muslin version for your dress."

"The dress we had agreed not to make?"

"Yes, that one," Adeline confirmed and Daisy nodded. She couldn't wrench her gaze away.

"Now, it could always catch fire, or be left outside during a storm, or flung down an elevator shaft at the Fifth Avenue Hotel. These things happen," Adeline said.

"It's terribly dangerous out there for a dress," Daisy murmured her agreement.

"I just had an idea of a gown for you and for your wedding, in particular. And then I had some free time—" This was a lie; the wait time for a House of Adeline dress was significant. "So I pulled this together. Just try it on. Just see."

Obviously, Daisy had to try it on.

It would be rude not to. Adeline was her friend.

It was just a muslin. It wasn't the real dress. It was just pretend. Like the color on her lips and the pink on her cheeks. Like her engagement.

Against her better judgment, Daisy tried it on.

It was immediately clear that this dress was nothing less than a work of art. It was not a gown that could be subjected to arson, neglect, or the perils of an elevator shaft, coal bin, or railroad track, or any other hideous fates one might imagine.

Adeline had ignored Mrs. Swan's dictates about *more* and also *even more!* Instead, she had created a gown that highlighted the best of Daisy herself. Every stitch and seam was placed to enhance and support, to create a gown that she could move freely in—as much as one could, given the fashions of the day.

"The lace will go here, on the bodice, and on the skirts. But any embellishments will be kept to a minimum. You have a strong face, Daisy. You mustn't try to hide behind ruffles and other distractions. A simple cut will suit you best."

"It's beautiful. And this is just the muslin."

"A beautiful dress for a beautiful woman."

"You don't have to . . ."

"Shhh. Look." Adeline pointed Daisy's attention to the mirror. She was riveted by her reflection. She felt beautiful in this dress and it showed in the light of her eyes, in the head held high. It wasn't just the dress though. She loved the color on her lips, the hint of pink across her cheeks. She loved what those things symbolized to her: daring for more, daring to make her dream come true, daring to show the world that she was worthy of adornment.

"It will have pockets, of course." Adeline's signature design feature was pockets in dresses. For love letters, for handkerchiefs, for lip paint. For a train ticket and coin if she needed to run away. Because she had always planned on doing whatever it took to stay unwed.

But this dress dared her to imagine that she might stay and marry Theo.

With this gown on, Daisy could now start to picture what it would be like to walk down the aisle of Grace Church and to stand up beside him and promise to love him. And didn't that make a

real blush deepen on her cheeks. To show everyone who had thought so little of her—everyone
who had *quacked* at her—that she was a tower of
strength, beautiful if not pretty, and loved.

In her fantasy, he loved her.

Daisy had spent a significant portion of her
time scheming and plotting how to get out of the
wedding. This was the first time that she really,
truly imagined actually going through with it.

Now she had reasons to consider it, beyond
the dress.

They had made love. That mattered. They
had created something—a burgeoning little
business—that would bond them together anyway. Once they had stopped bringing out the
worst in each other, they started bringing out
the best. They were conspirators who shared
kisses. Did she dare to chance that they could
be more for each other?

If they did wed, would they do so for love or
because they could not agree on a scheme to get
out of it? These were questions Daisy didn't have
answers for right here, right now. But if the answer was *yes* or *I do*, she wanted to be wearing
this gown for the moment.

"The wedding is in less than a month," Daisy
said. Less than a month to make up her mind to
alter the course of her entire life. But the moment
to decide if she wanted this dress was now. "Sup-
posedly. Allegedly. Rumor has it."

"That doesn't leave much time to make this into a gown," Adeline said. "It will take my girls many, many hours. Twelve-hour days."

Daisy had put her body and reputation on the line to protest seamstresses being required to work *ten*-hour days.

"If we make the dress, I hope they will be compensated accordingly."

Adeline smiled. A twinkle in her eye.

"Of course. We value women's work here."

"And what if I end up not needing the dress?" Daisy asked. It had to be asked. Because wanting to stand up in front of Manhattan society in a pretty dress, loved by one of their favored sons, was not a good enough reason to get married. Because one night of passion and a business entanglement were also not good enough reasons to pledge forever. Because Daisy wanted independence more than anything. Maybe even more than Theo. Definitely more than this beautiful, gorgeous, one-of-a-kind, made-for-her dress. "For who will want a jilted wedding dress, made exactly to my measurements?"

"I can always burn it. Drown it in the East River. Shred the fabric and use it to stuff pillows." Adeline shrugged. "But who says you won't need the dress?"

Chapter Twenty-Three

One is prepared to support the ladies'
club movement as long as the women
focus on matters that pertain to the
realm of women. Anything else would be
shocking, sensational, and scandalous.
—*The New York Post*

25 West Tenth Street

$\mathcal{I}$t was with great optimism and a heart full of
hope that Daisy climbed the stoop at Miss Harriet Burnett's town house for the weekly meeting of the Ladies of Liberty Club. Today she had
something to share.

Something shocking.
Something sensational.
Something scandalous.
Something pretty.

It was her newly created line of Dr. Swan's Cosmetics. Daisy was confident in her formulations,
which were a blend of science and creativity that

had been tested by the girls in the shop, as well as some of the actresses at the Empire Theater who had volunteered. And Theo had really outdone himself by sourcing small, stylish metal boxes labeled with the same lavender paper of all the other Dr. Swan products.

They both had every expectation that this would mimic the success of the Midnight Miracle Cream, which was flying off the shelves. They had even expanded into the Morning Miracle Cream, a lighter version. Once a few brave women had dared to buy it publicly, once the newspapers had reported on it, once friends had discussed it, once it seemed commonplace enough, the sales took off. Daisy expected that once again, the Ladies of Liberty would be instrumental to her success.

Daisy knocked on the door at the town house using the heavy bronze knocker cast in the shape of Medusa's head. So very Harriet. Miss Burnett's butler opened the door to her and gestured toward the drawing room, where Harriet, her erstwhile companion Miss Ava Lumley, and other ladies of the club had already gathered and were doing serious damage to a pot of tea and tray of sandwiches.

There was no pretense about lady appetites at club meetings. If one was famished, one ate a sandwich. Or two.

"Ah, Daisy! There you are!" She hoped everyone would notice the cosmetics she had applied—a soft pink tint to her lips, a similar dash of color to her cheeks. She'd taken great care in her application to achieve a look that was subtle but noticeable all the same. Then she had to wait for her mother to leave for her charity luncheon so that she could escape with her carefully made-up face intact. Her mother would have a fit if she saw it. Then Daisy would be really delayed, if not banished to her room, and she was *so* excited to share her newest creation.

For the very first time, she *wanted* to be noticed for her face.

But Harriet just waved her in and said, "We are discussing the issue of restaurants."

"Particularly the fact that women are not allowed in them without a man," Ava added.

"And then one is not expected to display much of an appetite when dining in the company of men, so what is even the point?" Elsie said. The clubwomen's gazes drifted toward a tray of sandwiches and cookies that had been demolished.

Daisy availed herself of a spot on a plush pink velvet upholstered settee and accepted a cup of tea. The satchel full of promise and products rested at her feet.

"This rule, this *expectation*, is just another way in which women's sphere is limited," Harriet said. "We fear for our reputations should we venture out alone, so we stay in or merely travel from drawing room to drawing room. Which raises the question, why is it so terrible that a woman go out alone?"

"It's dangerous. Our virtue might be . . . compromised," Elizabeth said.

"Or people might only think our virtue has been compromised. Which is almost worse than being actually compromised," Elsie remarked.

There was a ring of truth to this. It brought to mind the sneaking around she had done the other night. It didn't matter what she had done, as long as she wasn't seen doing it. As long as no one gossiped about it, it might as well have never happened.

But why, she wondered for the first time, was it so very terrible that people would think she was a woman who'd been made love to? She was either labeled a hopeless spinster or bride-to-be or wife; anything else was dangerous territory.

"Never mind that it's exhausting moving around in all the skirts and fripperies that a woman must wear," Ava said.

"I'm working on solving that one," Adeline said to the group's gentle laughter. "It won't be long before hemlines are shorter. Mark my words."

"Until then, there is nowhere to go and it's too difficult to get there and one risks their reputation in doing so. One might as well stay home."

"I do believe that is the point," Elsie said dryly.

"How are we supposed to upset the natural order of things from home?"

"Again, I do believe that is the point," Elsie said.

"Daisy, what is on your face?" Harriet asked.

All the women turned to face her. Finally!

"You might be noticing my lip color." Daisy smiled. "It's specially formulated to mimic the look of a woman who has just been kissed." Daisy paused for *oohs* and *aahs* that were not forthcoming. Nevertheless, she persisted. Because they were definitely intrigued and definitely looking. "With my proprietary blend of waxes and oils, plus specially crafted mixtures of pigments to create flattering shades—"

"Never mind all that!" Elsie interjected with a wave of her hand. "Who have you been kissing?"

Miss Lumley answered for Daisy. "Theodore Prescott the Third, obviously. Her fiancé. Obviously."

"Her fake fiancé," Harriet corrected. "Whom she has told us on multiple occasions that she loathes."

Eunice snorted at that. "It didn't look like she loathed him backstage at the theater."

Daisy's cheeks turned a shade of pink that Theo might have called *upstanding spinster romanced by a rogue and embarrassed in front of her friends.*

"What were you doing backstage at the theater?"

"Research. For this . . ."

Tea things were promptly cleared away from the

table—they had vanquished a tower of sandwiches and petit fours and drained the teapots—and in that space Daisy created her display of products she carefully removed from her satchel. There were small pots of lip paints in varying hues of pink and red and little powders for cheeks.

A hushed silence fell over the ladies present as they examined everything, some women even daring to pick them up and examine them. It wasn't that these things were utterly foreign. They had been around for decades—centuries, even—but for as long as anyone in this room could remember, they were only worn by certain kinds of women. The ones of questionable virtue.

Rouge was something for actresses and prostitutes; women who earned their own money.

The ladies with reputations of impeccable virtue, such as the ones in Harriet's drawing room, were not usually at liberty to openly browse and experiment with these products. They were high society wives and daughters or respectable middle-class women. But they were also daring to push the boundaries of what proper ladies could do. They pushed the limits, in the most ladylike way. They owned and operated their own businesses, they earned their own way as reporters, they were doctors and activists.

Proper ones though. Not a smidge of lipstick was to be found on their lips.

"Do I have a volunteer to try it?" Daisy asked.

"Will it come off?"

"Of course. Regular soap and water should do the trick, but I have also been working on a special solution that will help remove it."

No one clamored for the opportunity. The women were silent. But Daisy recognized the expression on their faces: it was of a woman desperately keen to try it but determined not to appear thusly. A similar expression was to be found on the faces of wallflowers in ballrooms all over town; girls who wanted to dance but did not appear to want to dance.

Because then what would people say about a woman who obviously has desires?

To be obviously *wanting* was unseemly in a woman.

"I'll give it a go," Harriet said gamely. She was always one to support her friends. Daisy gave her a grateful smile.

"We'll start with the rouge. It's a loose powder lightly tinted with pink to provide the illusion of having received a delicious compliment from a suitor one likes."

Blushing at receiving a compliment was ladylike enough. The women curiously appraised Harriet's now delicately pink cheeks.

Daisy carried on, reaching now for just the right shade of pink for Harriet's complexion.

"I have formulated a few different shades of

lip paint. I think this color is a little more daring, but I think it would suit you, Harriet."

It was a shade of red that Theo called *Lady Rebel*.

Daisy carefully applied the lipstick to Harriet's lips and moved back to admire her work and let everyone see. Had everyone not been watching the application process, they might not have noticed the difference. Daisy had not used a strong hand—they were not under stage lights in front of an audience of thousands, after all.

Harriet looked just like she always did, just ever so slightly *more.*

Except for her mouth. Her reddened lips were shocking.

Or sensational.

Or scandalous.

The pigments on her face issued a command: *Look at me. Look twice. Notice me.* It did this in a world where women went about their day clad in full-length gowns that covered nearly every inch of their bare skin and often even hid behind a veil. In other words: *Do not look. Nothing to see here!* Women were supposed to make it easy to forget about their existence. To hide the fact that they were flesh-and-blood humans who wanted things.

In such a world, it was best just to stay home, then.

After all, the only women who wore face paints

wanted people—men people, particularly—to look at them. It was actresses and prostitutes who dared to attract a gaze, to hold it, own it, and demand to be seen and recognized.

Or perhaps women who wanted to change the world and challenge the world to notice them.

"Daisy, do you really mean for respectable women to wear all this out?" Ava asked softly.

"Adeline has spoken often of the power of an excellently made dress to make a woman feel comfortable and confident as she ventures out of the home and into the world." At this there were murmurs of agreement. "What if these cosmetics also functioned to give women confidence? The attention I have received has not always made me feel my best. I am so happy with myself but why can I not have this little *something* that makes me feel even more confident?"

This elicited more intrigued chatter from the group of ladies. They, too, were aware of tired eyes or dull complexions or loath to leave the house due to a blemish, so aware that the world was evaluating them upon their face. "What if being able to make oneself feel prettier made one also feel more confident to go out into the world? Then imagine what she might accomplish."

The women burst into conversation. Agreeing and disagreeing passionately. One voice, Elizabeth's, rose up.

"I don't know that I would feel confident with

a red mouth like that. I'd be terrified that everyone would be looking at me."

"And questioning my virtue," another woman added.

"And once it is in question . . ."

"Would it really be the worst thing in the world?" Daisy asked. It was a question she, who was earning her own fortune and determined to be a spinster and had the protection of an engagement to Theodore Prescott the Third, could afford to ask.

"Why should women in those professions be demonized anyway?" Elsie asked. "Especially by women like us? They are only trying to support themselves and their families. Are we really so very different? Aren't we all just people trying to succeed with the opportunities available to us?"

"It would not be the *worst* thing but . . . a woman's good reputation is what enables her to find a good husband and to move in good society. What is more important than family and friends?"

"Our good reputations are what enable us to advocate for other women. Our efforts are only taken seriously because we are virtuous, upstanding models of ladyhood."

"Or because we *appear* to be," Harriet corrected.

Daisy wanted to protest "it's just lip paint!" but it wasn't. Alone in her lab, it was just mixing compounds and materials and it was just science. And then it became much more significant. She had only aspired to make herself, and other women, feel beautiful. She never thought it would be making a statement, too. She could see now that it wasn't just lip paint at all.

"If enough women wore it, all at once, society couldn't possibly decide all of a sudden that all women were compromised and that such a significant group of women should all be ostracized from good society. If it were a common enough thing . . ."

"But someone will have to be first."

Daisy knew it would have to be her.

Chapter Twenty-Four

For the first time ever, Theodore Prescott the Second is opening his doors to Manhattan society to show off the size and opulence of his ballroom and the immensity of his wealth. The occasion is a party celebrating his son's upcoming nuptials to Miss Daisy Swan.
—*The New York Post*

The Prescott Ballroom
901 Fifth Avenue

*T*onight Daisy's face was one that would, if not launch a thousand ships, at least turn heads and get society talking.

Not just because they were all in attendance at a soiree to celebrate her looming wedding. It was her mother's idea for Prescott Senior to host a party to honor the match and make it even more impossible to get out of. Prescott Senior obliged; Evelina Swan was hard to say no to. Even Daisy and Theo didn't complain when they both immediately spied the opportunity it presented.

It was a chance for Daisy to step out wearing cosmetics. It was a once-in-a-lifetime chance to attend a party where she would be the center of attention, celebrated for the man on her arm and the respectability he conveyed, and a party where everyone would have to notice her *and* be nice to her.

She was going to take full advantage.

Daisy emerged from the ladies' retiring room with lips distinctly redder than when she'd entered. In full view of her fellow females she had leaned toward the mirror and applied a sheen of her *Lady Rebel* lipstick. Before she left the house she had oh so subtly darkened her eyes and highlighted her cheekbones with a dusting of her *Fair Maiden* blush.

She looked sensational. A little rebellious.

Not pretty but quite possibly beautiful.

She looked like a new woman.

With a quick, satisfied smile at her reflection, she slipped the small jar of lip paint into the pocket of her gown, ignored the open-mouthed gasps of her fellow attendees of the ladies' retiring room, and strolled back to the ballroom.

Miss Daisy Swan was a respectable young woman—so much so that marriage to her was penance and a chance at redemption for the Four

Hundred's wayward, scandal-plagued golden boy. If any one woman could pull off lip paint in a ballroom at her own engagement party and be invited out again tomorrow, it was she.

Daisy "Ugly Duck" Swan.

Theo was waiting for her with a smile on his lips, ready to escort her into the crowds. He was as boyishly handsome and exceptionally dressed as ever. The man did know how to wear a tuxedo. But what made her a little bit breathless was the deeply appreciative way he looked at her. Like she was beautiful. Like he was lucky to stand beside her. Like they were co-conspirators and he liked it.

"Hello, Daisy. You look sensational tonight."

"That is part of the plan, isn't it?"

Her gaze locked with his. She felt that now-familiar heat of wanting for him. She reminded herself that this was just an advertising scheme. It was Theo's idea. They would trade on their good standing in society and their notoriety as a couple to take the shock and scandal out of the sight of a respectable lady wearing lipstick.

They would make it acceptable.

Then they would sell it. And break up. And live happily ever after?

"Shall we take a turn around the ballroom?" Theo asked, and Daisy linked her arm with his.

"We are here to cause a scene after all."

Her years of good behavior had to be good for

something. She was ready to trade her past for her future. And so she stepped into the crowd, confidently on the arm of one of the most adored men in Manhattan.

People took notice. Perhaps it was her gown. Her face. Him. The two of them together. Whatever it was, people looked twice. And then they turned to their neighbor to discuss the sight of Theodore Prescott the Third *happily* strolling through the ballroom with Daisy *Ugly Duck* Swan. Except she wasn't so ugly, really.

"She looks . . . different."

They couldn't help but overhear as they moved through the crush.

Daisy held her head high. Because she hadn't changed her appearance that much. Just a little splash of color, really. Her nose was still a trifle too much, her eyes a smidge too close. Her mouth might not be fashionable—yet. But hers was a face that would now turn heads and she felt good about it. That made all the difference in the way she moved through the ballroom, in the way she dared to lift her head high and meet people's gazes.

Arm in arm, Theo and Daisy kept walking. She was almost enjoying herself. This almost felt *right.*

"They're noticing," he murmured.

"You do tend to draw attention," she said.

"I think it's you."

"I daresay most of them wouldn't have noticed me in a fully made-up face if *you* weren't on my arm. It's you. And me. Us. Together."

Theo handed her a glass of champagne from a passing waiter and she was glad because the conversation was verging precariously close to the topic which must be avoided until . . . later. The *what is going to happen to our fake engagement* conversation. She was loath to have it. Because even though she liked him and what they created and the way his kiss and his touch thrilled her . . . Daisy didn't love the feeling of *needing* him. She still dreamed of her freedom, and wasn't ready to marry him.

Daisy had the impression it might hurt him to say so.

Not just his reputation, either.

She did not want to hurt him. She cared enough about him for that.

"Is she wearing . . . lip paint?"

"Yes! Blanche saw her apply it in the ladies' retiring room. In full view of everyone!"

A chorus of shocked female voices. They could not believe she would be so brazen. And forward. So wanton. And untoward.

"Only certain kinds of women wear cosmetics."

And then there was that. And there it went. Her unquestionable virtue. Gone forever on a whisper in a ballroom.

"Well, they are engaged so . . ."

"The more they discuss it, the more publicity we get," Theo murmured.

"But the more they talk about it, the harder it will be to break the match," Daisy said. This, she realized now, was the flaw in their plan.

"But if a little lip paint is what it takes to snare a man like Theodore Prescott the Third . . ."

Daisy and Theo turned to each other, bright eyes and smiles. Because there it was, the first glimmer of possible acceptance. The first hint that their plan was working. The first indication that maybe all of their efforts hadn't been for nothing.

But then the tenor in the ballroom changed, suddenly, as if a cold wind swept through. The uproarious chatter quickly became somber as voices dropped to just whispers and murmurs and the sickening sound of grave concern. As if a president had died or a bridge collapsed.

Her mother came rushing toward her.

Daisy knew something terrible had happened when her mother didn't flirt with Theo or express the slightest outrage over her daughter parading around a ballroom in a full face of cosmetics. She didn't even bat an eyelash.

"Daisy, we have to go. Immediately."

"What is it?"

"It's all over, is what it is. We need to leave *now.*"

Oh. This. Was. Happening. Now. Tonight. Of all nights. Daisy had known this was coming;

something bad with her father's business that would ruin everything, for everyone. It was why Daisy had to find protection—or a way to stand on her own. It was why her mother schemed and pushed to get her daughter married. It was all a race against the clock and they had lost.

One of the evening's guests, Mrs. Waverly, cut through the crowd with her sights set on the Swan women. Thick coils of pearls were roped around her neck, tumbling over her bosom, falling to her waist. Her complexion was ashen. She clutched a flute of champagne, which sloshed over her fingertips and she didn't even notice.

She stopped a foot from Daisy and her mother and tossed the contents of her glass in their faces.

Daisy shrieked in shock. If there had been any doubts that she'd been wearing cosmetics, there were none now. There were dark streaks and clumps of rouge and powder running down her cheeks. Not her best look. But no one looked at Daisy anymore; they were more interested in Mrs. Swan.

"Is it true, Mrs. Swan? *Is it true?*"

But her mother stood still, champagne dripping from her face. Theo handed her a handkerchief, which she accepted.

"Mrs. Waverly, please. This is *not* the time for theatrics."

But Mrs. Waverly begged to differ. "I asked you if it was true, Mrs. Swan. Is your husband's

brokerage firm a sham? Has he really been stealing from new investors to pay returns to everyone else? Is it true that this nefarious scheme has
collapsed?"

Daisy felt her lungs constrict so much that it
was impossible for air to move in and out. She'd
had hints. She'd had her suspicions. She just hadn't
known for certain. Now here it was, the moment of
truth. Awful, ruinous, disastrous truth. It was far,
far worse than she had suspected. Her father was
a fraud. Worse—his victims were their friends
and acquaintances.

She dared to lift her gaze to Theo.

He was plainly shocked by the sudden turn of
events.

Once the shock wore off, she detected betrayal.
She ought to have confided in him and she regretted that she hadn't.

"I don't know what you are talking about, Mrs.
Waverly." Her mother forced a little laugh. "You
know society wives like us don't bother with
their husband's business."

She tried to laugh it off. But no one was laughing because if it was true . . . if it was true . . . the
truth was too unbearable. There was an unnatu-
ral silence in the ballroom. The ease and laughter
that had been there a moment ago had now van-
ished, leaving something cold and hardened in
its place. They had all trusted their fortunes with
him and reveled in the wealth he'd showered

upon them. A genius, they had called him. Now they were revealed as unfortunate fools.

"They are saying that his entire company was a sham. That new investments paid off previous investors. That the funds have all been taken and spent. That all our money is *gone*. Do you know what that means for the families in this ballroom?"

No one needed to explain. Everyone understood that the party was over—literally and figuratively. Her family was finished in this town. Many others would be taken down, too.

Daisy watched as ashen-faced men turned to leave. Wives and daughters trailed behind—their vibrantly colored gowns and ornate jewels a mockery of the present moment. Fortunes were lost. Families ruined. Lives over.

Not the least of which included her own.

Daisy turned to Theo to say something, but any words died on her lips. He still looked so shocked and *hurt*.

"Did you know about this, Daisy?"

"Yes. No. It's hard to explain. Not exactly."

"I see the urgency for us to wed now," he said quietly. "It wasn't about you and me at all."

She watched as he put the pieces together—he wasn't just a pretty face—and understood the reasons that Mrs. Swan was so insistent they wed. And why Daisy was so determined to earn her own fortune.

While everyone in the ballroom moved numbly toward the exit, one man strode determinedly through the crowd and halted before them. He leveled them with a stare that made Daisy grip her mother's hand tightly. That stare was positively lethal. That stare made Daisy question her very existence.

Theo stepped away from her. An almost imperceptible step away from her and toward his father.

Theodore Prescott the Elder spoke: "It should go without saying that if this evening's revelations are true, this match no longer has my support."

Once upon a time, Daisy had made a list of ways to get out of the wedding and *this* had not made the cut.

> Did you hear about the scandal
> with the Swans?
> —Everybody in New York, practically

Later that night
854 Fifth Avenue

EITHER NEWS TRAVELED fast or the servants of the Swan residence had been given orders earlier to start packing once Daisy and her mother left for the ball. When they returned, their town house was frantic with activity as servants rushed to and fro to pack one steamer trunk after another.

Mrs. Evelina Swan was leaving town. Indefinitely. And she would be taking anything that wasn't nailed down—and anything she didn't want seized by the authorities. Jewels. Paintings. Silver. Whatever solid gold trinkets were lying around.

Daisy nearly tripped over her own satin shoes trying to make sense of it all.

She had expected a scandal tonight.

Just not this one.

She had known *something* was coming—some news that would shake her equilibrium—but she had not anticipated a scandal of this magnitude. Some bad investments, perhaps. Not a carefully constructed web of deceit that involved many of their family's friends and acquaintances. This was the sort of scandal that didn't just blow over in time. It was the kind that blacklisted a girl forever.

It seemed her mother knew it—and had known it all along.

"I have passage booked on the HMS *Majestic*," her mother said. "We sail for France tomorrow morning. We can't possibly stay in New York now."

"But I don't want to leave New York."

Her mother gave her a sympathetic smile. "I know, darling. But what choice do we have?"

No wonder she had insisted that Daisy marry sooner rather than later and that she marry someone like Theo who, in theory, could offer Daisy the wealth, connections, and security she needed to weather a storm like this and to stay in the city she called home.

It was *love* that made her mother force the marriage.

The revelation took Daisy's breath away.

"The news hit a little sooner than anticipated," her mother admitted. "But I think we shall be able to set sail before anyone comes for us. I managed to switch the tickets I had reserved for your honeymoon. Why would anyone want to come for us anyway? We are just some silly women."

Her mother fluttered her lashes. With a little pout she instantly transformed into a sweet, brainless woman who was best just sent out of the way of the men and their important business.

"Oh, dear God."

That was how her mother was going to get them out of any interrogations or repercussions. She would play the role of ditzy society darling who spent her days just spending money with no questions asked about where it had come from. Daisy saw that, in a way, her mother was just as much of an actress as the ones on Broadway.

"Go on, Daisy. You must pack your things. We haven't any time to spare." She glanced at the blank space on the mantel where the clock used to rest. "Our ship departs tomorrow and we must be on it."

"What about Theo?"

"What about him?"

"The wedding. The church. The champagne and the roses?"

"There can't be a wedding now, darling."

"But you reserved the church. Invitations have been sent. You have been planning a reception for a thousand people at the Fifth Avenue Hotel."

"It's too late for that now, Daisy. We can't stay here. Theo can't protect you now. His father will not stand up for you. I think he might have been one of your father's investors—I don't know. I *refuse* to know. At the very least, I'm certain many of his friends were. He will not countenance a match between you and his son now. I think it's safe to say the wedding is off."

"But . . ."

This is what she had wanted. Desperately.

Her mother smiled at her. "You are free, Daisy."

This was the reprieve she had hoped and prayed for. Yet here it was, falling right into her lap and she didn't want it.

"I should think you'd be happy about that, no? After all your hemming and hawing about marrying him in the first place. Now you're free to make a really advantageous match."

"Mother . . ."

"Once we land in Europe we'll set about landing you a lord. An earl or a viscount or something. Like your sister Camilla. After a few years, when the scandal will have died down, we can return to the city. Nothing like an aristocratic title to open doors that were previously closed."

"You have it all figured out, don't you, Mother?" Society was a game of chess and Daisy was her pawn.

"I can't believe you would think otherwise, Daisy."

And with that, Daisy was dismissed to go pack up the contents of her life. She paused in the doorway of her room where Sally had already begun packing her gowns, gloves, underthings, shoes . . . The things she would need to land that earl or viscount, while the things Daisy loved that made her *her* would be left behind.

Books for her classes at Barnard sat on her bedside table. Her chemistry supplies remained untouched in the corner of her room. And all her samples of lip paint and rouge were scattered across the top of her dressing table. Little cast-off hopes and dreams that would be swept away as Daisy set sail for a new life in Europe.

A new life in which she sacrificed herself on the altar of a loveless marriage so that in a few years' time her mother could have what she loved and wanted most in the world: the adoration of society. Evenings at all the most glittering parties.

Why would she *not* do this for her mother, who

gave her life, tried to protect her, and stood by her for everything? She was the one who'd soothed and comforted Daisy after Theo and his friends cruelly teased and taunted her. She was the one who had persuaded her husband to support Daisy's college ambitions. She had supported her daughter in so many ways, and for so long.

Evelina Swan wasn't some flighty society lady; she was a woman who played the hand she'd been dealt. And she was a mother who loved her daughters fiercely. She'd only been trying to protect Daisy.

And so how could Daisy deny her this one thing?

How could she leave her mother to face this uncertain future alone?

Their ship sailed tomorrow morning for a new life in Europe. There was no good reason for Daisy Swan not to be on it.

Except for Theodore Prescott the Third.

Who had never said he loved her.

Chapter Twenty-Five

New York society is reeling from the demise of Jack Swan and his fraudulent investment scheme that has decimated many of the city's fortunes.
—*The New York Post*

The Prescott Mansion
The library, specifically

*D*awn broke on the Prescott mansion to reveal a house still wrecked from the party the night before. Champagne glasses and stray pearls were strewn among all the art and antiques. Servants went about the task of cleaning up in muted silence.

By now, everyone had heard the news.

Legendary investor Jack Swan had defrauded dozens of investors with a scheme that took from new infusions of cash to pay off previous investors. The victims of his deception included some of Manhattan's most-storied families, senators, and former presidents, and even the church.

And Theodore Prescott the Second.

Prescott Senior spent hours in the library, in hushed meetings with advisers and partners to ascertain the extent of the damage.

Theo wandered the halls. Thinking. Wondering. Trying to make sense of everything. *Had Daisy known?* She must have known. She must have had a reason like this to push so hard and fast to make their business a success, so that she'd have something to fall back on when everything collapsed around her. Theo couldn't be mad about it because he also had his own reasons for joining her.

He just wished she would have confided in him. If he was honest with himself, the lack of trust and confidence in him was what hurt the most. To think of all the intimacies they'd shared. Except for this one.

He didn't know what it all meant for them now.

What would happen to him and her?

What did he *want* to happen with him, her, the two of them together?

Theo didn't know yet.

Theo knocked on the door to the library. For once, he did not wait for his father's bid to enter before he strolled into the room. He just accepted that he had a right to his father's attention and strolled in.

Theodore Prescott the Second sat slumped in his chair, a cigar burning in the ashtray on his desk, sleeves rolled up, hair in disarray. He looked rough, like the young steelworker he'd once been.

But he also looked defeated.

"How bad is it?"

"Bad."

"Will you be able to keep the steel company? The house?"

These were questions Theo never, ever imagined he would ask. Strangely, he didn't fear the answers. The reason was that he had something of his own now—a company he'd helped build from scratch and his own income. And even if those things were gone now, too, Theo still had his new-found confidence and knowledge in building a business. He still had connections, his education. For better or worse, whether deserving it or not, a man like him always had a chance to succeed.

He could be just fine on his own.

He could afford to take a chance on love.

He sent a silent prayer of gratitude to Daisy. He could only see these truths because of her.

"Well, it won't bankrupt me." Prescott Senior laughed bitterly. "Thomas, Cavanaugh, and the church bore the worst of it. But it's bad."

Theo had to wonder what hurt more: the blow to his father's bank account or to his pride in his reputation as being the richest, the most powerful, the most untouchable.

"No matter what, not *all* is lost. I have money."

"How cute. My son offering his pocket money. Which *I* gave him."

Theo waited for the sting of his father's mockery.

Ah, yes, there it was. But it faded as quickly as it had come. Because his father didn't know the truth. While Theo regretted the present circumstances, a part of him was glad for the opportunity to stand up and be the hero. He had earned it.

"My business is on track to generate a million dollars this year, Father. I know, it's just one million. But you must admit that's not too bad for the first month."

His father looked up with narrowed eyes.

"Your business. *Your* business?"

"Yes. Dr. Swan's Apothecary. Maybe you've heard of it? It's all the rage among society ladies. There's been nothing like it ever before."

"What the devil is that, even?"

"We sell a revolutionary new complexion balm. Soon we'll be launching cosmetics."

It so happened that there was something worse than his father's legendary stare. His father's laughter. His rich, uproarious, mocking laughter that wasn't even muted by the thick carpet or books on the walls. It could echo in a boy's soul and head forever, that laughter.

Theo discovered that now. He almost wanted to press his palms against his ears to drown it out. Instead, he stood still and tall and faced it.

"This is not the time for jokes, Theo."

"Why do you think I'm joking?"

"Because no son of mine will have gone into business making face cream for society ladies."

Except he had. And he was good at it. And he liked it. It made him happy. Didn't that have to count for something?

"I thought you wanted me to find a purpose," Theo said, fighting to keep control of his voice. Because all these feelings—years and years and years of feelings and unspoken words—were ready to make their debut now. "An occupation. Some focus and discipline. Something that will make me a man we can both be proud of. And I have done it."

"No, you haven't. You're just selling face paints for prostitutes." His father took a long inhalation of his cigar and exhaled. "I get it. You're just doing something to get out of your marriage with that Swan girl. It's safe to say that match no longer has my blessing. So you can give up on your little business."

His father waved him off. Literally a wave of his hand, like his own son was some employee to be dismissed. Like he had every expectation that Theo would do his bidding. Like Theo wasn't his own man.

But he was.

His voice was steady when Theo simply said, "No."

"No? The girl or the business?"

Theo didn't even have to think about it. He was sure of the answer. "Both."

"Tell me, *son.* How much humiliation am I

supposed to take?" His father leaned forward now, eyes narrowed. "We are Prescott Steel, forged in fire and the backbone of Manhattan's legendary skyscrapers. And you want to make toiletries for ladies and marry the daughter of the man who nearly bankrupted me and my friends? Hell, no. My word is final. You'll come to work with me. I should have insisted on that from the beginning."

"I see. You never wanted me to find *a* purpose or occupation. You wanted me to follow yours. You thought forcing me into an engagement with Daisy would be such an awful prospect that I'd come running to Prescott Steel, ready to do your bidding. To become just like you."

"You could do worse. You have done worse. You are not the son I'd hoped for."

And there it was. His father had never said the words aloud, but Theo had always felt the weight of them. And now the air rushed out of his chest. It took a minute, a real minute, before he remembered that the world was still turning and he should probably keep breathing.

The thing he had feared most in the world had just happened and not only had he survived, Theo also realized that it wasn't the thing he dreaded most. Not anymore. Losing Daisy. Losing what he had with her. Losing the man he'd become because of her. That was now the fate he feared.

Finally, Theo found the words he'd always carried around but couldn't quite articulate. Fear of his father's mockery and disapproval always kept his true feelings unspoken. But now Theo knew beyond a shadow of a doubt that he didn't have anything to lose by saying them.

"I only wanted your approval, Father. I only ever wanted to make you proud of me for who I was. I only ever wanted your love. But now I wonder if you are even capable of it. And now all I want is to be with Daisy."

Theo turned to go. His hand was on the doorknob when his father's voice stopped him.

"I won't let you do it. I won't let you embarrass me with that business or that woman."

"The thing is, Father, you can't stop me."

Some are wondering if the match between
Theodore Prescott the Third and Miss
Daisy Swan will go on. One cannot imagine
it would, given the circumstances.
—*The New York Post*

Later that morning
Central Park

THIS TIME WHEN they met in the park, it was planned. The weather was cool and crisp, the sky gray-tinged; it was a no-nonsense kind of New York day.

"You." Theo said the word because there was so much he wanted to say and he didn't know where to begin.

"You," she replied in kind.

For a moment they just stared at each other. Once upon a time Theo had said she wasn't his type, but now he couldn't imagine a face that he wanted to gaze at more than hers. Beauty was her luminous skin, the quirk of her smile, the bright intelligence of her eyes. Pleasure was her lips, the softness of her skin. Delight was every moment with her, not knowing what would come next.

Their worlds had collapsed around them and yet here they were in the shadow of that duck pond and the gazebo and all their worst moments together. Everything had changed.

"Of all the ways on our list to get out of the wedding, I never saw this one coming," he said. "Did you know, Daisy?"

"I knew my father was up to something not good. I never imagined it would be this bad. It is why my mother forced and rushed our wedding. She wanted me to be protected."

"Why didn't you tell me, Daisy?"

"First we were enemies. And then I was too busy kissing you."

"I can't say that isn't true." When does one find the perfect moment to confess that Something Bad Was Going To Happen? Especially when one had so many other things to talk about. There was so much kissing one could do. Theo harbored no grudge that she hadn't told him. "What happens now?"

"They are transporting all our trunks to the docks right now," she said. Suddenly, he couldn't breathe. Suddenly, his knees felt weak. "We'll sail for France this morning. We haven't booked return tickets."

"Of course. What else would one do the morning after a scandal?" Theo quipped because he didn't trust himself to say anything else. She was *leaving*? She couldn't leave now. He . . . needed her.

"Apparently, one sets sail to France and plans to stay forever."

"No one stays in France forever," Theo replied. "It's where one goes for flirtation, fashion, and a quick jaunt to gaze at some art so one might lay some claim to culture. But then one returns home, to Manhattan, with a better wardrobe."

Daisy smiled in spite of herself.

"We certainly can't stay *here*," she said. "Well, my father will be staying. In jail."

"Not quite the Fifth Avenue Hotel."

"Not quite," she agreed. "But my mother and I will go. She has some idea that if I just marry a count or an earl, all will be forgiven and we'll be welcomed back into New York society. Eventually."

"So the wedding is off," he said.

"Allegedly."

"Rumor has it."

"People are saying," she replied. And people were saying. It was in the newspapers this morning that they couldn't possibly marry now.

"You've gotten everything you wanted," Theo said. "The wedding is off. Our business is successful and on track to be more so. You will be free to enjoy your spinsterhood and all the freedom it entails. I have no doubt that Dr. Swan will be all the rage in Paris. In fact, it might be easier to sell there than here."

"If I go to Paris."

"You can't stay here, Daisy." The truth of it was a suffocating weight on his chest. He knew what she would endure to stay here; it would be brutal. Because he loved her, he couldn't ask her to suffer that. "You can't stay," he repeated even though the words tasted like ash in his mouth. "Not after what your father did to everyone. Your reputation . . ." Theo couldn't stand to see her insulted in the newspapers, cut by society, and shunned by her friends, and their business suffer.

"Why, Theo, you almost sound like you want me to go."

"No, Daisy—"

"Do you really think I'm going to let some scandal run me out of town?"

Theo cracked a smile. Because there were

words he needed to say. Words that were pent up in his heart. Words that were his feelings. He didn't want to keep them to himself.

"I don't want you to go. I want you to stay in New York. With me."

Chapter Twenty-Six

New York women are a little less radiant and
significantly more irate due to the sudden
demise of Dr. Swan's Apothecary. How else will
they obtain their Midnight Miracle Cream?
—*The New York Post*

The next day
27 Union Square

*T*heodore Prescott the Second did not waste
time in proving that he could and he would put
a stop to Theo's business. Because nothing was
more important than an old man's pride. Not a
young man's dreams, not a young woman's ambitions.

Theo had told Daisy of his father's vow to
ruin them before Daisy said goodbye to her
mother and ordered her trunks to be removed
from the carriage headed toward the docks and
to the ship.

His honesty and timing had been the stuff of a
true hero and gentleman.

However, Daisy, foolishly, hadn't really believed that Theodore Prescott the Second would spare the time to ruin them. After all, he was such a busy and important man.

Silly her for underestimating what a man will do to protect his reputation.

What really burned was how little effort it took for Prescott Senior to grind everything to a halt with nothing more than a word, a letter, a well-placed connection for the New York Society for the Suppression of Vice to shut down the shop. Someone there just happened to have heard from a "trusted source" that the cosmetics were just to signal to "certain kinds" of women that they were really selling contraceptives. It went without saying that was all manner of illegal.

The landlord found this suitable reason to terminate the lease.

And so Daisy and Theo stood before the empty storefront where their shop used to be. The contents had been confiscated. Heaven forbid such dangerous and lethal products as ladies' toilet preparations be available for purchase.

Dr. Swan's Apothecary was gone. And with it, their sole means of supporting themselves.

"It's not too late for you to join your mother in Europe, Daisy. I'm sure you could launch the business in Paris without any troubles."

"I could go this evening," Daisy agreed.

"Paris is lovely this time of year," Theo remarked.

"But it's not New York." Daisy sighed. The truth of this merited a moment of silence. She and Theo and Dr. Swan belonged in New York City, a place for schemers and dreamers. Once one fell under the thrall of New York, no other city would do. Not even Paris.

Daisy was prepared to do battle for her right to stay—on her terms.

"Daisy, I'm so sorry. This has to be my father's doing." Theo paused before continuing. "He swore that he wouldn't let me embarrass the Prescott name with a business like ours. If I had just quit and gone to Prescott Steel . . . or if I hadn't taunted him . . . It's my father's doing, but it's my fault."

"No, Theo. One might say it's all my fault. I brought you into this mad scheme. I'm just sorry that he can't appreciate your talent. And my genius. And what we achieved together."

Right there on the busy street, Theo clasped her hand and squeezed. Right where anyone could see. There were definitely perks to having one's reputation being in tatters; one could hold hands in public with a handsome man and just enjoy it.

As much as one could enjoy a romantic moment while standing before the wreckage of one's destroyed hopes and dreams.

"You stayed for me. For us. For this." Theo gestured at the empty storefront. Their sign had been hastily boarded over. It hurt to look at. She glanced up at him and Theo turned to face her. He gazed deeply into her eyes.

"Daisy, I promise to you that I am going to make this a success so that when I propose marriage, you have a choice." Her lips parted. She hadn't expected this. "I love you. And I will marry you in an instant for protection or reputation if you just say the word. But I have some notion of you saying yes with your whole heart and being able to afford to say no. And I will do everything in my power to make sure you truly have a choice."

Her heart was thundering even though she was standing still.

Theodore Prescott the Third was somewhat proposing and it was the most romantic thing she'd ever heard. And all she could think of to say was . . .

"Oh, Theo . . ." She sighed. "And just to be clear, that's *oh, Theo* in a good way. You've left me speechless."

Right there on the busy street, in the shadow of their former shop, he laughed. Because it was him and her and they were in love. Not even Theodore Prescott the Second and the New York Society for the Suppression of Vice could stop it.

"Paris *is* lovely this time of year," Theo said.

"You sound like you have an idea."

"We go to Paris. Reopen a shop as Madame Swan's. The Parisians are so much more . . . open. It won't be long before we're more successful than we've ever imagined."

Daisy didn't answer right away because she was giving the matter serious consideration. As much as one could amidst the bustle of Union Square. Paris was beautiful. The French would certainly embrace Madame Swan. Her scandalous reputation wouldn't follow them. She and Theo would be together. Who knew what kind of happiness they could make?

But . . .

"You're not going to let him win, are you?" Daisy burst out. "We can't let him *win*."

"It's not like that . . ."

"It's one hundred percent like that," she said. "You have threatened his dominance so he must reassert it. You have challenged his pride and so he has to crush yours. Well, I won't tolerate it and neither should you."

"Think practically, Daisy. He is wealthy and powerful—so much so that even your father's fraud can't bring him down completely. He just said *a word* and our business is gone. He can still afford to stop at nothing to make sure I don't embarrass the family name. He has all the power to get what he wishes."

"Except he doesn't," Daisy said impatiently.

She felt a grin tugging at her lips because she had an idea. She would *not* relinquish her dream, her lover, or her city. "What he refuses to see will be how we succeed."

"What are you talking about?" Theo, bless him, was so good-looking even when he was so clearly confused.

"What is your father oblivious to? What is beneath his notice? Who will he refuse to do business with? What is our secret weapon that your father can't control?"

Theo stared at her blankly and she thought maybe he *was* just a pretty face. Except she knew better. And she had an idea. And he trusted her.

"Women, Theo. Women!"

Moments later
25 West Tenth Street

THEO HAD NO more urgent and pressing business at that moment besides following Daisy on an errand she refused to explain. She led the way to an unremarkable town house a few blocks south of their shop. After a brief knock, the butler opened the door, took one look at the two of them, and said, "I'll see if Miss Burnett is at home."

"Thank you, Hollis. I appreciate it."

Theo deduced that this was the home of Miss Harriet Burnett, one of Daisy's friends who had joined them at the theater to give the appearance of chaperoning them. He racked his brain trying to think of what he knew of her, which was very little. She was one of the women who never sought out his attentions and so he hadn't paid much attention to her.

"My friend Miss Burnett has graciously offered me a place to stay while I am still in between residences," Daisy said. He had wondered, but she had assured him her accommodations were secured.

"She is a good friend to you," he said.

"She is an excellent friend to me and many women."

The butler returned. "The ladies will see you now."

And just like that the doors to the drawing room were opened to reveal a smattering of women, some of whom he recognized and many whom he did not. They all sat in a circle while some sipped tea, or sewed things, or leafed through Bibles open on their laps.

"I'm so sorry to interrupt like this," Daisy said.

"It's just a little gathering of the Charitable Ladies' Auxiliary Club," Harriet said with a smile. "Is everything all right?"

Daisy sat right down and poured herself a cup of tea. Theo stood uncertainly behind her and all the ladies.

"No. We need help. Allow me to explain."

Daisy told them about *her* father's scandal,

which everyone already knew all about. She apologized for it. Then she told them about *his* father's underhanded, behind-the-scenes scheme to ruin their prospects together by ruining their business.

Daisy commanded their rapt attention. They all spared him the occasional glance. He felt . . . ornamental. Superfluous.

But also very curious.

Because Daisy said she had a plan and thus far her plans had been good ones. If they needed to enlist the Charitable Ladies' Auxiliary Club, that was fine with him. Whatever it took for him to be able to propose to her.

"Prescott Senior has the whole town under his thumb, as we can surmise," Daisy continued. "What he doesn't have is *us*. If we can rally the women . . . If we can promote it in places he won't think to look . . . If we can operate beneath his notice, literally and figuratively . . ."

"Then we have a chance," Theo said as he realized what she was plotting. "A fighting chance."

"I like that," one woman said. "Taking the town by storm, right under his nose."

"I would take some delight in that."

"Excuse me," Miss Ava Lumley interrupted. "Are we going to talk about the fact that Theodore Prescott the Third is here?"

"He is my business partner," Daisy said. "That's the only reason I brought him."

"The *only* reason?" Miss Lumley persisted.

"And . . . possibly more than just her business partner," Theo added. It seemed like what they wanted to hear and it was the truth.

"I thought the wedding was off," Miss Burnett said.

"Allegedly," Daisy answered.

"Rumor has it," Theo said.

"People are saying."

"I see." Harriet glanced from Daisy to Theo and back again.

"It is just Theo and me now," Daisy said to the group at large. "I declined to join my mother on her great husband-hunting expedition in Europe. I'm not ready to give up on my dreams. Or New York." She glanced up at him and said, "Or Theo."

That elicited a tremor of murmurs from the women.

"What do you need to make this work?" Miss Burnett asked.

"We'll need a place to make the Midnight Miracle Cream and other preparations. The process is not complicated. We already have the ladies we need to do it. They only need space to work," Daisy said. "And we'll need a store, as well."

"We don't need a store," Theo cut in. "It's too easy to target—either by going straight to the landlords again or by staging protests. We only need a way to connect with our potential customers, especially those who might be interested in our products but wary of being seen purchasing them."

"I have what you need," Harriet said. "I have a kitchen table and an address."

"And we can assist," one of the other women said.

"But," a woman started, "it is cosmetics. And the risk to our reputation and the work we do—the charitable ladies' auxiliary work—wouldn't that all be threatened if we did this?"

"We don't *all* have to do it."

"But it reflects on *all* of us."

And just like that, the Charitable Ladies' Auxiliary Club descended in a fierce—but polite—debate. Then voices started rising. Politely, of course. They were ladies after all. But the pitch was high and getting higher. These women had dearly held opinions and weren't afraid to share them or to clash with their friends and fellow club women.

Until finally, finally, Miss Burnett put a stop to it.

"Oh, it's just lip paint!" Harriet cried out and the women fell silent. "To be honest, I don't like the way it feels on my lips or the way the rouge feels on my skin. I don't care if everyone wears it or no one wears it. But I will fight to the death for a woman's right to have the choice."

There was a long moment of thoughtful silence.

"If you wish to participate in this mad dream

of mine, please do," Daisy said. "But if you do not wish to, then you don't have to and there will be no hard feelings."

And with that, the meeting came to a conclusion. Bibles and sewing things, whatever they were called, were put away.

"We will name our firstborn Harriet," Theo said solemnly.

"Let's not get ahead of ourselves," Daisy said. "One day at a time."

"Should you be so blessed, I would cherish my namesake."

"We should get started."

"But first there is one last order of business to take care of," Ava said. She clapped her hands to get everyone's attention. Somehow they all knew to swarm around him, a cloud of taffeta and wool serge and brooches that could double as weapons. Their gazes were narrowed and sharp. Everything about them somehow communicated a lethal threat to his well-being.

They were just ladies but . . . they weren't. They were more.

Harriet stepped right up to him, toe to toe, nose to nose. She was rather tall, so she could look straight into his eyes and deliver quite a threat.

"I speak for all of us women when I say that you were never here, this meeting never happened, nothing was ever discussed. If we are ever introduced you will pretend you don't even know us. If you ever speak of this, we will see that every door in this town is closed to you. Forever."

Theo glanced at Daisy, who just shrugged and replied, "What she said."

Chapter Twenty-Seven

Ladies and gentlemen of New York, the
infamous Annabelle Jones has arrived.
—*The New York Post*

Days later
The Fifth Avenue Hotel

*W*omen. That was the secret to success according to Daisy. When it came to putting their plan into action, Theo would be starting with one woman in particular.

The infamous Annabelle Jones. She was an actress of some renown for both her talents on stage and backstage. She was most recently famous for her role in the Saratoga Scandal, in which she played the part of Scandalous Woman and Terrible Influence upon one of Manhattan's most beloved bachelors.

She had been lying low after the uproar, only somewhat by choice.

Now this infamous actress arrived in the city

to some fanfare. The newspapers greatly anticipated her arrival and she did know how to create a scene to ensure that all eyes and obsessions
were focused on *her*. She and her retinue—and
her many, many trunks—proceeded directly
from the train station to the Fifth Avenue Hotel,
where anyone who was anyone booked a suite
on the top floor. She had two.

The spectacle of her arrival in the city was
widely reported and well attended—people
paused on the sidewalk to watch her go by.
There was an audience outside the hotel. So
many people desperately wanted a glimpse of
her while also feeling some need to snub her
because she was an actress and everyone knew
about actresses.

Inside the lobby she stopped to take tea with
her longtime friend and partner in crime, Theodore Prescott the Third. They sat in full view of,
well, everyone. The greatest performance of their
lives was pretending not to be the slightest bit
aware of how many people were watching them
and talking about them.

"Hello, Annabelle."

"Theo." She smiled at him and extended her
hand for a kiss. "The last time I saw you, the
police were dragging you away after our wild
escapade. And now here you are. More handsome and more scandalous than ever before."

She poured him a cup of tea with the grace of any debutante.

"You look well, Annabelle. Much better than when I saw you last."

"Well, I'm not on death's door anymore. Thank God." She paused to lift her eyes to his. "Thanks to *you*."

He remembered that night. He and his fellow Rogues had arrived at her residence with some intention of seeking their pleasure with a woman who was renowned for providing all sorts of entertainments. But it was not to be an evening of making merry, no matter what the papers had said. She was in bed, feverish and ill from an *operation* gone awry, and left on her own by the man who had gotten her in such a condition.

She knew it. He knew it. They were the only ones.

"Anyone would have done it."

"We both know that's not true," she said. "Because not anyone did. That doctor, the housekeeper, those idiots you call your friends. They all left. Not one of them cared about my life. Except for you."

Theo lifted his eyes to hers, finding them bright and brimming with feeling. He saw not an accomplished and scandalous actress, but the young girl who had run away from the family farm out west and the woman just trying to get by in the world by whatever means available. He did not judge her for this. If anything, he had admired her gumption and determination. Even then, he had envied it.

"You didn't deserve to die. Not like that." Some idle rogue—not unlike Theo—had gotten her with child. And some idle rogue—not Theo— demanded that she do something about it. The impossibility of her position meant she had agreed. A doctor had been willing to help her—but not once the fever set in.

Penance, the physician had said. It had been up to Theo to save her by whatever means necessary. He stole a horse and carriage—the first he could find, Cavanaugh's open two-seater, so all the world could see them. He wrapped her in a blanket and set off with her to find another doctor by the most direct route possible—which was directly through town. She didn't die. But they both sacrificed something of their reputations so she could live.

"No woman deserves to suffer as you did."

"And that is what makes you worth it, Theo. It's not your pretty face or your turns of phrase. It's that you don't turn your back on women. You don't leave them to fend for themselves."

Like some men do. The words did not need to be said.

"How are you doing, Annabelle?"

"I'm fully recovered, if that's what you're asking. I'm ready to take the theater world by storm. I have the lead role in *The Importance of Being Earnest*. It's the most anticipated production in the city. We'll play on stage at the new Olympia Theater. All the newspapers are desperate to feature me."

"Of course they are. You're a beautiful, talented, and scandalous woman. You'll be the toast of town. You won't be invited to the high society parties, but they won't miss your performances. They certainly won't miss reports of your goings-on in the papers."

"Nevertheless, I'm surprised you asked to see me. And so publicly, too. I thought I heard word of a fiancée."

"It's complicated. But Daisy and I . . . we have an understanding. I am here with her full knowledge and support."

"Well, now I'm intrigued," Annabelle murmured and sipped her tea.

"I admit, I've come to ask a favor."

"Anything."

"Wait until you hear it."

"So tell me."

"Daisy and I have gone into business." He explained about the Midnight Miracle Cream, of which Annabelle was already a dedicated user—and she hadn't even known of his involvement. He also explained about Daisy's ambitions to launch cosmetics and his father's determination to thwart them.

"And I'm wondering if you'd be so kind as to wear our lip paint and perhaps mention it in an interview or—"

"Do you have it with you?"

"Yes, but—"

"I'll do it right now."

Theo paused at the shocking proposal. When had he become so propriety-minded? Women didn't wear cosmetics and they certainly did not apply them in public, especially the middle of the Fifth Avenue Hotel lobby. It wasn't done and he wanted to stop her from ruining her career on stage over some lip paint. She had so much promise; she had worked so hard.

"Annabelle—"

"I know my own mind, Theo. I don't know if it will help you for the likes of me to be seen applying lip paint, but I can guarantee that it will get people talking about it. At the very least, the theatrical people might start using it."

"Talking about it is all we need."

Daisy had explained her idea to him. If they could just harness the power of women—their connections, their conversations, their ladies' pages in the newspapers, then everyone they wished to appeal to would start talking about it. And so here was Theo with Annabelle Jones, whose forthcoming stunt might make an appearance in the gossip columns. Daisy and Harriet would prevail upon their newspaper reporter friends to include favorable mentions of it in the ladies' pages they wrote and edited for.

It was entirely possible that Theodore Prescott the Second would never hear of it.

Because ladies' stuff was beneath him.

While Theodore Prescott the Second could shut down a store, he had no say in the manner in which Miss Harriet Burnett used the mailing address of her privately owned town house. They could run the Dr. Swan mail-order business from her kitchen table and there was really nothing Prescott Senior could do to stop it.

There was a way forward.

It depended entirely upon women.

Women like Annabelle Jones, ready to put her lips on the line for him, his lady, his love.

He handed her the little pot of lip paint he brought for the occasion.

"Compliments of Dr. Swan herself," he said, sliding it across the white tablecloth.

The outside was lavender paper. Inside, the color was red.

But red was so insufficient a word to describe this hue Daisy had created. When Theo looked at this shade of fierce crimson, of hot vermillion, he thought *full-scale rebellion*. He thought *last night's scandal*. It was a thoroughly unapologetic, take-no-prisoners shade of red.

It was shocking. Scandalous. Sensational. Downright revolutionary.

The ones they had first experimented with were pale pink—light, sweet, verging-on-innocent pink. They were sorry for being daring; they were politely inquiring for an opportunity to go out discreetly, during daylight, with a chaperone. If a traditional, respectable matron was going to wear a lip color it might, one day, be that shade of *maybe pink*.

But perhaps he hadn't understood the who and the what and the why he and Daisy were attempting. The woman who was going to take a chance on wearing color on her lips in this day and age was not some high-status, proper matron. It was a woman who wasn't afraid to flirt with scandal, break the rules, or be the subject of conversation. The woman who would take a chance on this had nothing to lose and everything to gain. This was a red for women who wanted more from the world and fearlessly reached out for it—no matter the cost.

Theo watched in shock and in awe as Annabelle held up a small silver tray on the table—polished to a high shine—and in that murky reflection, she brazenly applied the lipstick to her lips. She pressed them together. Puckered her lips. Blotted them on a linen napkin.

Theo was aware of a hush stealing over the room. His back was to everyone in the room but that silence told him everything he needed to know without turning around to look.

She applied Dr. Swan's Lip Paint in full view of everyone in the restaurant.

Which is to say she had, essentially, performed this scandalous act in full view of everyone in New York. Theo had hoped she might *mention* it in a newspaper interview or *maybe* convince the theater to use it. This dramatic display left him speechless.

"How do I look?"

Beautiful wasn't the right word. *Pretty* wasn't, either. Theo didn't know if he liked what he saw or not. He only knew that he couldn't look away from her full, red lips. She looked *arresting*.

"Who knew such a little pop of color on a woman's lips could cause such an uproar," Theo mused.

"Oh, it's not just a pop of color."

"What is it, then?"

Annabelle smiled as she pocketed the container of lip paint. "It's the suggestion of pride in one's appearance. It's a suggestion that a woman believes she is worthy of adornment and feeling beautiful and put-together. It's the suggestion of money of her own, probably that she earned. It's not just lip paint. It is a declaration that a woman is not content with what God gave her and she believes that she can do better.

It's a command to look at her mouth and listen to what she has to say. And that is why it's so shocking."

There was another skirmish among ladies today, this time at Delmonico's . . .
—*The New York Post*

Meanwhile, at Delmonico's . . .
Fifth Avenue and Twenty-Sixth Street

ON WEDNESDAYS THE ladies went to protest. On this particular Wednesday, the Ladies of Liberty had conspired to protest the pesky rule that women were not allowed to dine in restaurants without a male chaperone.

Ladies could not dine alone. It simply was not done.

Not without questions being asked about their virtue.

And what could a woman do without her good name and impeccable reputation? Nothing good. Nothing decent. Or so it was understood. Because once the lines were blurred between Angels of the House and Fallen Women, how would one make sense of the world?

What if Fallen Women took up residence at home and what if Angels took the world by storm? The world would surely go upside down and topsy-turvy. But perhaps that wasn't the worst thing.

Harriet, Daisy, and their fellow club women were of the opinion that a woman ought to be able to dine in a restaurant all alone if she wished it, with no repercussions. A woman ought to be able to satiate her appetite, alone, in public, if she wished it. They were of the firmly held conviction that a woman was entitled to life, liberty, and happily-ever-after . . . however she defined it for herself.

Lunches out on the town, included.

"Remind me again why we are doing this?" Elizabeth asked the select group of women who had donned their finest and gone to Delmonico's at midday. They gathered outside the doors, waiting for everyone to arrive. It was important that they present a united front when they crossed the threshold. "It's just lunch, isn't it? Are we really putting our reputations on the line for a midday meal?"

"It is not just lunch," Harriet reminded her. "To forbid women to dine without a man present is to convey that a woman is insignificant and hardly has a right to exist without a man."

"It sends a clear message that women ought to stay home, out of sight and out of mind," Ava said.

"Well, I for one am ready to do this. If only because I'm famished," Miss Archer said to the laughter of the group.

Once ready, Harriet pulled open the heavy doors. They descended upon Delmonico's, dressed in their finest and most fashionable attire. To their smartly tailored day dresses they added statement furs, tasteful brooches, and hats, of course. One could not make a statement with one's appearance without a choice bit of millinery upon one's head.

They were the very image of respectable, well-to-do women. The epitome of Proper Ladyhood.

They were immediately confronted with the first adversary: Pierre, the maître d'. He was a distinguished-looking man of middle age who took no small enjoyment from the power he wielded by virtue of his position at the fine dining establishment to the Four Hundred.

Since its founding decades earlier, Delmonico's had been steadily moving to locations farther and farther uptown, as the fashionable fortunes had done. It brought its prestigious reputation with it. Pierre had been there every step of the way.

He stood at the entrance ready to decide who was privileged enough to enter the private, exclusive sanctuary that was the dining room—and who was not. Pierre lived and breathed to enforce the standards and had no trouble saying no when the situation called for it. He had once blocked a Rockefeller from entering because he lacked an appropriate necktie. *A Rockefeller.* He answered to no one and observed the rules of the establishment like they were the Ten Commandments, and God and Moses themselves were watching over his shoulder.

He was there when Harriet and her phalanx of ladies arrived.

"Good afternoon." He nodded politely at the group of women while scanning their ranks, no doubt looking for a man in their midst. "How may I help you, ladies?"

It was Harriet who spoke for the group. "We are here for lunch. We would like a table. There are ten of us."

Pierre treated all ten of them to a very apologetic smile. "I'm terribly sorry, ma'am. But we only seat complete parties."

Harriet smiled back at him. "As you can see, we are all present. All ten of us."

But Pierre was not fazed. "Are you certain no one else will be joining your party?"

"I should think we have enough," Harriet replied with a firm smile. She gestured to her companions. "As you can see, we are a large party."

"I would think at least one more would be necessary to join your party," Pierre replied coolly. In other words, would a man be appearing to dine with them and lend some veneer of respectability to this spectacle?

"Our party is complete," Harriet said firmly. Behind her, the Ladies of Liberty stood firm.

Daisy knew her heart was beating hard in her chest. She fully believed in their cause but there was nothing like a confrontation to get a girl's heart racing. "We are perfectly suitable, just as we are."

"I'm very sorry, madame, but it is our policy that women must be accompanied by a man in order to enter our dining room." Pierre did not appear to be in the slightest bit sorry. In fact, Daisy had the distinct impression that he thrived on moments like this when he could assert the authority of his position.

"And why is that?" Harriet inquired. Politely.

"Delmonico's has strict standards and rules. I am simply here to ensure they are maintained."

In other words, he was just a man. In a position of authority. What could he possibly do to change the ways of the world?

"Are you saying that Mrs. Johnson does not meet your standards?" Harriet inquired. Mrs. Johnson was married to a prominent preacher at one of the city's larger congregations.

Pierre's smile faltered.

"Or is Mrs. Collins not suitable?" She was married to a wealthy philanthropist who had recently made headlines for his sizable donation to the Metropolitan Museum of Art.

"My apologies. I did not recognize madame without her husband." Pierre paused to appear mournful. "I'm sorry that I cannot allow a group of women—respectable and esteemed as you all are—to dine without the presence of a male chaperone. It is only to protect the reputation of good women such as yourselves."

So now it was a *favor* to the ladies. He was only helping them not make a silly little life-altering mistake. The Ladies of Liberty erupted in disgruntled chatter.

And Harriet persisted with her questions. Good, honest questions.

"Do tell, good sir, what is occurring in your establishment that ladies will need male protection from?"

"We are a fine-dining establishment. There is nothing untoward occurring."

"It is more often the case that women need protection from men, not the protection *of* men," Miss Archer remarked.

"Or is it to protect the men from the women?" Miss Lumley quipped.

"Oh, yes, the mere presence of women might upset men's delicate constitutions and ruin their appetites," Mrs. Collins said.

A group of men arrived now, in their suits and clouds of smoke and masculine voices and expectations for a table, immediately, to satisfy their manly appetites. They were confronted by a swarm of well-dressed, rebellious ladies.

"What is this?"

"We don't have all day."

"Ladies, *please*," Pierre replied. "I need to seat the gentlemen."

But the Ladies of Liberty stood firm.

They were here for lunch. Should they not be accommodated they would cause a scene instead. This was becoming clear to Pierre. His battle was lost either way.

"We are merely trying to understand why we may not patronize your establishment," Harriet said. "As you can see we are respectable women who merely wish to have lunch."

She dared him—dared him!—to declare that they were not respectable. She dared him to say out loud in actual words that a woman could not join the dining service. That a group of respectable matrons together could not embark on a decorous luncheon.

"What is this?" a man's voice called out. "We have a reservation."

The gentlemen now waiting were grumbling. Loudly.

The ladies were already ruining their lunch.

Just then another group of women arrived. Jennie Jones and a cohort of lady reporters for the various papers all burst in, breathless, with their reporters' notebooks and pencils in hand.

"Sorry we're late. Did we miss it? There was a fire downtown and a murder uptown. Quite a morning in the city."

"Not yet," Daisy replied. "We are on the verge of storming the dining room. And then the real show will begin."

"Phew. We all rushed from other stories to get here in time. Something is always happening in Manhattan."

Something was always happening and people here were always in a rush and nothing, nothing, was more important or valuable than one's time. Especially a businessman of the sort who lunched at Delmonico's.

Finally, a consensus emerged. "Oh, for God's sake, just seat the ladies, Pierre!"

Finally, they were seated at a large round table, cheeks flushed with success and raising a glass to their determination. Their orders were placed—for Delmonico's steaks, especially. Disrupting the status quo did give one an appetite.

And then in small groups they excused themselves to visit the ladies' retiring room, from which they emerged with their lips painted red. Bright, unapologetic, shockingly red.

Each woman wore Dr. Swan's newest product—privately manufactured, not yet available for purchase—a lip paint in the shade of *Rebellious Red*. They were wives of clergy and philanthropists and robber barons. They were daughters of politicians and financiers. They were independent women of rank and respect. And each one of them was respectable enough to be seated for lunch in the Delmonico's dining room without a gentleman at their table.

If they were already going to cause a scandal by simply going to lunch, why not cause one more with just a dash of lip paint?

Chapter Twenty-Eight

Dr. Swan's color enhancements for the
lip available in Scarlet or Pink.

Some like to play it safe . . .
And some like it scandalous.

From the makers of the
Midnight Miracle Cream.

To purchase, send $1.50 to Dr. Swan at
25 West Tenth Street, New York

—Advertisement in all the best
New York newspapers

A few days later

*T*he newspapers dedicated inch after column
inch to the shocking occurrence of women, both
high status and low, donning lip paint in public.
There was Annabelle Jones, applying the stuff in
full view of the other guests in the Fifth Avenue

Hotel lobby. To say nothing of the scene at Delmonico's. Theo casually dubbed it The Scarlet Scandal and the press printed it and reprinted it.

Scarlet: the color of rebellion and transgression, but also love and passion.

The more the scandal was reported on in the paper, the more it was discussed and thus the more coverage in the press it merited, and all of a sudden it was everywhere, all at once. It started to become commonplace.

Once it was discussed around the breakfast table, it could hardly be declared a total and absolute taboo.

Funny how scandal had a way of lessening the scandal.

To capitalize on the attention, Theo took out an advertisement in the best newspapers, to run alongside all the gossip columns and opinion pieces discussing The Scarlet Scandal. The advertisement was a simple illustration of a woman at her dressing table, a variety of Dr. Swan's toilet preparations before her. Theo had composed the text.

The envelopes came in a trickle and then in a rush. Harriet had offered her kitchen table and address and both were put to good use. All day long the house was bustling with the work of a half-dozen lady chemists and assistants creating the preparations to fulfill the orders. It would be difficult to claim obscenity when all the best newspapers printed the advertisements, when all manner of women were purchasing the products and daring to wear them to church or charity luncheons—not just the stage or other "unsavory" places.

And so, thanks to Theo and Daisy's friends, her creations made the world a little brighter.

At night though, the house was still and quiet. And Daisy and Theo definitely had something to celebrate.

Theo came to call on Daisy at Harriet's town house, where she was staying indefinitely. If anyone would understand about needing a place to stay while trying to make her own way in the world, it was Miss Harriet Burnett.

"I am not usually in the habit of entertaining gentlemen callers at any hour, let alone this one but . . . Ava and I will be out for the evening," Harriet said as she adjusted her hat and bid good-bye to Daisy and Theo. "We expect to be late."

Daisy was not exactly invited out these days.

There was nowhere Theo would rather be.

They were gloriously unchaperoned. Daisy was now a scandal-plagued spinster of a certain age, so firmly on the shelf that of course she could—and would—idle away the evening alone with the bachelor of her choosing.

This was the freedom she had always wanted. She was delighted to spend it with Theo, seated side by side before the fire. She raised her glass of champagne to cheers with his.

"We did it," she said.

"We did *something.*"

"I think I have been involved in more scandal in one week than most people experience in a lifetime," Daisy remarked, settling against Theo.

"And to think, the night is young. We are still young. Who knows what else we might do?"

"Speak for yourself. I'm a scandalous, on-the-shelf spinster," she said with a laugh. "I couldn't be happier."

His gaze met hers. His blue eyes, sparkling.

Daisy didn't miss how he said *we.* She didn't miss how that mention of *we* made her heart skip a beat. Theo had told her that he would propose to her when she could afford to say no.

It seemed that she could afford to say no. It seemed that their business would find a way to survive and perhaps even thrive in these circumstances. If nothing else, she had friends who would ensure that she landed on her own two feet.

She truly had a choice.

So Daisy couldn't help but wonder if Theo would propose to her now. Tonight. While they were blissfully alone before this roaring fire and feeling exhilarated from gambling big and winning.

"We could do anything we wanted," she said.

"We could do whatever you want," Theo replied. She knew what she wanted.

"I want you to kiss me, Theo."

He didn't need to be told twice. His lips found hers for a slow burn of a kiss. Because they had all night.

Or forever? The thought didn't just occur to her. It'd been in the back of Daisy's mind ever since he said he would propose, eventually. But instead of considering all the reasons why not, she found herself considering all the reasons *why yes.*

Theo clasped her face in his hands, threading his fingers through her hair. She leaned into him, letting herself sink into this kiss and all the sensations rocketing through her. The wanting to feel his bare skin against hers. The yearning. The *loving.* His touch. His mouth. His words, his wit, his daring. Theo all day and this Theo at night.

If this was what forever could be, she was seriously considering it.

But was he considering it?

If he was, wouldn't *now* be an excellent time to say so?

Instead, Theo chased away these thoughts with kisses, finding that particularly sensitive spot on her neck that just chased all the thoughts from her head except for the really wanton ones.

She didn't have to be afraid of those now.

She was a scandalous spinster. She could kiss

Theo all night if she wanted to. And tomorrow morning, too. She would. Because being a scandalous spinster felt an awful lot like being a woman who reveled in her own pleasure and freedom.

"I just have to say . . ." Theo murmured between kisses. "That I definitely appreciate this new style of dress."

It was a tea gown, explicitly designed for ease of movement and to be worn without a corset— and removable without the assistance of a maid. Adeline had come up with the design but refused to share her inspiration. Daisy had some idea.

This. Theo pushing the folds of crimson silk off her shoulders, slipping the layers aside to reveal her breasts.

Yes, she wanted her freedom. But she really wanted it for this. His mouth, hot on her bare, feels-like-a-dream skin. This passion, with this man. The one she wanted. The one she loved.

Loved.

Daisy gasped. Was it at the realization that she loved him or the way his tongue teased the pink centers of her breasts? Or both. Definitely both.

And *this*. The way the folds of the skirt fell aside so he could skim his fingertips along the soft, sensitive skin of her inner thighs. She trembled.

He found that exquisitely sensitive part of her and touched her there, just how she liked it. Because she had shown him, and he had learned from her, and when a woman found that . . .

First, she moaned from the pleasure of it.

And then she entertained thoughts about forever and always.

Because they were so damn good together. Her. And him. Them, together. By day or by night, they were some sort of miracle.

The hour was growing late and they quit the drawing room and stumbled up the stairs to her room. Layers of clothing were strewn around. They fell onto the bed. Hands clasped, fingers entwined, mouths connected for a long, deep kiss. Theo's skin was hot against hers and she felt his arousal, hard and wanting.

Why didn't he ask her . . . ?

Because talking was too much to ask at a moment like this, when there was almost too much to feel. But really, *why didn't he ask her?*

"Yes," she gasped to a question he hadn't asked. But she wanted him to ask.

"Yes," she gasped to him as he pushed inside her. *"Yes,"* to the connection of their bodies and hearts and everything, anything. *"Yes,"* she gasped to the ferocious feelings of pleasure building inside her as he thrust in and out, and in and out, harder and faster as their desire spiraled out of control. *"Yes,"* she cried out as he reached his own climax. *"Yes,"* she cried out because they were home, alone, and she wanted him to know just what effect he had on her.

"Yes," she whispered as she lay in his arms,

after. Hearts pounding. Breathing unsteady. She wanted to say yes to a question he hadn't asked.

What was he waiting for?

What was *she* waiting for?

Daisy had no good answer to that. So she turned to him and said, "Theo, I love you. Will you marry me?"

The next morning

OF ALL THE strange and unexpected places Theodore Prescott the Third had woken up, in bed with Daisy in the guest bedroom of Harriet Burnett's town house was definitely the strangest and least expected.

Yet there was nowhere else he would rather be.

It was, however, just a bit awkward descending the stairs in his wrinkled suit, which had spent the better portion of the evening on the floor. He was known for his stylish attire and now he was presenting himself thusly. Also, his hair was a mess.

Daisy was hastily attired in a soft blue day dress, her skin luminous, and she had attempted to style her hair.

"I see congratulations are in order," Harriet remarked when they appeared in the dining room where she and Miss Lumley were sipping tea.

But she was also eyeing the large stack of letters—product orders—that had arrived in that morning's postal delivery. Some of it would be irate letters lamenting their work of the devil, the downfall of morals of young people these days, etc., etc. But some of it would be orders and cash.

"Our scheme seems to have worked," Daisy said.

"Which one?" Harriet asked.

"All of them, it seems," Ava answered. She could scarcely conceal the smile behind her teacup. "Honestly, Harriet. Just look at them."

"'Just pretend to be engaged,' she said," Theo remarked. "'We'll go our separate ways,' she said."

There was mirth in his eyes and laughter in his voice.

"And then I asked him for real," Daisy said. Then she dropped onto a seat at the dining table and poured a cup of tea. As if ladies proposed to gentlemen all the time and it was not remarkable in the slightest.

"I gather he said yes," Harriet remarked.

"Oh, I had hoped this would happen . . ." Ava gushed happily, her eyes bright and cheeks flushed with joy. She did love a romance.

"He said yes," Daisy answered her friends, but her gaze was fixed on Theo.

"I said yes," Theo said, again. Because when the woman you wanted to spend the rest of your life with asked you to do just that, there was only one thing to say. Yes.

"Before or after she saw this?" Harriet asked as she handed that morning's newspaper to Daisy. "Page six, halfway down the page."

It was a paragraph in one of the three gossip columns in the paper. It had undoubtedly already been read by a significant portion of Manhattan by the time Daisy set eyes on it.

The wedding between Theodore Prescott the Third and Miss Daisy Swan had been scheduled for this Sunday at Grace Church. The groom would like it to be known that he intends to be present to say "I do" and hopes from the bottom of his heart that the bride will be there, too.

"Well, that doesn't leave much time to get a dress," Daisy said with happy tears in her eyes.

"Never mind the dress. I'm just going to take it off," Theo said with a rakish grin. And then he earnestly spoke the sweetest words. "You are always beautiful to me, Daisy, no matter what you wear. I love you. I want to make you the happiest girl in New York."

Epilogue

Five years later

*A*fter their wedding at Grace Church, Daisy and Theo first opened a new shop on Fifth Avenue. After that was sufficiently successful, they let an apartment at a new building uptown. The Dakota was a newly constructed building of apartments that had attracted well-to-do professionals like themselves. They felt right at home with their new baby, a girl named Harriet.

It was just another morning in their household—the baby, nearly a year, gurgling in her crib. Daisy and Theo dressing for the day—they had spent the previous evening undressing each other and now their clothes were all strewn about the room. Sally, her longtime maid, would arrive soon to help with the household and the baby. But for the moment it was just Daisy and Theo and everything.

"Where are my favorite shoes? We are launching the new rouge today and I would really like to have my favorite shoes. I was wearing them last night because . . ."

"I know you have a launch today. I placed advertisements for it in all the best newspapers, remember?"

"Of course I remember."

By mutual agreement, Theo had left Dr. Swan's to start a business of his own, one that created and placed advertisements for various companies. It was a particular passion and talent of his that more and more businesses sought out. Of course he left Dr. Swan's in Daisy's immensely capable hands and she brought on some particularly ambitious and talented friends from the Ladies of Liberty Club.

"Do be home early if you can. My mother is coming to dinner tonight."

"Is she bringing the earl?" Theo asked.

Mrs. Evelina Swan had obtained a divorce. Given the fraud perpetuated by her husband, it was really the sensible and least scandalous thing she could do. As a single woman abroad, she flitted from house party to house party until she landed an earl of her own. He even had a castle.

"She never leaves home without him," Daisy replied.

"That's a good line. I should use it," Theo murmured.

"Theo . . . Shall we invite your father? Try to make it a family affair?"

They regularly invited his father to dine with them. His secretary always replied that unfortunately Prescott Senior had an engagement that could not be missed. Theo still wasn't just a pretty face; he understood that meant his father still didn't respect him.

Which was fine. Sad, unfortunate, and a terrible waste but . . . fine. Because Theo had true love and a family of his own. He had something else to fill his heart and his days and sustain him.

"Why not send him an invitation? One of these days he might even say yes."

Theo could also afford to be generous. He was outrageously successful professionally. But that paled compared to the fact that he'd found a woman who loved him for who he was.

He had found happily-ever-after and it was this: he and his wife getting dressed for the busy day ahead, tending to the baby, planning for family suppers . . . It was the simple little things, but with love.

"Oh, and on Wednesday I shall have to miss supper," Daisy said. "The ladies and I are protesting."

"What are you protesting now?"

"The lack of women's suffrage, of course. They are planning a parade. I think perhaps I'll even hand out samples of lip paint to the women marching. I've just created the most perfect shade of red. I'm calling it *Lady Be Bold*."

"Perhaps I'll join you," Theo said, pressing a quick kiss on her red lips. "You know I'll always be by your side."

Author's Note

*I*f one is going to write a series about girl bosses of the Gilded Age (as I have set out to do), it seemed inevitable that I would include cosmetics. But I was hesitant to write a novel about makeup, given what a fraught topic it can be among women—then and now. Does it perpetuate unrealistic standards of beauty or does it empower? Once I gave myself permission not to know and to just explore it, I found ample historical material to support Daisy's dream of launching a cosmetics company in the Gilded Age—with the help of a man.

I was first inspired by the book *War Paint: Madame Helena Rubinstein and Miss Elizabeth Arden: Their Lives, Their Times, Their Rivalry*, which detailed the invention of the modern-day cosmetics industry through the life stories of Helena Rubinstein and Elizabeth Arden. While their husbands were involved in their businesses, these women really ran the show.

But before Helena and Elizabeth, there was

Harriet Hubbard Ayer, one of the great beauty and business entrepreneurs we've never heard of. In the 1870s, she was the reigning queen of Chicago's social scene who spent her time throwing parties and redecorating her houses. But by the mid-1880s she was a destitute, divorced single mother supporting her two daughters in New York City. She sought employment from Sypher's, an antiques dealer whom she used to make all her purchases from. Given her extensive knowledge of both antiques and their clientele, she was an incredible success. On one of her business trips to Paris, she bought the recipe of a face cream reportedly used by the famous French beauty Madame Recamier. Back in New York City, with a loan from a man named James Seymour, she launched Madame Recamier's Toilet Preparations, Inc., at her kitchen table.

It was a runaway success, in no small part due to the advertising copy she composed, paid endorsements by actresses, and the allure of her high society status. In *Some Like It Scandalous* I have given these talents to Theo.

Harriet's life provided a template for Daisy's—up to a point. James Seymour wasn't content with having his loan repaid to him; he went on to have her committed to a sanitarium in an effort to seize control of her business (which Theo would NEVER do). She escaped and went on to reinvent herself as the editor for the women's pages of Joseph Pulitzer's newspaper, *The New York World*. She died at just 54 years of age—after helping launch the modern beauty, advertising, and women's media industries. Her life story is a fascinating one and you can read more in her biography *Dispensing Beauty in New York and Beyond: The Triumphs and Tragedies of Harriet Hubbard Ayer* by Annette Blaugrund.

As I have been researching the Gilded Age and reading biographies of forgotten women, I began to notice something: all these impressive, successful businesswomen kept popping up in each other's stories and they were doing the most fascinating, successful things and living incredibly vibrant, dynamic lives. We tend to assume "a young lady would never" when in fact so many women *did*. We just never were taught about it in school. With all of my historical novels, and this series in particular, I hope to shine a light on the history that's been hidden from us.

On that note, the professional women that Daisy mentions in early chapters are real (with the exception of Adeline Black, my heroine in *Duchess by Design*, who is inspired by the real-life Madame Demorest who created and oversaw a veritable fashion empire in the later half of the nineteenth century). Fun fact: she was besties with Jane Croly (see next page). Even a side character like Eunice at the theater has a real historical counterpart in Bessie Marbury, a theatrical agent and producer in this time period. Fun fact: in real life Bessie was also friends with Elizabeth Arden. They are *all* connected!

The character of Harriet Burnett is inspired by the real-life Jane Cunningham Croly, the journalist who founded the Sorosis Society, which is the real-life model for the Ladies of Liberty Club. According to *The New York Times* this club "inaugurated and epitomized the women's club movement and was itself one of the most influential organizations for women in late nineteenth-century America." Their purpose was to further the educational and social opportunities of women. The members included activists, writers, female physicians and ministers, a fashion magazine editor, businesswomen, and even Emily Warren Roebling, the woman who oversaw the construction of the Brooklyn Bridge. While Sorosis membership tended to be upper-class white women, I have made the choice to diversify my fictional ladies' club with the inclusion of the real-life African-American millionaire businesswoman Madam C. J. Walker (she has an amazing story—look it up!).

Jane Cunningham Croly founded the club in 1868 after being barred from a New York Press Club dinner—at Delmonico's. She responded by showing up with her fellow lady club members and disrupting the men's lunch (horrors) at a time when it was considered highly improper for women to dine in restaurants without a male escort. To the credit of Delmonico's they did let the women dine and even hosted their anniversary meeting each year. But a stigma about women dining without a man persisted. In fact, it was the 1969 protest of the Plaza Hotel's Oak Room's refusal to serve women lunch that introduced Gloria Steinem to the women's movement.

Speaking of scandals in restaurants—the scene where actress Annabelle Jones applies lip paint was inspired by the famous French actress Sarah Bernhardt, who in the 1880s scandalized people by applying lip paint in public. But it also got people talking and helped pave the way for the use of cosmetics in the theatrical world and then on film. From the beginning, actresses had been relied on to help promote cosmetics and other products.

Lastly, what really got me fired up to write this story was a scene that never made it into the final version. Legend has it that lipstick only really took off in 1912 when Elizabeth Arden herself handed out samples at the suffragist marches, thus making the bold red lip as much a symbol of women's empowerment as the white suits the suffragists wore.

So perhaps it is not "just lipstick" after all but a symbol of all the young ladies who dared— along with all their friends.

Acknowledgments

I would like to thank my wonderful readers! Your enthusiasm and encouragement means the world to me. And a big thank-you to Tony, Nathaly, Sarah, Eve, Lucia, Lou, Helen, Jonathan, Antonia, Penelope, and The Wing for a safe space to write rebellious and romantic lady books. Special thanks to my mom for everything, including not minding too much when I "borrowed" her make-up and lipstick. ;-)